"Grisham and Turow remain the two best-known writers in the genre. There is, however, a third novelist at work today who deserves to be considered alongside Turow and Grisham. His name is John Lescroart." —*Chicago Sun-Times*

## Praise for the Novels
## of John Lescroart

### *Betrayal*

"*Betrayal* is provocative . . . a tour de force of a legal thriller . . . easily usurps the latest from Grisham and Turow." —*The Providence Journal-Bulletin*

"Lescroart dispatches courtroom scenes with crisp efficiency." —*Entertainment Weekly*

"Adrenaline-infused . . . A first-rate addition to the author's ongoing series, this should please both long-time readers and new fans." —*Publishers Weekly*

"Extremely satisfying." —*Library Journal*

"A great read." —*Booklist*

*continued...*

### The Suspect
## The American Authors Association
## 2007 Book of the Year

"An intriguing puzzle. . . . Developments in Stuart's case will keep the reader guessing until the very end." —*Richmond Times-Dispatch*

"*The Suspect* is one smooth ride, and a fine legal thriller to boot." —*Philadelphia Inquirer*

### The Hunt Club

"A fast-paced tale of high-society intrigue and street-savvy suspense." —*The Washington Post Book World*

"Stakeouts, fake-outs, make-outs and shoot-outs. . . . [Lescroart is] a terrific yarn spinner." —*Chicago Sun-Times*

### The Motive

"Surpasses anything Grisham ever wrote and bears comparison with Turow." —*The Washington Post*

"Unfolds like a classic *Law & Order*." —*Entertainment Weekly*

### The Second Chair

"Lescroart gives his ever-growing readership another spellbinder to savor." —*Library Journal*

### The First Law

"With his latest, Lescroart again lands in the top tier of crime fiction." —*Publishers Weekly*

### The Oath
### A *People* Page-Turner

"A TERRIFIC CRIME STORY." —*People*

### The Hearing
"A SPINE-TINGLING LEGAL THRILLER."
—Larry King, *USA Today*

### Nothing but the Truth
"RIVETING . . . ONE OF LESCROART'S BEST TALES YET."
—*Chicago Tribune*

### The Mercy Rule
"WELL-WRITTEN, WELL-PLOTTED, WELL-DONE."
—Nelson DeMille

### Guilt
"BEGIN *GUILT* OVER A WEEKEND. . . . If you start during the workweek, you will be up very, very late, and your pleasure will be tainted with, well, guilt."
—*The Philadelphia Inquirer*

### A Certain Justice
"A West Coast take on *The Bonfire of the Vanities* . . . richly satisfying."
—*Kirkus Reviews*

"A gifted writer. . . . I read him with great pleasure."
—Richard North Patterson

### The 13th Juror
"FAST-PACED . . . sustains interest to the very end."
—*The Wall Street Journal*

### Hard Evidence
"ENGROSSING . . . compulsively readable, a dense and involving saga of big-city crime and punishment."
—*San Francisco Chronicle*

### Dead Irish
"Full of all the things I like. Lescroart's a pro."
—Jonathan Kellerman

# SUNBURN

## JOHN LESCROART

A SIGNET BOOK

SIGNET
Published by New American Library, a division of
Penguin Group (USA) Inc., 375 Hudson Street,
New York, New York 10014, USA
Penguin Group (Canada), 90 Eglinton Avenue East, Suite 700, Toronto,
Ontario M4P 2Y3, Canada (a division of Pearson Penguin Canada Inc.)
Penguin Books Ltd., 80 Strand, London WC2R 0RL, England
Penguin Ireland, 25 St. Stephen's Green, Dublin 2,
Ireland (a division of Penguin Books Ltd.)
Penguin Group (Australia), 250 Camberwell Road, Camberwell, Victoria 3124,
Australia (a division of Pearson Australia Group Pty. Ltd.)
Penguin Books India Pvt. Ltd., 11 Community Centre, Panchsheel Park,
New Delhi - 110 017, India
Penguin Group (NZ), 67 Apollo Drive, Rosedale, North Shore 0632,
New Zealand (a division of Pearson New Zealand Ltd.)
Penguin Books (South Africa) (Pty.) Ltd., 24 Sturdee Avenue,
Rosebank, Johannesburg 2196, South Africa

Penguin Books Ltd., Registered Offices:
80 Strand, London WC2R 0RL, England

Published by Signet, an imprint of New American Library, a division of Penguin
Group (USA) Inc. Previously published in a Pinnacle edition. Published by
arrangement with the author.

First Signet Printing, June 2009
10  9  8  7  6  5  4  3  2  1

To Leslee Feinstein and to Pat Gallagher.

I would like to thank the San Francisco Foundation for its encouragement and support.

For this new edition, I'd especially like to thank Barbara Sawyer, who is responsible for its resurrection.

There is something bittersweet and wonderful about seeing an old, long-out-of print book re-emerge back into the light of day.

It's bittersweet because the person who wrote the book has changed into an entirely different being from the idealistic and ambitious young man who set out to write what he hoped would be the first book of a long literary career. My initial, naive vision of the writing life never considered the possibility of a sustained oeuvre, which has now reached the majestic total of twenty books. I thought that the way it worked was you wrote one novel so unforgettable, so true, and so sweeping that everybody in the world read it (think *To Kill A Mockingbird*), and then after that, you were somehow, magically, transformed into an Author for Life. Little did I realize back then that authors who made a living at this noble profession tended to write a book every year or at least every couple of years. So, since *Sunburn* was going to be my one shot at literary immortality, I felt I had to throw everything I had into it.

As I first set down the blank pages next to my typewriter (yes, a typewriter—it was that long ago!), I dared for the very first time to let myself imagine that I might be creating a real book, something important that would have a life beyond my own. And if that was what it was going to be, I wouldn't be satisfied with a pedestrian story told in the "regular" fashion. No, I'd of course first have to set it in Europe, à la Hemingway and Fitzgerald. Then I would tell the story in a stylistically intricate way—using a narrative voice in first, second, and third person. No one had ever written a book like the one I was contemplating. It was not only going to change my life—it might actually change the literary world itself. Needless to say, *Sunburn* did none of the above.

Hence, bittersweet.

Although *Sunburn* did win the San Francisco Foundation's Joseph Henry Jackson Award for best as-yet unpublished novel by a California author under thirty-five, publication did not follow for another four years. And that initial publication was after the book had gathered the proverbial drawerful of rejections. Finally, when it did come out, it was as a paperback original with a cover that was misleading and tasteless at best, and semipornographic at worst.

So now I approach the occasion of the reissuance of *Sunburn* with a mixture of joy and trepidation: joy because for a writer it is always wonderful to see one of your very early efforts have a new chance to come back into print and to reach an entirely new audience; and trepidation because the book in question is so far removed from the kind of story, and the style of writing, of the rest of my published work that a part of me halfway fears that it might disappoint my loyal readers.

So for those readers, and also the new ones, who are now holding *Sunburn* in your hands, I offer you not an apologia, because I remain extremely proud of this book and believe that there is much to recommend it, but an explanation of the first stirrings of a writer's instincts that drew me to this story in the first place.

So what did writing this book teach me? How did it help to turn me into the writer that I am today?

One of the conceits that accounted for my early rejections was my then-held—and long-held— belief that the act of writing was such a sacred artistic endeavor that it should flow unimpeded from the brain to the page. The idea of rewriting struck me as impure, sacrilegious. So I wrote slowly, self-consciously, forming whole sentences at a time before I would commit them like precious brushstrokes to my canvas. If a conversation failed to sustain interest, or a description fell flat, I would be tempted to let the words stand because they were natural. I thought they were more real, not realizing that "real" in fiction, as in sculpture, is an artifice. When I finished my first draft, every instinct in me wanted to call the book finished for good.

But then I asked myself, what if it could be better? Would revision lessen the book's power or purity? The answer, of course, though painful to admit, was no. The answer to that question is always no. The cliché is that there is no good writing; there is only good rewriting. And this is the book that taught me that. I labored and labored over the words of the second draft, removing what made me cringe, adding flashes of poetry or insight. And all of these changes made the book so much better. Still not perfect, but well on its way to readable.

The other major problem as I set out to be a writer was that my focus was almost exclusively on character, and this in spite of the fact that I had not yet learned two crucial lessons: one, André

Malraux's dictum that character is fate, and two, that character is revealed by action. It was in the actual writing of this book that these twin pillars of fiction came to have some meaning to me. I wanted everyone to talk about ideas and to represent ideals, but I found as I tried to formulate scenes that unless the characters in them actually did something—and, more than that, something interesting or unexpected!—that there was no life, no vibrancy, no drama.

The power of the first scene, of the very first words—"It wasn't what you'd call a clean kill."—introduces action as revelatory of character in a specific scene, and it's this sense of scenes building on one another, of people interacting and revealing themselves, that drives the story forward. Story is so much more than mood, but until I put characters into action and into conflict, I had been blind to this lesson.

As I've intimated here, I've done another small revision on this edition of *Sunburn*. I've removed a few inconsistencies, added some motivation, deleted excessive and cringe-inducing verbiage. What's left is the best book I could write at the age of thirty, and one that taught me much of what I've come to know about writing.

Now, rereading the novel myself for the first time in nearly thirty years, I was alternatively pleased by my audacity, by some flashes of verbal dexterity, by the depth of tone and the complexity of the plot itself, and chagrined by many glaring motivational failures among my characters and an embarrassing overabundance of cliché and profanity (most of both of these flaws hopefully excised in this printing). In the end, I was happily surprised not by how much revision the book needed, but by how little. The story still works. The characters are alive and real. The setting is genuine. I would be surprised if many of this book's modern readers did not have to stifle at least a lump in the throat in the final pages. I know that I did.

—John Lescroart

# PART I

# One

It wasn't what you'd call a clean kill.

But then, it was only meant to be theater, and judging from Kyra's reaction, a comedy at that.

She was sitting on the stone wall laughing, and I hurried out from the woods next to the house to see what was so funny. Her squeals drowned out the squawks from the chicken until I'd come into the courtyard.

I noticed at the same time that she was wearing no underwear, and that the chicken was bleeding from its back, not its neck. Sean was standing over it, one leg holding down its legs, the ax in his one hand, ready to swing again. The chicken fluttered its wings madly, trying to free itself, pecking randomly, crazily, at Sean's foot. Kyra laughed again, and I stood transfixed while he brought the ax down three more times, finally severing the head. Then he removed his foot and the body began running in its last, hopeless freedom. When it dropped, Sean looked up at his audience.

"I told you I could."

"And you did. You were wonderful."

"Close your legs," he said. "You're pretty visible."

"You've got blood on your pants." She dropped from the fence. "Here's Douglas. Did you see him?" she asked me. "Wasn't he splendid?"

I walked over and picked up the chicken by its legs. "I don't get it," I said.

"It's dinner," said Sean, no longer triumphant.

"I gathered that, but why didn't you let Berta kill it, or me, or even Lea, for God's sake. I just don't see the point."

Kyra put her arm around his waist, and lifted her breasts at me. "I told him he couldn't do it with only one hand. He'd been going on about how he could do anything anyone else can, even if he didn't have two hands, and I bet him he couldn't catch a chicken and cut off its head. And what are you so sore about, anyway? It's only a chicken."

"I guess I don't have the same stomach for blood that you do," I said, and walked into the house, holding the limp and bloodless bird.

\*     \*     \*

# SUNBURN

The vacation had been Lea's idea, and at first it had seemed like a good one. We'd been stagnating at our work for a year or more, and it had been time to get over the inertia and move anywhere, so we had decided to visit her brother in Spain. He lived out behind the little town of Tossa de Mar, which is about halfway to France along the coast from Barcelona, and it had seemed far enough away to make it a real change.

Her brother, Sean Mallory, had bought the house about a year after his accident. The insurance company had paid him a fortune for losing his hand in a press, and he decided to see something of the world with his newfound riches. He'd only gotten as far as Spain before he decided he'd found paradise, and he'd bought this house and settled down. Since then, we'd received letters about once a month extolling the wonder of Iberia, and they'd sold us on going over.

Now he spent his time trying to write novels. He was, for the most part, an entertaining and generous host who left us alone when we wanted to be. Occasionally, he'd become intolerable and yell at everyone in the manner of someone who's grown used to getting his own way, but it would always pass quickly, and it seemed a small price to pay for an otherwise idyllic Spanish vacation.

I had supposed at the time, since Kyra and

novel-writing commenced simultaneously, that there had been some link between the two. From his descriptions, I had imagined her to be interested in art and artists. This was not the case, and though there must have been some connection between this new vocation and his life with Kyra, I couldn't fathom it.

She was a well-built woman and knew it, and whatever power she exerted over Sean I suspected lay in his adoration for her body. She exposed herself subtly but often to inflame him with jealousy, and he exploded into rage every two weeks or so. Once, he'd even gone so far as to throw her out of the house, though on that occasion she hadn't even made it out of the courtyard when he'd called her back, begging forgiveness. As far as I knew, she'd been faithful to him since she'd moved in, which had been about six months before our arrival.

When we'd left Los Angeles we had no idea of what Spain was like, or who peopled this paradise called Tossa. Lea had wanted to get out of the ad game, and I had thought, what the hell, maybe I'd write a novel. I had given up fiction after three years of poverty had been neither as romantic nor as fulfilling as I'd hoped it would be. The magazine articles I wrote had provided a good living, but I, too, had felt it would be good to have a change. I'd become bored putting words together as if I were macramé-ing something. This I say in retrospect. I hadn't really noticed that I wasn't content until Lea had put the bug in my ear. Since we'd arrived, I hadn't written a word.

Berta was standing by the kitchen door when I came inside. She had looked to me, at first, like every other Spanish woman older than a girl, always dressed in a black dress and black stockings. But as I'd come to know her, I realized that she was not so much unattractive as lacking in glamour. Her features were strong and her smile really wonderful. She probably wasn't much beyond forty-five, and before too long, we'd become friends in broken English and Spanish.

Now she leaned with a weary smile against the doorpost. *"Muy loco,"* she said, motioning outside.

I laughed. *"Sí.* You want the chicken?"

She took it and walked into the kitchen. Sitting on a stool near the table, she pulled over a can and began plucking, talking quietly to herself all the while.

After a few moments of watching her, I went upstairs to where Lea was napping. She lay curled in the bed, her back to me, the solitary sheet down around her waist. When I opened the door, she turned over, half-awake, and yawned.

"What was that awful noise?"

I sat on the bed. "Puberty rites, I suppose. Sean had to prove his manhood to Kyra."

"What? Again?"

"Again."

"What time is it?"

"About six, I guess. You sleep well?"

"Must have." She put her head on my leg, and curled herself around me. She had the slender and, I thought, beautiful body of an underdeveloped girl of twenty, and she was nearly twice that. Still, I felt that lately she'd come into bloom. She'd never been shy about her body with me, but now she exuded a certain pride in its lines. Before we'd left, she'd stood one day in front of the mirror and looked at herself, naked. "I'm so glad I've never had big breasts," she'd said. Then, later, "I'm beginning to feel like a beautiful woman. Should a woman my age feel that way?"

"Douglas," she said, "I'm not that way with you, am I? I don't test you all the time?"

I leaned over and kissed her. "If you do, I don't notice."

"Because I think it's terrible. If only poor Sean would see . . ."

"But he does it himself. Even if he doesn't see it, it must come out in other places we don't know about."

"I wish she'd leave."

"Now, now . . ."

"Well, he is my brother."

"And he is no kid." I lay down beside her and kissed her again. "*Basta*, OK?"

"OK."

We began making love. Downstairs we heard a car pull up and honk, and we stopped.

"Not more guests," she said.

"No fun eating alone, you know."

She put her head back on the pillow, and sighed.

"Are you glad we came?"

"Sort of."

"It's weird, though, isn't it? Sean and I used to be so close, and now he's distant even while he's being the warm host. I can't seem to approach him, though I feel like if he'd let himself slow down for a minute, it would be all right. But he's—I don't know—almost crazy to keep going. But not in any direction. Like maybe he's afraid that if he stops he'll stop for good."

"Maybe he is."

"Do you want to go away?"

"No. Things might change. It's only been six weeks, you know."

"I know. But I wonder . . ." She stopped.

"What?"

"Well, if it'll get to us. I mean all this free time, so much time to think about life. I wonder if it's a good thing, if Sean's just keeping so busy to keep himself from thinking about himself. And Kyra's just . . ."

"And they're neither of them anything like us," I said. "We're here for a vacation, remember? It's what we wanted—some time to think things over."

"I know." She put her arms back around me. "I know, but sometimes I just get afraid."

"Do you want to leave?"

"Oh, I'm not sure. I just don't want things to change with us. And sometimes I think too much, and think I feel different."

"About us?"

"No, or a little. I don't know. Just tell me you love me," she said, and rolled on top of me. "I love you, you know. I really do."

Objectively, if we had wanted to get away from California, we couldn't have picked a worse spot than the Costa Brava. I'd never seen one landscape so closely resemble another. There were the same pine trees, the same slightly red earth, the same hills, even the same sky, though of course you could see it more clearly than you could around L.A.

Tossa itself sits in a little cove near the most blue

water imaginable, but we didn't stay in the city. Actually, very few people lived in the town proper, especially between September and May. Sean's house was back up in the hills behind the town, and with its white front and red tiled roof, it could have been transplanted whole from one of the canyons or Beverly Hills. However, it was supposedly rich in tradition, having been a Basque stronghold during the Civil War. A few bullet holes testified to the truth of this legend, but they could have as easily been made by an imaginative real estate man. In all probability, the Realtor's (and Sean's) claims were true. God knows, the house looked the part.

Driving up from the town, we passed several acres of cork trees and stubby vineyards, interspersed randomly. When we had arrived in late summer, the colors had been predominantly yellow, green, and red, with the sky a deep and constant blue. The road itself wound like an Indian trail—dip, weave, and bend, hopelessly banked—as it worked its way back from the coast. Our first trip up to the house, by taxi, had been harrowing, but Sean and Kyra had kept us laughing as we drove. We'd since made it a point, however, to drive ourselves whenever we'd wanted to go back down. It wasn't much better, but it was better.

Off the road, we turned into a rutted road of red clay, which ran between some vines, into a cork forest, and into a clearing, all in less than half a mile. The house was surrounded by a rock wall, not a fence, which was overgrown in places with ivy, but was mostly bare. The overwhelming impression, especially after coming out of the cork trees, was of a dazzling whiteness—a Spanish, blinding, pure white which seemed to transform heat into color, so that you felt rather than saw the harsh whiteness of the place. It was the white from which visions arose.

The house was a U-shaped, two-story structure, made thick-walled for coolness against the Spanish summers. The bottom of the U faced the gate of the courtyard and contained two doors—one to the kitchen, the other to the living room. Behind the kitchen stretched a hall and Sean's office. Our rooms were upstairs over the kitchen and office, and directly over Sean's bedroom, on the other leg of the U, were Berta's rooms. Downstairs, the living and dining rooms abutted the kitchen, and there was a small library down the hall beyond Sean's bedroom. Alongside the library, outside the house, seemingly carved there, was a stone walkway to the roof. One of the beams here protruded several feet and, according to the legend, had been the site of many hangings. From the roof, the town of Tossa was just visible over the trees.

There was also a back courtyard, which was

mostly a flower garden. An old toolshed stood out beyond the cleared section, and chickens pecked here and there, but it was a pleasant enough spot in the early evenings when the sun had just settled into the foothills behind us.

One of the peculiarities of the house was the acoustic quirk between Sean's bedroom and ours. At certain times during the afternoon—just at dusk, most often—we could hear Sean humming or muttering to himself. We could in fact listen to anything he might be doing, all unwittingly. Sometimes, in that hour before dinner, the quiet would become so intense that it was palpable. We would hear his door opening and Kyra's voice, and then a long, almost nervous silence, broken by a sigh, or by a shutter being hastily drawn.

# Two

Denise Hanford grew up in West Orange, New Jersey. She went to a Catholic girls' high school until she was sixteen, when she became pregnant. She wanted to have the child, not because she loved either the father or the idea of having it, but because she simply couldn't imagine the alternative. Her parents, however, were more realistic, as they had put it, and the pregnancy was aborted in the third month. Later, Denise told the few friends who had known that she didn't want to be bothered with the stretch marks.

She transferred to a public school, then went to college in Maine, where she graduated in 1971. By March of the next year, she had saved enough for a flight to London, where she began calling herself Kyra.

By degrees she worked her way south—three

months as an *au pair* girl in Paris, four months teaching at Berlitz, again in Paris, a move to Corbière, her first job as a barmaid, a fight with the owner of the bar, who was also her lover, and finally her arrival in Tossá.

A woman with her looks never had to be out of work or alone, but after Corbière and three years of working and saving, she craved a rest and some solitude. Tony was an attractive and, miraculously, intelligent man who had one night visited some friends at her *pensión*. Kyra—by now the name was her own—had been invited to share some wine, and had found herself talking to him most of the night. He hadn't tried to sleep with her, and that had so impressed her that she decided to be his friend.

In London and Paris she'd had countless lovers, often sleeping with two or three men in a single day. In Corbière, she'd settled down to one man, but it hadn't lasted, and it had seemed only logical to her to have no one in Tossa. At least it would be worth a try. After meeting Tony, she moved into a different circle, and though she might have appeared promiscuous, she abstained.

She found herself changing in other ways. Always before, she'd been constantly active, going from bar to party to work to sleep to party again. Now she could sit and do nothing, or read for hours at a time. As the winter ended, she went for long swims and sought deserted beaches.

For all of Tony's influence on her social life, they remained only friends. For her, it was an odd relationship, but she didn't want it any other way. She needed a rest from men. When men had been her great concern, she'd been more strident, bitchy, narrow, and now she was feeling almost serene. She intimated to interested men—and there were several—that she had a lover who would be arriving soon.

Though perhaps she felt serene, no one would have described her that way. With others around, she was rarely quiet. She painstakingly avoided giving the impression that she was ever introspective. Let them think I'm completely callous, she said to herself. That's fine. Let them think there's nothing inside me. She had all her moves down, alluring and aggressive, ready to take sex and take it lightly. Tony suspected that she wasn't what she seemed, and asked her why she put on the act.

"Everything I do is me," she answered fiercely.

Tony described her to Sean as the "sexiest virgin I've ever met."

For as long as she could remember, sex to her had been more a matter of power than of desire. She'd learned early that she would be abused if she did not use, and so use she did. She didn't think that she hated men, but she would never let anyone near her. She'd slept around as much to keep herself from getting involved as to keep men aware of her independence. She'd slipped up in Corbière, almost caring about her lover, whom she had only used, after all, to get a job in the first place. But finally he had ignored her moment of vulnerability, and she hadn't and wouldn't forgive him for that. So she'd moved and again built up her facade of invincibility.

Sean shattered that facade, without any effort, in one evening.

He hadn't planned to attend Tony's party that night, but he'd written all day and felt bored and stir-crazy. He'd given Berta the day off, as he often did on Saturdays.

When he entered the room, Kyra immediately noticed him. He was older than nearly everyone there, and evidently well-known, though she'd never seen him before. Before too long, she had Tony introduce them. She liked the way he walked, casually, with one hand always in his jacket pocket. She found herself hoping he wasn't married. Isn't that ridiculous? she thought. He was a big man, not handsome and not ugly. She wanted him.

There was an aura about him that struck her so sympathetically that it scared her. He was funny without trying to be a comedian. He seemed to know exactly what he was, and to like it. His laugh, like hers, was a little too loud. He didn't seem to take her at all seriously.

"You see, my dear," he said in a mock British accent, "I'm frightfully rich and it makes no sense at all to worry about anything, since I shouldn't have a care in the world, what?"

He drank immoderately, but didn't get sloppy.

"I can't talk so well to people when I'm sober. I keep feeling I have to observe them if I'm to be a phenomenal writer. But when I drink, you see, I realize how absurd it is to want to be a phenomenal writer, and so I don't observe at all, but have a hell of a lot better time."

"What do you write?" she asked.

"Cookbooks. You?"

They left the party to go for a walk. The early spring night had just a trace of chill. She realized that Sean was a bit tipsy, though he walked steadily. The air smelled of blossoms.

"Did you ever think," he asked, "that the fragrance of a night like this, wrapped up in the breeze, is like a string of flowers braided through a woman's hair?" Then he laughed.

But as they walked, he became quiet until suddenly he stopped and leaned against the side of a building.

"Wait a minute."

"What is it?"

His face in the half-light seemed transformed. No longer was he the bon vivant or the comic. His features held no sign of either self-pity or of malice toward her, not a trace of a phony romantic look, nor any other of the cheap tricks she'd come to expect from men who desired her, and who didn't want to wait.

"I'm ridiculously sober, and I don't talk good when I'm sober."

"What do you want to say?"

He thought a moment. "Nothing, I guess. Nothing." His tone was matter-of-fact. "It's just words, anyway."

"You seem quite good with words."

"Oh, I am. So what?"

"It's just . . ."

"Come here."

He put his hand behind her neck and drew her to him. They didn't kiss. She stood passively, leaning slightly against him while he held an arm around her.

"I think . . ."

"Shut up," he said gently. "You don't want to say anything."

She realized that he was right. They remained, not quite embracing, for several minutes. Finally, she stepped away from him and looked at his face again. It was impassive yet tender. It looked like his natural expression, although she imagined it must have grown strange even to himself through lack of use. The muscles were relaxed. He looked at her not passionately but with interest, and she wondered if her own face reflected that same calm interest.

She kissed him.

As they walked back to the party, he began talking lightly again, and she was strangely relieved, as though she'd been let off the hook. She was on more solid ground with his insouciance. She was amazed at how vulnerable she had been for a moment there, and now she could be herself again, as he was. He was just another man and she wouldn't go making an ass of herself for him. Her face once again adopted her smile, and she walked easily beside him, elated and relieved and grateful.

But she knew that something odd, out of character for both of them, had happened, and that they'd retreated from it in the same way. There was an unsettling comfort in that.

She put her arm through his.

"Watch out for that arm. There's no hand on it."

"Are you serious?"

"Perfectly."

His smile was completely natural. "You don't

think I became rich because of my talents? Here," he said, "come around the other side and hold my hand."

Below the window, they heard the sounds of records and laughter.

"Do you want to go up?"

For a moment, she was terrified of staying another second with him. She knew that they wouldn't go anywhere to talk. They would walk until he stopped again and then he would touch her and she would want him.

"No. Let's walk some more."

The next couple of months were hell. For the first time in her life, she desired someone. After that night when in fact they had made love in the backseat of Sean's car, she hadn't seen Sean again for two weeks. She even thought of leaving, going farther south, and forgetting this interlude.

Her solitude became unbearable. She was constantly out on the town, going to the discos, drinking and sleeping around. She wouldn't have him think that he was anything special. Yet she found that she couldn't leave town.

Then one day she met him in the street. The season was just beginning in earnest, and the streets were more crowded than they'd been, or she'd have seen him and ducked out of his way.

"You're avoiding me," he said calmly. He didn't seem the least bit upset. "I just wondered why."

"I haven't been home, is all."

"I noticed. I came by twice."

He steered her into a café and ordered.

"Why should I be home, then?"

"You shouldn't. A young and attractive girl like yourself should be out getting all she can."

"That's none of your business."

"I know. Just an observation. Do you want me to ask you for a date?"

"No."

He shrugged. "Suit yourself. Enjoy your coffee."

He got up and left, never having raised his voice or lost his smile. She nearly jumped from her chair to follow him.

"Sean."

He stopped and turned. She ran up to him.

"I'll be home Thursday night."

"That's nice."

"If you want to come by . . ."

"I'm sorry. I'm busy Thursday."

"Well, pick a day."

"For what?"

"Goddamn you, I won't beg."

"Neither will I. How about today?"

"Tonight?"

"Today. Right now."

\*     \*     \*

She couldn't change, try as she might, and he didn't become any more insistent. When they were together, they either fought or made love. There was no repetition of the peaceful joy they'd taken in each other on that first night, and yet it was that first night that had brought them back together again and again. In some undefined way she knew that, and knew that it was true for him too. Still, she was not able to rest. She was more promiscuous than she'd ever been.

Occasionally, after they made love, they'd go out to dinner or a cabaret. Sean would drink too much. Even when they weren't angry, their words took on a sparring quality. He would never spend the entire night with her. She never went to his house.

Then, in early July, after he hadn't called on her for a week, she was sitting at a table outside a small German café just in front of the church, and Sean drove up in his black Peugeot and parked in front of her. Getting out, he walked to her table and sat down.

"This has got to stop. I want you to come live with me. If you don't, I won't see you again. And if you do, make no mistake, it's the end of your fucking around."

As she looked at him, she once again saw that

clarity in his face, a look of nearly total uninterest in her. He'd made up his mind. If she didn't go, he was gone. She finished her pastis.

"Help me pack my things."

After Douglas left the courtyard with the dead chicken, she turned to Sean.

"Why don't you kick them out?"

"I like them."

"Just now?"

"So what? Doug's pissed off. It happens."

He was embarrassed, and disgusted with her for the moment. She watched him walk into the house.

"Where are you going?"

He stopped in the doorway. "To do some writing, then clean up. Tony's coming over for dinner."

"All right. I won't bother you then."

"Good," he said. "Don't."

Despite their greater intimacy and half a year of living together, things between them had declined. Nothing really had changed since she'd moved in. At first they'd had quiet times—nights sitting before the fire, finishing off their dinner wine, talking, or just lying watching the flames. But always, the next day, she would provoke him, and the fighting would start again.

She'd lived constantly hoping that he would

throw her out, or that she would tire of him, and terrified that one of these things might happen.

When his sister and brother-in-law had come, she had wanted to run away. It had not been so much that she had disliked the visitors as that she had resented their intrusion. Before they arrived, there seemed to be endless time to work things out, to change slowly to suit each other, and though it hadn't worked, she still felt hopeful that it would. But when they'd come, she'd felt, in a real sense, back in society.

Sean had begun having parties, and their private lives had stopped evolving. They became victims of their friends' expectations.

There had always been in her a need to appear consistent in front of others. This was why she'd always changed locations before she'd changed her actions. She couldn't explain why this was true, but it had always been so. And Doug and Lea had arrived when she and Sean had been fighting and challenging. They'd both fallen into their public roles, and their already tenuous private lives, which had brought them together, were buried under this hail of momentum.

Still, she couldn't stop herself. Though she knew it was poisoning all that was good between them, she continued to taunt and belittle him, while he remained detached and, realistically, on guard.

At least she had been faithful to him. Other men didn't interest her, though she pretended otherwise, and she knew that here Sean would draw the line, as he'd said.

But now, as she watched him enter the house, she felt physically sick. She turned and looked at the surrounding woods, and slowly walked out through the gates into the trees.

She had gone too far. Douglas had been right. She'd been pushing too hard for weeks now. Leaving the road, she walked back between the trees, which were beginning to turn for autumn. She kicked at scattered leaves on the ground, then leaned back against one of the trees. Her stomach felt hollow and she crossed her arms and leaned over. Suddenly, she felt her frustration like a force moving up from her stomach. She began to cry, at first softly, and then threw herself headlong on the ground and sobbed uncontrollably.

After a time, she stopped and lay quietly. Then she got up and walked back to the house, through the front room, and back to their bedroom. She took a shower and put on a terry-cloth robe, then walked back through the house to Sean's study.

He sat in his chair in front of his desk. His right hand cradled his head and covered his eyes. He might have been sleeping.

"Sean."

He looked up. She crossed to him and knelt on the floor beside him.

"It's not working, is it?"

He stared silently ahead.

"Because I want to tell you that we have to start over, and not be afraid to admit or show that we like each other. It's like we've gotten so that anything but fighting is out of the question between us, and I don't want to fight you anymore. I really don't."

He put his hand on her head and smoothed her hair. He looked impassive, bitter.

She put her head on his lap and whispered, "It just seems that ever since we started, it's been one or both of us afraid to be ourselves. I don't know why. But it's been like there's this . . . I don't know, this force making a travesty of us living together. Like we never really wanted to try, but something made us. You know what I'm saying?"

He nodded, gently rubbing her neck.

"But now it's gotten horrible. I don't care, now, if you hurt me. If you want to, then go ahead, but I won't be a bitch anymore. We don't have to be this way."

"I know."

"So let's not. Let's stop."

"What have I been doing?"

"Hiding."

27

"From what?"

She stopped looking up at him. "Let's just leave it at that. There's more to you than you show me."

"There's more to everyone than they show anyone."

"You showed me more our first night."

He was silent.

"Come on. Stand up." She was smiling now. "Do you want me to help you change?"

"I can change myself," he answered.

"I know. Do you want me to help you?"

Gradually his features softened. He smiled. "Let's have a kiss," he said. "Then we'll see."

# Three

We stayed in bed until the sun had nearly gone down. Below we could hear Sean and Kyra speaking with the guests, who had come up from the town, I assumed. The window in our room looked out over the courtyard and to the trees beyond. It was a beautiful evening. We had dozed and I had wakened before Lea. Lying on my back, I enjoyed the weight of Lea's head as it rested on my chest, her leg thrown carelessly over mine. Sean's earlier foolishness was forgotten. I even felt kindly disposed toward Kyra.

Berta rang what we called the half-hour bell, telling us when dinner would be served, and I pulled gently at Lea's hair.

"Food," I whispered.

"Uhhh."

"Dinner bell just now."

I took my arm from around her and sat up. Automatically, it seemed, she reached out and scratched my back.

"God, I'm lazy."

"So it seems."

I got up. "Coming?"

"Minute."

The upstairs showers had been installed the previous spring, but had not been connected to the water heater, so showering was more of an ordeal than I'd been used to, but I was getting to like it. At least it was impossible to emerge drowsy.

While I spluttered and groaned, Lea came in and sat on the bidet, which was, if possible, colder.

"How do you do it?" she asked.

"Clean living," I said. "Hand me a towel, huh?"

She shivered. "Still."

"Should I shave? Sean tell you who's coming?"

"You know anybody with a white Citröen?"

"No."

"Then I don't know." She had a towel wrapped around her hips, as a man might, and combed her hair abstractedly. She looked at me in the mirror. "Don't shave. You look good."

We dressed together, husband and wife, talking like it, and went downstairs.

\* \* \*

Of the three guests, I had met Tony before. He was getting a doctorate somewhere in Spanish literature. He'd been up to the house several times before, and I liked him. He wore dark slacks, loafers, an open shirt. A handsome Spaniard, he was olive-skinned, slim, with a woman's hands, and yet not effeminate, but somehow rugged. His voice was abnormally deep. I remember having been surprised when I'd learned he was a student, so far was he from the scholarly type. The last two times he'd been by, we'd all gotten drunk and told filthy stories. Now, when Lea and I entered the room, he rushed to embrace us both, laughing contagiously.

"Come," he said, "meet my friends. Tonight we'll be more sedate, eh?"

"He means under sedation," Sean put in.

The woman was young, possibly not yet eighteen, and very pretty, dressed in a white shift and sandals, medium-length dark hair surrounding her face.

"Marianne is just in from France. She studies anthropology. And this," said Tony, presenting the other guest with a smile, "is Michael Barrett, our chaperon."

"He is not that," said Marianne. "We don't need a chaperon."

Tony winked at us. "Ah, innocence."

We all laughed politely and began making small talk, but shortly I noticed that Michael had sat back in his chair, seemingly content to be left out. He was an American, from Seattle originally, who'd been in Europe for several years. Somewhere in his early twenties, I imagined. He was rather tall and well built, with dark hair that was long but not unkempt.

I thought it odd that someone so young should be so reserved. It might have been shyness, but there was more a brooding quality about him—an inner quietness, maybe even a sense of solitude. When he did speak, he was, to my mind, forcedly polite, and in Sean's relaxed front room it was out of context, leaving a tension like an unresolved chord.

Lea must have felt it, too. She was in a positive hurry to help with the drinks.

Of course we all had gin and tonics. No other drink, even sangría—especially sangría—is so typically Spanish. We drank from tall glasses filled with ice and a wedge of lime. Outside, it still hadn't completely darkened, and a slight warm breeze came through the open front door.

Lea was over talking to Sean, Kyra was in the kitchen getting more ice, and Michael, now Mike, sat sipping his drink. Marianne harangued Tony about something in French, then got up from the couch and crossed to where I stood, near the liquor cabinet. She really looked enchanting.

"Why are you standing over here alone?" she asked.

"I'm an observer," I said.

She turned and looked at Mike, now talking with Tony. "We have too many of them here already. Come over and talk to us." She reached out her hand to me—cool and very small—and led me over to the sofa.

"What shall we discuss?"

"Anything you like," I said.

Tony stood next to her and put his arm around her waist.

"Would you get me another drink?" she said to him. Then, to me, "No one seems to pay much attention to the women here, *n'est-ce pas?*"

At that moment, Kyra came back in from the kitchen with the ice. She was wearing a floral print which fell loosely from her neck to the floor. It was open at the sides, clasped by a pin just above the waist, and she wore nothing under it. She was a fine-looking woman, if only she would not flaunt it so blatantly. She walked over to Tony, who was fixing Marianne's drink, and hugged him from behind. Lea and I looked at each other and shook our heads, and when I turned to continue talking with Marianne, she had crossed over to Tony and stood possessively clutching his arm.

I sipped my drink and joined Sean and Lea. Mike had gotten up and now the younger people were standing in a group and talking.

"Have you known Mike long?" I asked Sean.

"We were just talking about him, too," said Lea.

"Met him a few times. There is something about him, though, isn't there?"

Lea stared at him. "He seems a bit . . . I don't know. I can't place it at all."

Lea took my hand and squeezed it.

"He works at a bar in town," said Sean. "I'm not sure if he's the bartender or waits tables, but he's a nice enough guy. Plays a hell of a game of chess."

"So you do know him."

He shrugged. "The way one knows people here. He happened to be having a drink with Tony when I ran into them and asked them up."

"He seems perfectly normal now," said Lea, "but just when he was sitting there, so quietly, it was . . . it was eerie, I suppose."

Sean laughed. "It's this Spanish twilight. Alters all the shadows until they're not quite recognizable."

"Or creates shadows out of nothing?"

He remained smiling. "Maybe. But that's the romance of this place. You sense a shadow, a mood, a mystery somewhere, but when you examine it, you find it was either the sun, or the heat, or the gin."

"There's no real romance here, then?" I asked.

"Depends on what you mean by real. It's all real enough at a distance, so the trick, if you're after romance, is to keep it there. If that movement in the bushes seems somehow strange, don't walk out to the woods and find out it's a bit of cloth dangling from a branch. Stay by your window and believe it's a demon watching you." He took a long drink. "Also depends on what you want to see."

Lea spoke. "So we imagined whatever it was about Mike?"

"Just what was it you might have imagined?"

"Well." She paused. "I can't really put my finger on it."

"Doug?"

"I don't really know, either."

"There," he said, "you see. But go on believing anything you want. It makes life so much more interesting. And now, if you'll excuse me, I think I'll go hurry Berta." He bowed, and disappeared into the kitchen.

Lea looked at me. "I suppose he's right, but it did seem . . ." She stopped. "It seemed, whatever it was, real enough to me."

# Four

He turned out of the rutted backstreet and into the main road. Beside him on the seat was an open bottle of *tinto,* and from time to time he'd tip the bottle back as he raced along the curving road. He was anxious to get to the main road that ran out of Blanes, and get to his destination near Perpignan before daybreak.

Already it was nearly four a.m. The bar had closed up late, and Victor, their singer, had stayed around to drink and swap songs for nearly an hour. Mike finally had to get him drinking Pernod laced with illegal absinthe, so that he'd get drunk and leave. Then there'd been the usual checking up to see that the *graffa* bottles were corked and ready for tomorrow. Luckily, it had been a quiet night. No one had been exceptionally drunk or obnoxious.

That, at least, had been a relief. When he'd

last gone to Perpignan, he'd spent all his closing time cleaning vomit from the floors. This cheap liquor really wasn't the best thing to get drunk on. He took another swig of the *tinto,* and the trees whizzed by.

Occasionally he'd see lights approaching and have to slow down. He didn't know whether he preferred the private cars that tended to drift over into his lane, or the taxis that would always turn on their brights as they came closer, leaving him half-blinded as they sped past.

He was no slouch behind the wheel himself. Even with the oncoming traffic to contend with, he made it from Tossa to Blanes in around twenty-five minutes. Then he hit the autoroute and really began to move. The white Citröen compact wagon quickly got to cruising speed; then he set the throttle, had a long drink of the wine, and lit a cigarette. Looking at his watch, he smiled. Should make it now, he thought.

When he reached customs at the French border, the eastern sky was already light gray. There were no problems, of course. He got out his passport, and had it stamped, talked to the guard briefly and was passed through and into France. He drove a few more miles, then turned off the autoroute and up away from the sea flats into the foothills. On either side of him grew carefully tended stretches of vineyards. The sun came up behind him and lit up the countryside before him. Here and there patches of mist hung over the vineyards, and already he could see the workers moving in the rows.

Presently he rounded a slight curve and came upon a group of small white structures huddled up against the side of a hill. In front of them stood two men smoking cigarettes, stamping their feet against the cold.

Mike pulled up and braked too quickly in front of them, skidding along for ten feet or so over the graveled road top. Then he opened the door and got out.

"Hey, 'Ligio."

One of the men walked over to him and they shook hands. With a minimum of words, they went back into the huts and took out two long, heavy boxes. These they put into the back of the Citröen, under the floor and carpet. In less than ten minutes, Mike was back on his way out of the foothills, heading down to Perpignan, and then to Barcelona.

This was not the best way to deliver guns and ammunition, but larger quantities were correspondingly dangerous. The fewer people involved, the less chance of being caught, and if it took longer than large-scale shipments by, say, fishing boats, it was nevertheless almost foolproof. Also, if any one person were caught at the border or on the road, only a few guns would be lost, as opposed to a shipload.

In spite of the speed of the operation, which was to be expected anyway with experienced men, this morning had not gone well. The guns were all right; he'd seen to that. But the whole feel of things had been wrong. They had not taken his money, as they always had before, but rather had given him an address in Perpignan proper where, they'd said, he should go and find Monsieur Leclerc, obviously a phony name, and pay him.

He was tired. He rolled down the side window, squinting into the sun, and lit himself a cigarette.

No, something was wrong.


At twenty-five, with quite a bit of hard living under his belt, Michael still was a strange mixture of awareness and naïveté. People constantly described him as close-lipped or mysterious, but to his own mind he was merely cautious. No one would have called him a warm person, yet a stubborn romantic streak would occasionally surface. And it was this romantic part of him, he knew, that really controlled his life.

When he'd first arrived in Spain, he'd been attracted by the idealistic fanaticism of some of his

Basque acquaintances. Being a bartender, he met more people under looser conditions than he would have under other circumstances.

They would sit in the bar until closing time, drinking wine and brandy, toasting themselves and the coming death of Franco, when there would be revolution and finally independence for the Basques. He couldn't help overhearing most of what they said, and they gradually came to trust him. Eventually, more to give himself something to do than out of any political convictions, he volunteered to help them deliver guns to their comrades.

He had his own reasons for this step, even though it was motivated by his sense of adventure. He wanted to become familiar with parts of the Mediterranean underworld, and he thought that this would be a good place to start. Why he wanted to do this remained a mystery even to those who thought they knew him. But he did his job quietly and well, and no one really cared about his motives. They remarked, however, on his fearlessness. He seemed to be pursuing death at every turn, never quite going so far as to attempt suicide obviously, but driving recklessly, almost tempting the police to pull him over and discover the carload of guns.

Once a Gypsy knife thrower had come into the bar, and Mike had volunteered to be the target.

The Gypsy outlined his body with knives thrown into the wall opposite the bar. He hadn't flinched, and afterward had tipped the Gypsy one thousand pesetas. His fearless acts were not done with the careless bravado of the drunk or the show-off, but rather with a calm concentration that made them all the more impressive, an effect he couldn't have cared less about.

Another time he had been up at the fort above Tossa during a winter rainstorm with some acquaintances, and had decided to walk the parapet, about a foot wide, which circled the fort and dropped sheerly to the water three hundred feet below. They tried to persuade him to stop, but he had mounted the wall and started walking.

"The wind is too strong," they said. "The walls might crumble with your weight. It's too slippery."

"It doesn't matter," he said. "Leave me alone."

Dying was one thing, but being caught and spending twenty years in jail quite another. He pulled over to the side of the road and got out of the car. There was a tree nearby and he went and sat under it.

No, he didn't like it.

It made no sense to him, and that, in turn, made him nervous. The sun was fully up now, and beginning to get hot. He took off his sweater and smoked two cigarettes. Then he got up and back into the car.

In Perpignan, he parked just inside the city limits and walked into the first café he came upon. He ordered a double espresso and a shot of brandy, then looked at the newspaper until he'd finished both, trying to think of nothing until he felt refreshed. The piece of paper they'd given him with the address on it was stuffed into his front pocket, and he took it out and flattened it on the table. He was to pay Leclerc at 10 Avenue de la Gare, #3 as soon as he could. He memorized the simple address, then set fire to the paper and watched it burn in the ashtray. Leaving change on the table, he left the café, but did not walk in the direction of the car.

It was still quite early in the morning, but many people were about. He arrived at the Avenue de la Gare almost immediately, as it ran along the outskirts of the town, then turned inward. Number 10 was almost all the way downtown, but he enjoyed the walk, and arrived within a quarter of an hour. A gendarme directed traffic at the intersection, but otherwise he saw no police.

Walking back to the car, a feeling of unease stayed with him. He got in and turned on the road away from town. Making mental notes where he was going, he took several back roads, avoiding the main highway, until he came to a restaurant he knew that sold pottery in the surrounding lot. Driving on for another two hundred yards, he finally stopped by a huge oak in a small grove. Here he unloaded the two boxes from the back, being careful to keep them covered by debris.

He cared not at all for the Separatist movement, though he'd been happy enough to be involved in it for the adventure of it all. Now, when it threatened him, he decided to get out of it. He wasn't even sure that there was any danger, but today, after nearly a year of it, it felt wrong, which meant that somebody had slipped up, and he wanted no part of it. He would return the money in Barcelona and tell them where the guns were hidden, and if someone else wanted to come and get them, and pay Monsieur Leclerc, whoever he was, then they were welcome to.

He was back in Tossa by two, and slept until nearly six. After going for a swim, he was at work behind the bar by seven, slightly more gregarious than usual. When Tony came in, he was happy to see him. They had a drink together and were talking about soccer when Sean came in and joined them. After a while, Sean left to meet his girlfriend, but not before he'd invited Mike and Tony up to dinner in a few days.

In bed that night, he couldn't sleep. Now that he'd quit working for the Basques, he wasn't doing anything but passing time, and he knew it. He thought of packing and moving on.

He went to the window. The moon reflected off the water, and he stared at it for a long time. It seemed so calm out there.

Suddenly he knew what was so wrong. He felt empty. Nothing was happening in his life. He started to tell himself that it didn't matter, but then he stopped. That was all he'd been saying now for six or seven years, ever since . . .

Again he stopped his thoughts. It wouldn't do to think about it. Maybe he'd had enough of things not mattering. Maybe he should pick something, at random, to care about. But he was too honest with himself to do that. It wouldn't work for him. Absently, he picked up his guitar and started playing, then as abruptly, put it down. He lay back down on his bed and closed his eyes.

Mustn't just latch onto anything, he thought. Something real has got to happen. Don't go fooling yourself just because you're alone.

But he was more than alone, depressed, and tired. He had decided to give up. It was all so meaningless, anyway.

If only something would happen, he thought.

Almost anything. He wouldn't be picky. He turned onto his side and pulled the pillow over his head. But he had to watch that he didn't fool himself. He'd had something he believed in before. Maybe he could resurrect that.

As long as he didn't fool himself. That was the main thing.

# Five

We all had time before dinner for another gin and tonic, and so by the time we sat down, any ominous overtones had disappeared. Sean came back in with several bottles of very chilled white wine and set them out within everyone's easy reach. The round, heavy wooden table easily sat the seven of us. I sat across from Lea, between Tony and Marianne.

It could be argued that the chicken in Spain is the best in the world, and Berta was a genius at preparing it. She would roast it on a spit in the kitchen, turning it in front of an oak log fire, letting the drippings fall into a pan, to which she'd then add sherry and garlic and a few secret spices. With that as the main course, and the fresh bread always smeared with olive oil, salt, and tomato, the lettuce and onion salad, and a large bowl of pinto beans, dinner was a great pleasure. By the time we'd all finished, we were euphoric. We had drunk nearly all the wine, and everyone was talking animatedly.

Outside, it was black dark. The living room, with only two small shaded lights, was dim, and we adjourned there for the brandy that Kyra was bringing around. It was Fundador brandy, which didn't taste good, and yet we drank it after nearly every meal. Everyone knew it wasn't good brandy, and still we all drank it. And there was good brandy to be had. It was a small mystery, and one that I never understood. Sean once had told me that Spain didn't make good brandy, but did make Spanish brandy, as though that had explained it. He'd been drunk at the time.

When Sean wasn't drunk, he was always ready to discuss anything: sports, art, politics, gossip. He was a great talker, and I had almost immediately found that I loved his company. When he was drunk, though, it was another story. All he would talk about on those occasions, which were not infrequent, was Kyra or drinking. I had earlier formed the impression that those two things were all he really cared about, and I had seen nothing to change that opinion. Still, I liked him immensely.

I sat with Tony and Marianne, and the talk turned to Franco, who had been in a coma for several days. Everyone was wondering what Juan Carlos would do about the Spanish Sahara crisis, and Tony started arguing with Marianne, who was surprisingly, I thought, very pro-Spanish.

"They shouldn't let the Moroccans take one step onto Spanish land," she said.

"It's not our land," said Tony. "It's African land."

"It's yours. You've had it a long time."

"But we took it."

"And so, then, it is yours, *n'est-ce pas?*"

Tony then reached down quickly, and took off her shoe.

"Is this shoe mine?"

"No. It's mine."

"But I have it."

"But it's mine. Give it to me."

"If I kept it for a week, would it be mine?"

I laughed.

"No. It's mine."

"A year?"

"No."

He laughed and gave it back to her. "You're a fool."

"But it's not the same."

"Ah, but it is."

"It's not," I put in.

"What would you do then?" Tony asked me.

"Shoot them," said Marianne.

I laughed again. "Perhaps a little extreme. They are, after all, unarmed. I don't know. I wouldn't shoot them, and neither would I give it to them. I can't agree with you that it's already theirs."

"Why not?"

"Just because you did already take it. If you can't hold on to your possessions, they are de facto no longer yours. That's tough, and it's not very moral sometimes, but it is the way things go."

Sean came by with the brandy. "Profound thoughts being uttered?"

"Hardly," I said. "Pour me some more."

He sat down cross-legged on the floor in front of us, and the talk drifted away into other things. Across the room, Lea and Mike sat on two easy chairs and talked quietly. Kyra evidently had gone to bed.

After some minutes, Tony and Sean got back to Franco, and Tony once again became intense.

"Do you have the bottle?" he asked.

"I do." My brother-in-law stood and crossed to the old chest where he kept the liquor. Going to his knees, he reached far back into the recess and pulled out an old bottle of champagne. He turned and showed it to Tony.

"Good."

"I think I've had enough," I said.

Tony had leaned back with his arm around Marianne. We were all relaxed now, very much friends again. "That's not for drinking now. Maybe tomorrow."

"What is it for?"

"When Franco dies."

A hush fell over the room. Lea, from where she sat, spoke. "Put the bottle away, Sean. It's dangerous."

I wondered how Sean could have become so patriotic in so short a time, but later that night Lea told me that Tony had given him the bottle to hold for him.

"Why would you want to celebrate?" I asked. "There'll be no change with Juan Carlos."

"It will change," said Mike, from over by Lea. "There is always change."

And again there was that strange and silent aura around him that we'd felt before dinner. Sean returned the bottle, and then Marianne asked him if he had a guitar. "Mike plays, and I want to dance."

Sean went and got the instrument and we waited, talking. Once again the atmosphere became light and convivial.

I'd noticed time after time in Spain that the attitude toward performing or dancing or simply singing aloud was completely different from back home. Here there was none of the self-consciousness with which people approach their own talent in the States. People dance here. I'd passed houses in the town where a lone couple would be dancing to the music on the radio. The discotheques thrived. Maybe I'd just been meeting a new type of person, but I didn't think so. I suspected that these same people wouldn't dance in another setting. Though not clumsy, I had never been a notorious rug-cutter, but many times here I'd danced until covered with sweat and then, exhausted, had fallen into an easy chair for an hour, or bed for the night. I knew it hadn't all been the impetus of the gin or sangría.

A few weeks before, I had been in town with Lea having coffee in a bar, and we had met a young woman who'd told us that she was a poet. After asking us if we'd like to hear some of her work, she took out a sheet of paper and read us some of her poems, with great feeling, oblivious to the other patrons. She had been, as far as I could tell, not at all drunk, and at the time it had seemed a completely natural thing to do. Sean had become the same way. He'd walk out from time to time with a few papers in his hands and, sitting down, would begin to read us what he'd written, sometimes for criticism, but mostly just to share it.

So when Sean returned, Mike didn't protest, but took the guitar and proceeded to tune it. Marianne stood up and took off her sandals. A few chords in a minor key, and then a flamenco flourish: Mike was no virtuoso, but he knew the rhythms. He played easily, his right hand moving constantly while his left alternated between two chords. Of course it was not real flamenco, but it was what one most often heard, and to our ears it passed for the real thing. Marianne whirled in the center of the room while we all clapped the time.

Another song in another key. Tony suddenly leaped up, yelling, "Ai, Ai, Ai," and began singing a Spanish song they'd obviously done before, his deep voice perfectly suited to the roughness of the melody. Marianne danced and danced, and before long we were all into it. Sean got a few more bottles of white wine, which we passed around without benefit of glasses. The songs changed. Whoever knew them sang along. Lea got up with castanets.

I found it hard to keep my eyes off Marianne. She was really lovely. Had my daughter lived, they would have been about the same age. Her white shift seemed to glow in the room, and as she turned, it spread out, letting the dim light through a bit, silhouetting her body.

From time to time, I looked across at Mike who, it turned out, played better than I had first thought. Seeing my gaze, he would smile. But somehow again he didn't seem to fit in. His was the music that had brought us together this way, and yet he himself was detached. It was not that he was unfriendly—he seemed, in fact, to be happy playing for us—but the music didn't seem to affect him. Perhaps that had been the resonance I hadn't gotten from him all night. He seemed devoid of joy. Somewhere back in his eyes there was something missing, so that even when he laughed, you felt an emptiness; you were suspended.

But these thoughts were fleeting. The women danced and we drank wine and more wine, singing happily and crazily. Happily and crazily.

Finally, Lea and Marianne collapsed in unison to the floor. Mike stopped playing and leaned back in his chair.

"Vino," he said, mock-weakly.

Lea stretched out to full length on the floor, and took the half-full bottle from between Tony's feet. Then, in a gesture that would have been lewd but for her grace, she twisted her body to face Mike and passed the bottle up to him, after first taking a drink herself. It seemed an immensely intimate act between them, but I'd had a lot of wine.

*"Gracias."* He took the bottle and emptied it in a long swallow. *"Muchas gracias."*

He put the bottle down. The moment was over, and Tony began making noises to leave.

But then Mike took the guitar again and started picking slowly, not flamenco, a melody. Marianne leaned back against my legs as I sat on the couch, and Lea stretched out full again, on her back, eyes closed. No one spoke.

It was a soft melody, indescribably melancholy. The notes seemed to hang in the room and make it dimmer. It captured for me in that moment what I'd been trying to define about Mike all night. It was his signature piece. It was clear he'd written it. It was elusive, subtle, unbearably sad, understated. He played it through twice, then stopped and put the guitar down.

"That's beautiful," said Marianne.

Lea was near tears. "Is that yours?" she asked softly.

He nodded.

"What do you call it?"

He looked uncomfortable, as if he didn't want to answer. "Must I call it something?" Not belligerent, defensive.

"I think so," Lea said.

"Yes," he said. "To myself, I call it 'A Prayer to No One.'"

"And is it to no one?" I asked.

"It certainly couldn't be to God," he answered with great bitterness. But then he smiled, as though he had caught himself at something. "Come on, it's time we leave."

We saw them to the door, Lea standing with her

arm on my shoulder. She pressed her head against me. "God, I'm tired. I'm going right up."

After she'd left, Sean and I stood at the door until long after the noise of Mike's car had faded away.

"I could use a real drink," he said finally.

"Me, too."

We walked back in and sat down in the melody-haunted living room.

It's hard to get American bourbon in Spain, but Sean had found an outlet and laid in a supply of Jack Daniel's. We drank it neat in large tumblers. He sat on the corner of the couch under the one light we'd left on. He had a creased, rugged face under hair that was light red flecked with grey, going bald at the top. He let it grow a bit overlong on the sides. His body was big—broad shoulders, powerful arms, a slight paunch. His legs had once been muscular, and still looked it. Wearing a plain white shirt and brown slacks, with his stumped wrist tucked into the pocket of a brown checked sports coat, he looked the picture of the successful, middle-aged artist. Though we were both pushing fifty, he looked older than me.

He put his drink down on the end table, pulled a cigarette from a pack, and lit it with a Zippo lighter. I was always amazed by the way he could perform these little acts with his handicap. He took a drag, then leaned back and closed his eyes.

"I want to apologize for this afternoon," he said wearily.

I waved it aside, but he went on.

"No. I don't know why . . ." He stopped. "I don't know what makes me act like that. Oh, I do know, really. If she would just cease with the taunting for a while. She teases all the time." He took a sip of his drink.

"Well . . ."

"Oh, I know. You're going to ask me why I take it, why I'm such a fool to let myself be bullied by her. And you should probably ask since you're a friend of mine. But you're lucky, you see, because of Lea, who's not a hard woman. I'm not saying she's not a good woman, or intelligent, but she's just not a challenger, a ball-breaker like that bitch is. So you're lucky, because it doesn't much matter after you're hooked if the woman's a bitch. And Lea isn't one. But believe me, if she was, you'd still be with her, taking it all . . ."

"You're getting led around by your dick, is all, Sean."

"We all get led around by our dicks."

"I think not."

"Oh, ho, we've got some learning to do here."

He was getting drunk, and I probably should

have said good night, but I was not the model of sobriety myself.

He went on. "You just better hope it doesn't come down to the crunch, 'cause you'll find I'm right, and you won't like it." He didn't say all this with any venom, but with the quiet slur of drunken certainty, and all at once he calmed down. "But shit," he continued, whispering, "shit, shit, shit."

"Is it all so bad? Because if it is, maybe you should kick her out."

"No. No, it's great. I don't just mean the sex, but she does something to me. I feel like I matter more or something. Why should it be her? I don't know. Why anything? She came along and I changed, felt things I hadn't let myself feel for years now. There are depths to her, but she hides from people, especially you. You intimidate the shit out of her."

"Me? I've always been . . . I've always gone out of my way to be nice to her. Except for times like today, I mean."

"And you don't think she feels that? That you're going out of your way?"

"I don't much care. What's the alternative? Be an out-and-out asshole to her?"

"But the condescension gets to her."

"Well, her attitude gets to me. So what? That's not the point either, you know. She makes you do things that aren't you, that make you hate yourself. How good can that be?"

"But that's not constant. It's not even normal. She's good to me, good for me."

I didn't buy that, but it wasn't the right time to disagree. "Well, Sean, I just wish it didn't have to hurt you."

"It's not all bad," he repeated.

"I'm convinced."

He sat silently. "Another drink?"

I shook my head no.

"Should I go away for a while, you think?" he asked.

"What for?"

"I don't know. Sort things out."

"I didn't think things were that bad."

"It's not that things are so horrible. It's that I feel I'm in over my head, like I'm not controlling anything between us. It's all her. Sometimes I feel that her goal is to get me to love her, so that she will have all the power. And the hell of it is, Doug, that I'm powerless against her. I don't want to fall so hard that I won't have any choices left if she betrays me . . ."

"What do you mean by that?"

"I mean that if I fall as hard as she wants me to, then I wouldn't be able to live without her, and I mean that literally."

"That's a bit extreme, don't you think?"

He stopped and thought a minute. "It's true as hell." He paused. "But you know, I couldn't live with her being unfaithful, either. I'd kill either her or myself."

"Oh, Jesus, Sean. Don't say that unless . . . ."

"Unless I mean it? OK. Let's just say I won't retract it." Suddenly he gave a halfhearted little laugh, and looking down, shook his head. "What's got into me?"

He got up and poured himself another shot. "I think that . . . that thing with the chicken today really got to me. Maybe I am being made a fool of. She really is so young . . . ."

"Maybe that's why you should give her more time."

"You think I should?"

He didn't want the truth, and I didn't give it to him. "Sure, talk to her. Tell her you feel like you've got to prove yourself constantly and it's getting you down. If she's understanding, she'll let up for a while."

"I don't want to lose her."

I wanted to ask him why, but instead stood up and yawned. "Bedtime."

"OK. See you in the morning."

I left him sitting there under the lamp. Upstairs, I stood at the window for a moment and looked outside across the courtyard. The quarter moon had come up, relieving the absolute darkness. As I undressed, a melody seemed to hang in the air, but by the time I had curled my body next to my wife's in bed, it had vanished.

# Six

You are sitting on the wall that borders the beach in Tossa, sipping a beer and enjoying the hot sun overhead, and you can hardly help noticing the two women walking together out from one of the shops and on down to the beach. You know they aren't European, not so much from their dress as from the way they walk with each other. They don't link their arms as they talk, but step lightly, independently, oblivious to the crowds shopping and going to the beach. They don't notice you as they cross the street, even as they pass within a yard of you, sitting as you are by the entrance to the beach through the wall. Yes, even as they get closer, they are a stunning pair, more beautiful than they'd first appeared. There is no haughtiness about them, only the supreme self-confidence shared by attractive women. They talk casually, and you only hear a few words as they pass, but enough to tell you that they are Americans.

The thinner one is wearing a tangerine-colored shift that goes well with her complexion. She appears to be older than the other one, though not much. Look closer, though, and there are small wrinkles around her eyes. She might, in fact, be almost forty. Her skin is smooth and strangely light. Perhaps she hasn't been long in Spain. Her hair, reaching to her shoulders, is almost perfectly straight, and a shining deep brown. Her legs are her best feature—very long and not too thin. The shift is tantalizingly short, and shows them off well. She is like a boy on top, but there is something distinctly sensual about her. Her whole demeanor is amused and, somehow, challenging, though not in a harsh way. When the other woman talks, she listens carefully, leaning forward toward her. She's vulnerable, you think, though maybe it's only the contrast.

The other one is a beauty. Possibly she is much younger than her friend. She wears white pants and a halter top that make her seem to glow in the bright sunlight. Her skin is dark, dark tan as though she's spent the summer sunning herself, and her hair has started to bleach itself from the exposure. She laughs often, loudly. You can easily hear her after they've gone some ways down the beach, but the laugh is not shrill. On the contrary, it is inviting. Her nose is slightly too big but it gives her face the character it needs to keep it from being merely pretty. Her mouth is full, her eyes a kind of bright sultry—the youth has not quite worn off them. In a few years, her eyes will positively smoulder, but now they are almost schoolgirlish. Her body is large and slowly graceful, but her waist is fine. Nowhere has she begun to go to flab. Her pants sit low on her hips, and her exposed midriff is, well, perfect. You think you've never seen more attractive breasts. She turns around abruptly to see something and catches you staring after her, and winks, or do you imagine it? You finish your beer and get up to walk to the shade of the narrow streets between the glaring white buildings, and try to find a place to eat lunch.

Lea pulled the shift over her head, and placed it on the sand so that she could lie on it.

"Remind me not to get too much sun."

When they had arranged themselves, Kyra asked, "You were saying?"

"Oh, about Sean. I know now it's ridiculous to talk about him. In a lot of ways I don't know him at all anymore. Certainly you know him better, but it's funny. Though he's so different from the brother I've known all my life, in many ways he reminds me of how he was when I was a little girl.

"There's this part of him now that he's either purposely kept hidden all these years or has truly repressed, and now it comes out. I really don't quite know how to handle it, or rather my reaction to it. He's—I don't know—childlike almost, but that's not really what I want to say either. He's more like he was when he was younger.

"He was always the acknowledged leader in the family. Not so much because he tried to be, or even wanted to be, but he just always had so much enthusiasm. He was always planning, planning, planning, and getting things done. Even if they weren't anything special if you looked at them objectively, he made them special for us. He always got so excited about things, and made it contagious. I remember he used to put on these neighborhood circuses, which were really just a bunch of kids walking a two-by-four stretched between two packing crates, or arranging five of us into a pyramid when none of us thought we could do it. But it's funny. That's the circus I remember. It was much more real to us than any real circus.

"The amazing thing to me now is that we never felt bulldozed. It always seemed the most natural thing in the world to do whatever Sean had planned, not only to us in the family, but to all the kids near our age. Our age? When I think of it, all of Sean's friends were young teenagers when I became aware of all this, and still I felt somehow included, and my friends did, too. There was never any feeling that we were less because we were younger, but we just fit naturally into whatever plan we were carrying out. I suppose a lot of it was the stuff that none of the older kids wanted to do, but it was great for us because we were involved.

"God, I remember it so clearly now, thinking back on it. I don't think I've thought of those times at all in twenty years.

"There were probably drawbacks I'm forgetting, but I was only a small kid who was thrilled that I was noticed at all. You know, I don't think Sean was ever even aware that he might have been using people. It was just that everything was so much fun and of course his way was the best. He was always so surprised if somebody got mad at him or didn't like him. He was always being called conceited by one kid or another, but I guess anyone with that strong a personality makes enemies. And he'd always react by backpedaling to get liked by whoever it was again. But pretty soon he'd get back to his old self. He didn't feel comfortable when he wasn't flamboyant. It was his natural style.

"But still, he was sensitive. Oh, I mean obviously he tended to be carefree—to act carefree, anyway. That's the way we all were brought up. Why bother to make a big deal out of your problems? Problems pass. At least that's what we were taught. He used to tell me that if you act happy, you'll be happy, and it worked. I know, I know, bad psychology, denying your real self and all that, but it wasn't so much that he denied it as refused to show it indiscriminately. He just thought it was bad form for him, personally. That wasn't how the strong person acted, and that was always the main thing he identified with—strength. He didn't want anyone pitying him. Anything he got involved in he could get himself out of.

"They once played a game where they stuffed some jeans and a shirt with newspaper and waited behind a hedge for a car to drive by. Then they threw the dummy out in front of the car and Sean ran out, yelling 'My brother. You killed my brother.' Stupid game. But they were just kids. Well, turns out one of the cars is driven by a man whose son had just been run over. I never before saw Sean take anything so badly. At home he brooded for a month. Of course then he got back to being his old self. But that was the first time I'd seen him obviously different from his public self. I guess I really became interested in him then, and he noticed. We became confidants, more or less. At least he'd come and talk to me. I didn't understand most of what he'd talk about—I was only six or seven then—but he'd come in to say good night and sit and talk until I'd go to sleep. I think that was why he liked talking to me. I really cared but I'd always wind up going to sleep. He called that my honesty.

"Once he came in and started talking about what he was going to do when he grew up, and about going to war soon and the next thing I knew I woke up and he'd gone to bed. It was horrible for me. I felt so guilty, as though I'd really let him down."

She fell silent and closed her eyes, remembering. The night had been freezing cold. She hadn't been able to get back to sleep so she'd gotten up and sat on the side of her bed. She'd been in a frenzy to tell Sean that it was all right, that she hadn't meant to fall asleep, and that she really did care. Without knowing why, she'd taken off her pajamas and run down the hall to his room. She watched him sleep for a few minutes, then shook him and asked if she could get in bed with him and hug him. She said she was cold. He pulled back the blankets and let her in, and she rolled on top of him, stretching her arms around his chest. She remembered how good it had felt, with his heart beating so loudly against her ear. She apologized for having fallen asleep, and then, after just a moment, dozed again. Then he awakened her and told her she had to go back to her bed. He had an erection that she could feel with her legs, and she hugged him tighter.

"I don't want to go," she kept saying. "Why can't I stay here?"

He laughed. "You'll know all about it soon enough." And he got up and carried her back to her bed.

"You'd better turn over now. This sun can be murder." Kyra pulled her out of her reverie.

She turned onto her stomach and smoothed out the shift beneath her on the hot sand.

They lay in silence then for a while. A man selling frozen chocolates walked by them, squawking like a gull. He stopped near them and looked over.

"Ai, carumba! Ai lookee, lookee, chongo, chongo! Ai likkee-likkee." The little man ran around like a hairless monkey, screaming and dancing. "Ai chongo, hey chongo!" He came over to them, delighting the other people on the beach, and shoved a chocolate ice cream into Kyra's face. He put on an insane grin and looked directly at her breasts.

"Chongo, chongo?" he asked.

Both women laughed and waved him off, but he went on, cupping his hands under his own breasts. "Oooh la la. No chongo. Mucho chi chis. Eeee. Eeee."

His laughter echoed down the beach. Then someone called for him and he ran off, screeching.

"Could he be more obnoxious?" Lea asked.

"I never think so, but then he does occasionally outdo himself."

Kyra got up and ran lightly down to the water. Lea watched her dive in and swim out to the nearest buoy, about a hundred yards from the shore.

When she came back, she told Lea to turn over. "Do you want me to put on some lotion?"

They started talking about Sean again as Kyra's strong hands rubbed the oil into Lea's back. Kyra wanted to know when he had changed.

Lea sighed. "When he came back from the war, he was completely different. Where before he used to sit with me and talk about his future, now he seemed to not care about it, or about anything. I remember him just sitting around the house in the afternoons after he got back, drinking beer and staring out of the front window. Finally he got a job, but just an assembly line job, and moved out of the house. After that, I rarely saw him, and when I did, it was almost too much for me.

"Once I went to his apartment and was supposed to stay for a week, but the place was a mess. Just a bed and a couch and newspapers all over the floor. Coffee cups lying all around and overflowing ashtrays. I only stayed one day. After that, we were strangers for a few years, but then when I moved to California, we began writing occasionally, and gradually, at least in his letters, he started to sound like his old self.

"Oh, he always had that same bluff exterior. You would never have thought, just to talk to him, that there was anything wrong. Even people who thought they knew him were pretty well fooled. It wasn't so strange that people coming back from the war were hardened. But for a good five years, I don't think he cared at all about anything.

"Even when his letters started saying something, they always stopped just before I felt he'd said what he wanted. And he stayed at that same job for more than twenty-five years. I think he'd probably be there still if it hadn't been for the accident. It's not that the job was so bad, but I just felt it wasn't right for him. He had so much more to offer. At least now with this writing, he's trying to get back in touch with himself. It's almost as though he's lived these past thirty years trying to get back to where he was when he lived at home."

She stopped talking. The sun beat into her back.

Later, they went to Kyra's favorite café, where Sean had come and asked her to live with him.

They ordered some filter coffee and sat inside, away from the sun.

"And you never knew what happened in the war that brought about the change?" Kyra asked.

Lea shook her head. "Not specifically, but it was a betrayal of some kind. I'm pretty sure of that. And it had made him just stop trusting people. He even once wrote that the only reason he told me anything in his letters was because I was far enough away that I couldn't do him any damage. That one hurt, let me tell you."

She thought back to the letter. "Even my oldest drinking buddies are just people to pass the time. Any one of them would screw me if they had to. No, maybe that's too harsh. Let's just say if somebody had to get screwed, it wouldn't be them. And how can you trust somebody when you know they feel that way? I think sometimes I'm really a fool and have always been one. I used to believe that if somebody was your friend, then that was that. Look on it as a defense alliance if you will. There was a certain perimeter inside which you were safe. But then . . . well, let's just say I found that that wasn't true."

The letter had gone on. "The real world runs on the 'Asshole Laws' which are three in number, to wit: 1) If things get tough for me, things get tough for you. 2) I'd rather be an asshole than suffer. 3) If somebody has to lose, let it be you.

"*Voilà!* On this cheery note, I sign off, remaining yours in unfaith, etc."

She winced even now as she thought of it.

"What's wrong?"

She tossed her head to shake off the thoughts. "Oh, just thinking back."

Kyra sipped at her coffee. "You know, though, he doesn't seem unhappy to me now. I mean, I know he's moody sometimes, but I don't sense that he's fundamentally depressed. He's so outfront that I don't see how anything could seethe inside him. He just lets go when he's bothered, don't you think?"

"He's always been good at seeming carefree."

"But I've seen him without his guard up."

"Are you sure?"

"Well, reasonably."

"Then I'm glad. But I wouldn't be surprised if he were still watching out. Especially with you. You're his first serious woman, you know."

"He's told me that, but I'm not sure I believe it."

"It's true. Though I suppose he's not exactly been alone over the years. But you watch, and see if he ever is really vulnerable. Maybe people shouldn't be. I don't know. I don't think I am. But Sean has to be, you see. He believes in it. And still he doesn't let himself go. Maybe he's afraid that he couldn't handle another betrayal. We've all heard him say he couldn't—that he'd kill himself, even."

"He wouldn't do that."

"Then why does he say it all the time?"

"He doesn't."

"He says it enough to worry me."

Kyra ran her hand through her hair and rested her chin on her hand.

"Lea, I'm not going to betray him."

"But does he know that?"

"I'm sure he does."

"Then why all the testing and teasing?"

"That's just the way we are. It's not that heavy a thing."

"I think maybe you're wrong."

"Is that you or Doug talking? Sure, we keep on each other's backs, but in a way it's how we show we care. I really think he needs to know, for example, that I find other men attractive, so that the fact that I'm with him means that much more. And what am I supposed to do about his hand? Go around feeling sorry for him? He really can do almost anything anyone else can. And it has freed him, finally. Now maybe it's unfortunate that he couldn't have had it both ways, but I think—no, I'm sure—that he prefers his life now to the one he lived five or fifteen years ago. If we fight, it's because we're the kind of people who fight rather than let things build up." Her eyes softened as she looked across at Lea, her hands curled around her coffee cup. "I am happy with him. Really happy. I'd never do anything to hurt him, especially just by teasing him. This jealousy thing isn't so much the flirting I do, I'm sure. I don't want anyone else. I wouldn't be with anyone else. We're friends. He trusts me. I told him I wouldn't be with any other men, and he believes me."

"Do you mean he wants to believe you?"

"No, I think he does. I really am aware of how serious all this is to him. Which isn't to say it isn't also for me. I don't know if he'd kill himself, but I know that my faithfulness is a symbol to him, and I see its importance. I don't know what he'd do if I betrayed him, or he me. I'm not sure either of us could stand it."

What a coincidence that you should happen upon the same women when you come in for your afternoon cup of coffee. They sit well back in a darkened corner, but immediately you notice them. There is a table free near them and you can't help yourself. You take it, if only to hear them speak.

It's nothing very important, you gather, though

they seem to be engrossed in it. Some talk about one of their boyfriends. Women like them probably have hundreds of men.

The coffee here is usually excellent, and they also serve a pear pie with whipped cream that has become a favorite. Too bad you've got only a few more days of vacation. But then, you suppose, if you lived here, it would finally get to you. No, it will be good getting back to work.

Again you look at the women. They probably spend all their days as they've spent this one. They sunbathe, eat, talk of their little society-oriented world. It must get terribly boring. They'd probably grab at anything for a little excitement.

And yet there's something about the way they talk. There's an intensity that seems to remove them slightly from the strictly mundane. Or is it that you just like to think that women who are so attractive ought to have something to say?

Oh well, the coffee has cooled and you take a sip.

They get up to leave. The older one brushes you slightly and excuses herself. Then you hear her say, "I don't really think he'd do anything that extreme."

What is wrong with the coffee? It tastes as if someone put salt in it.

# Seven

Lea had already left the bed. I opened my eyes and looked out at the blue sky through the window. Normally there was a breeze in the morning, wafting over our bodies as we lay in bed, cooling the room, waking us gently. But today the room was an oven. I got up and walked to the bathroom, my head throbbing. For once the cold shower was welcome.

No sooner had I begun than I heard screaming from below. Without even shutting the water off, I ran toward the noise, grabbing a towel to put around me on the way.

Downstairs, Berta was standing in the middle of the dining room, fanning the air with a broom, screaming in short, hysterical gasps.

I saw something dart through the air, then toward the living room, and thought it must be a

bat. Berta followed with her broom, still shriek-
ing. I went in and took the broom from her. She
kept gesturing for me to hurry and drive the thing
out. Looking up, I spotted it in the corner, more
scared, if possible, than Berta. It wasn't a bat, but a
lone and terrified sparrow beating its wings in vain
against the stucco. It took only a moment to direct
it to the door and out to its freedom.

Berta stood in the doorway to make sure it had
flown away. I turned around to her. "It was only a
sparrow." I handed her back her broom.

She sat in one of the chairs, and looked at me,
still shaking.

"It is from God. A message."

"What is?"

"A bird in the house. You don't know? It means
a death in the family."

I sat down across from her. "That's nonsense."

She crossed herself. "No. *Es verdad.*"

Then she finally noticed my lack of attire, and
looked down.

"You're not dressed."

"I heard you scream."

She got up with the broom. "Please," she said,
and turned back to the kitchen.

I was tempted to tease her about her long black
outfit on such a hot day, but thought better of it,
and went back up to resume my shower. On the

way upstairs, I chuckled. So she was, after all, a woman, in spite of herself. I wondered if it made her nervous.

The bird had certainly upset her, but somehow, in Spain, superstition didn't seem so ludicrous as elsewhere. It was almost believable.

But these thoughts disappeared under the cold shower. In minutes I was back downstairs at the table, drinking *café con leche* with a bit of roll and butter. I asked Berta to come and sit with me.

"Are you feeling better?"

She nodded. "It is not a good omen, still."

"Probably just wanted to get out of the heat. Where is everyone today, by the way?"

"Señor Sean is not out of bed yet. The two señoras have gone to town together. Señora Lea said for me to tell you she would be back in the afternoon."

"Did she say where in town she was going?"

She shook her head no.

I thought that strange, but not exceptionally so, and let it pass while I resumed my breakfast.

Berta poured herself a cup of coffee and sipped at it, looking distracted. "Do you want to go into Tossa today?" she asked. "Because a taxi will be up soon. I am going in for shopping."

"Thank you," I said. "I'd like to."

\*      \*      \*

We bumped and swayed in the usual manner all the way down to Tossa. Berta and I sat in the backseat and talked, trying to ignore the ride as we weaved from side to side.

I was feeling much better, though still slightly hungover, and with the windows down, the heat wasn't so bad. I looked over at Berta and was surprised again to find her so handsome. She had a fine face, neither young nor old. I wondered if, before Kyra, she and Sean hadn't . . .

"Were you married, Berta?" I asked abruptly.

"*Sí.*"

"What happened?" I didn't mean to press, but suddenly I badly wanted to know.

She looked down at the floor. "He went away."

"Long ago?"

"Eighteen years."

The driver swerved, throwing her against me, but she stared hard, straight ahead at the road, and I was content to be silent as we wound our way past the cork trees and vineyards, back down to Tossa.

I got out at the main crossroads near the back of town, and Berta went on to the market to do her shopping. I decided to walk through the town to the *ramblas*. It was near noon and the heat was stifling, but I knew down by the beach it would be cooler. Also, I'd be more likely to run into Lea down there. I didn't normally come in to Tossa without a plan, but it was a good town to browse in and, despite the heat, I enjoyed winding through the streets, with their empty *graffa* bottles, their grand summer *pensións,* now for the most part closed up until the next spring, their stray dogs, and their faint but ever-present smell of urine and decaying garbage.

The season was over, and Tossa was once again a town of Spaniards. Prices had dropped markedly even since we'd arrived, and the shops were closing for the winter one by one. Down at the *ramblas,* though, most of the bars and discos were still open, and it was here that I expected to find Lea. I knew that Tony often hung out at a bar called the Tiki, where Mike tended bar. It was a good place, with a vined terrace fronting the sea. By the time I arrived, drenched with sweat, a light breeze had come up, rustling the vines overhead.

There were customers scattered about, but no sign of anyone I knew, so I sat down, pulled a mystery from my pocket, and made myself comfortable.

A white-jacketed waiter came up and asked me if I'd like coffee. I told him I'd prefer a beer. During the last months of the season, Tossa invariably runs out of fresh drinking water, and they let sea water into the city water supply, so that all showers, drinking water, and, hence, coffee, is slightly, or sometimes very, saline. It was an acquired taste that I had decided to do without.

The beer came, and as I drank it my head cleared.

It was pleasant, sitting there under the vines with the light breeze blowing across me. The beer was good. But I found myself falling victim to what Lea and I had spoken about the day before—all this free time. It bred thoughts which, while not exactly useless, were certainly impractical. Daydreams came and went apace. Chance feelings and vague uncertainties could ferment and grow into full-blown emotions. Else why had Berta so affected me this morning? Why had Mike's song?

Where the hell was Lea, anyway?

Where had I heard that phrase which now seemed so apt—burned out under the magnifying glass of introspection? Ha!

On the beach, a girl was being thrown into the water, and her cries carried back to me like a memory. My thoughts turned back to my earlier marriage, and to my child, Becky. I'd met, wooed, and won Nancy in a whirlwind six weeks. After the wedding, we settled into a quiet neighborhood on Long Island. I'd been making a good living doing small articles that I then thought important. She'd become pregnant immediately, and we lived happily, domestically.

I remember especially the summers, when we'd drive out to fish in the Sound, or go up to Connecticut. But there'd been only two of those summers. Becky had gotten polio in one of God's little jokes and had died a few months before the vaccine had been discovered. After that, Nancy, too, had begun to fail—stopped eating, laughing, caring, and, finally, living.

I finished the beer and got up. They were loading the one boat for Lloret de Mar, and I decided to take it. These thoughts were doing me no good.

There was a wooden walkway to within about fifty yards of the boat and, after that, one had to trudge through the gravelly sand. The small blue and white boat played tourist Spanish music—I will never forget "Y Viva L'España"—through a loudspeaker in front. In season, a small fleet of three or four of these craft traveled every hour or so to Lloret and back, but now there was only one. It pulled up right onto the beach and lowered a gangplank. It was a steep and slippery climb, and nearly every loading saw a sprained ankle or skinned knee, from which the crew members appeared to take great joy.

I managed the boarding, though, walked to an empty spot on the bench that lined the sides, and took off my shoes to pour out the sand that had filled them. There was an air of slapstick about the whole boat trip to Lloret, and I enjoyed it. My

spirits lifted and, as we began the ride, I sat hyp-
notized as I always was by the unfathomable blue
of the sky and water. Looking back to the land
and its bleached white buildings was nearly blinding. Then there was that pleasurable but incongru-
ous feeling of relief that I always got when pulling
away from anything.

The boat wasn't crowded, and we'd barely
cleared the small bay before I spotted Marianne on
the bow. She sat cross-legged in shorts and a halter top, tan and alluring. Ah, the irony, I thought,
smiling. Knowing I'd begin to brood again if I
stared at her, I got up.

"Marianne."

She asked me to sit with her, and I did. "I wanted
to tell you that I had a wonderful time last night,
politics or no."

"So did I," I said, "but we're only guests of
Sean's ourselves."

"I know. But I wanted to tell you." She smiled.
"What are you reading?"

"Just a mystery."

"You like them?"

I shrugged. "Some."

"Passes the time?"

"Why do you say that?" I snapped at her, surprised at myself.

She didn't seem taken aback. "I don't know.

There is that feel about you." The sea was dead calm. Some bathers waved to us from the rocks. She waved back, laughing. "It's beautiful today, *n'est-ce pas?* I thought the summer was over."

"It is nice out here."

We lapsed into silence for a moment.

"I wanted to tell you," she began, "that I'm not so bloodthirsty as I sounded last night. It's just that I like to argue and playact a bit. Tony is nice, but I'd scare him if I didn't act just a little dumb sometimes. You see, my English isn't really so bad either. But these Spanish boys . . . well, he is attractive, and not nearly so bad as most of them. You see? Yes, you do."

She laughed infectiously.

"I see." I laughed, too. "What did you mean, just now, about me passing time, that I had that feel about me?"

"Oh, it's nothing you say," she said, touching my arm. "Don't worry—you're not giving yourself away."

"Giving what away?"

"Now don't pretend. No one as controlled as you are isn't concerned about letting people see him. I mean, the real him. But you seem—I don't know—maybe too much the observer, as if you're just trying to make it until you see something that

will free you, but which you're not sure is there."
She stared toward the shore.

"You're a wise little girl," I said.

"Don't tell Tony." Her face brightened. "Here. Get out your book and let me put my head on your shoulder and close my eyes."

We finished the short trip to Lloret without talking. I pretended to read, but was always conscious of the weight of her head against my arm and the young, clean, intoxicating scent of almonds coming off her.

Strangely, there was no sexual undertone. I felt we were old friends, as though long ago we'd been lovers and it hadn't worked out.

The boat landed roughly, and we got up.

"Read much?" she said, smiling.

"Can't fool you, can I?"

We got off the boat and started trudging over the hundred yards of Lloret's beach.

"Why'd you come here today?" I asked.

"Meeting Tony for lunch. Want to join us?"

"I don't know."

"Oh, you do. What did you come here for?"

"No reason, really."

"Then join us."

I laughed. "OK."

"OK."

"By the way, Mike wouldn't be eating with you, would he?"

She stopped and looked at me. "No. Why do you ask?"

"Just curious," I said.

She saw Tony on the *ramblas* and waved. "Come on," she said. "Let's run."

We ate at the Calamic Tavern, which was really not a tavern at all. Owned by a Frenchman with a Spanish wife, it served the best steaks on the Costa Brava. Sitting outside and drinking the ridiculously cheap *tinto,* we spent a while talking among ourselves and to all and sundry who passed on the narrow street. Tony seemed to know everyone—Pedro, who owned the English bar down the street and who was being divorced by his wife for, in Tony's words, "countless adulteries"; Andrés, his Dutch bartender, famed for being the friendliest man in town and an incurable drunk; Lisa, who owned the disco around the corner, and who normally spent the winters coming down off the pills she'd consumed during the summer, though this winter she didn't appear to be bothering; another Tony, the cook across the street, trying to decide, according to our Tony, whether or not to go underground rather than serve in the military.

Ramon, more or less officially the town ombudsman, sat down and joined us along with Trish and Ilse, two prostitutes. When they'd all gone, I asked Tony if Ramon knew all that went on, all about the dope and insanity.

He patted my hand. "He knows, and he doesn't know. It's a resort town here. If he likes you, he doesn't know. If not, he knows everything. I've personally seen him smoke marijuana, for instance, but I wouldn't suggest joining him." He stopped to drink his wine. "But if you think this is a group with stories, you should be here in the summer. Then it's a crazy place, which is why I leave—go to Barcelona.

"You know Pedro we just met? His wife came into his place in August and threw their baby through the big picture window, I swear to Almighty God. Why it wasn't killed I'll never know. And the next day they walked hand in hand along the *ramblas*.

"And there was an English singer here during the summer, working at the Hof van Holland, across town. He was to be paid at the end of the summer, and the owners decided not to pay him. No reason. He nearly killed them both with a wine bottle. He's in jail now, and will be for a long time."

"But why didn't they pay him?"

"As I said, no reason. Happens all the time. He

didn't have a legitimate work permit, and he had no rights anyway."

"Even to his pay?"

He smiled. "He's lucky he wasn't working for Spaniards. If he'd beat up two Spaniards the way he did, he wouldn't be in jail now. He'd be dead."

Marianne spoke up. "Then why would anybody want to come here in the summers?"

"It's free, fast, and cheap. Lots of girls. And the English and Germans and Dutch get their vacations and want to party all the time. I suppose it would even be nice for a few days. It's mostly the people who live here, the summer people, who have the stories. They come for the money, and do their year's work in five months. And so it's all they think about."

"And so the normal rules don't apply?"

"What's normal? Everyone here knows the rules, and the main rule is that there are no rules, except don't cross the *guardia*."

At the bar inside, the wine was sold from casks, by the bottle. Tony went back to refill our bottle and stopped to watch the television. When he came back out with the wine and a chess set, he looked at us and smiled. "Franco worsens," he said.

He and Marianne began to play, and all the while he kept up a patter with the passersby. After a short while, I decided to get up and take a walk. I'd had a lot of wine, and I thought a walk might freshen me up. I asked Tony if he'd be driving back to Tossa and, if so, if he'd drop me off at Sean's. That settled, I told them I'd be back in an hour, and started off.

The heat was still oppressive, especially in the narrow streets between the white buildings, shut off from access to the sea. I stopped in at a bar and had a beer, then another.

I wandered out again. In a public square there was a fountain and I dipped my hands in to splash water in my face.

"Ai."

I looked up to see a member of the *guardia* coming toward me shaking his head no. Saluting, I turned and left, finally coming out by the beach. I walked down the white wooden steps and lay down on the sand.

When I woke up, it was much later. The sun was still up, but it just cleared the tops of the buildings along the *ramblas.* I sat up with a start, shook my aching head several times to clear it, then stood and walked back to the Calamic.

They were still there, talking over the chess board.

"Have a nice walk?" asked Marianne.

"I fell asleep on the beach."

They laughed and stood up. "Better get you home."

Half an hour later they had dropped me off at the end of the rutted road that led to Sean's house. The sun had just about set. When I got to the house, Lea met me at the door.

"Where have you been? You look beat."

"My dear, I am beat. I think I'll skip dinner. Where were you today?"

"Just in town."

"I wish you'd have told me."

"I got up so early. You were asleep. You're not mad, are you?"

"No."

I crossed the room. "Tell Sean I'm sorry I'm missing dinner, but I need a nap."

"Do you want me to come up with you?"

"No. I'm sorry. I drank too much."

As it turned out, Lea and Kyra ate alone. Sean was in bed in his room, nursing an earache.

The next day, Lea and I went out for a walk. Sean stayed in bed throughout the morning, and Kyra sat knitting in the living room. Her presence annoyed me. She said that Sean's ear was very bad, and she'd poured oil into it and let him try to sleep. He hadn't slept at all the last night.

Outside, we held hands and picked our way through the trees, up toward the vineyards that bordered the road. The heat had let up. We got to a low rock wall and Lea sat on it. She kicked at the red dirt.

"Are you upset with me?" she said.

"Why would I be?"

"Yesterday."

"Did I act so much like it?"

She nodded.

"Well, I drink too much. It seems that all there is to do here sometimes is drink. Get up, drink, walk someplace, drink again, and think about the passing of time."

"Are you so bored, really?"

I shrugged. "I love you, you know."

She was relaxed, leaning back enjoying the sun. Her nipples stood out against her white shirt. I reached out and rubbed her belly, and kissed her. She moved forward on the wall and I raised her skirt up above her waist. We kissed again for a long time. She reached for me, unbuckled my pants, and wrapped her arms around my neck. I entered her standing, picked her up and held her while her legs and hips enveloped me. When we finished, I fell back to the warm ground. She cleaned us off with her shirttail, tucked me back in, and lay down next to me.

"Drinking and thinking isn't all you do here," she said.

Fifteen or twenty minutes passed. The sun beat down on us.

"I ran into Mike in town yesterday," she said. "That boy fascinates me."

"Um."

"He had a coffee with Kyra and me, and again I felt that same something. I don't know what it is—a sadness, I suppose. Kyra and I talked about him on the way home. She said he'd been like that since he'd arrived here, evidently. A real loner. Scares people off, and doesn't much care."

"He seemed nice enough to me."

"Oh, superficially he's fine. But there's something, after you get to know him . . ."

"How long did you talk to him?"

"Just a short while. This is all according to Kyra. And you know what else she said?"

"You want me to guess?"

She laughed. "No. I'm sorry. But evidently Mike smuggles guns for the Basques, or used to, which isn't so amazing in itself, except that even to the Basques, he said he didn't care about the movement. Just liked the danger, he said."

"Did you ask him about it?"

"No. It's all what Kyra says."

"You realize that probably she's full of shit."

"Maybe. I don't think so, though."

"Why not?"

"Well, she says she found out from Tony, and he does have connections with the underground."

"Well, anything's possible, but I'd have reservations about anything I heard from Kyra."

"I don't know. I'm changing how I feel about her. After talking more with her, I'm starting to see that she's not so shallow. She's certainly not the tramp you make her out to be. You two just have bad chemistry, is all. I think, for example, that she really loves Sean."

"Ha."

"No. I mean it. She as much as told me that she uses his jealousy to keep him loving her at fever pitch."

"Then she's sick," I said. "The jealousy itself is bad enough, but using it for that is the worst."

There was a light breeze and Lea sat up. She reached for a cluster of dried grapes that had been left on one of the vines, and began eating them. She motioned toward the horizon. "Clouds."

I looked. It would be a while before it rained.

Lea chewed on a few more grape-raisins that, to me, tasted bitter and dirty. She spit the seeds into her hand. The smell of our lovemaking rose off her, sitting as she was. I closed my eyes.

"I don't think, Douglas, that you really understand her at all."

I nodded. "Probably not, but I don't like her enough to try to."

"Why not?" she asked sharply. "Does she frighten you?"

"What nonsense is that?"

"It's not. So what if she uses jealousy to keep her and Sean's love immediate? She wants to feel things. Not so much have a status quo she can always control, but live right out on the edge of things."

"She's breaking Sean's heart," I said.

"She doesn't see it that way. She says that it keeps him going, keeps him excited and stops both of them from stagnating. And little things seem to sustain them, you've got to admit. They don't seem bored, or as weighed down by time as you and I do."

"That's right," I said. "Bring it back to that. It always seems, lately, to come back to that theme, that I'm bored and—"

"You just said it yourself."

"That was before making love just now."

"Well, I hate to think that we do it out of boredom."

And that one hit so close we lapsed into silence.

She leaned down again and put her head on my chest. The cloud came nearer and covered up the sun.

Finally, I spoke quietly. "I just don't believe in all this frantic passion anymore, hon. We both know it's not the small events that wind up making any difference, but the way you live, the things you really care about every day."

"But don't you think," she said softly, "that all your drinking and complaining about time to reflect are your own way of telling yourself that those things like your writing, or our house back home, or any of what you call the little things, the day-to-day things, really don't mean so much? That we're both of us out of touch with ourselves and don't much believe in anything anymore? You say our love, but even that sometimes is like an old shoe." She smiled then, and ran her hand over my brow. "Just sometimes, but you know what I mean. Serviceable and comfortable, but that's all. You know? Not completely alive."

"Do you really feel that?"

"Sometimes I do, Douglas. I really do."

I put my arms around her and hugged her to me. She was right, though I couldn't admit it then. Nothing much did mean anything to me, and all the trappings of discourse and intercourse really were only that. In truth, nothing had touched me in years, and while I'd been busy working, I'd pretended so hard not to notice that I hadn't noticed. It became my style to be cool and aloof, and I was.

I thought back to Sean and Kyra and the episode

of him killing the chicken. Why had it incensed me so? It was cruel and bloody, no doubt, but also vital in a way I hadn't been since—since I can't remember, maybe ever. It could be that Kyra's taunting was her way of keeping Sean alive, and maybe that newfound vitality was the key to the connection between Kyra and his novel writing. Things had meaning to him now, and details were important. Maybe her teasing was a tonic to his closed-up, tight-assed, earlier self saying, "There, you bastard. Deal with this, and this, and if I piss you off, good. Explode, get mad, grow."

Bullshit, I said to myself. She's driving him crazy.

It started to rain, then hail. We got up and ran for the cover of the trees. Crouching between two oaks, Lea told me she'd made a date to see Mike that afternoon, and did I mind? I said I didn't, but that was a lie.

# Eight

Berta, as she did most Saturday mornings, got up early and caught the bus into the Blanes station. As always, it was crowded, mostly with tourists in bright-colored shirts and light pants, lining up for their tickets. Everyone was so wonderfuly carefree, she thought. It must be wonderful to take a vacation. It certainly was nice of Señor Sean to give her Saturdays off most of the time.

The station lay in a pocket of sulphur fumes just outside the city. It was a small, brown, squat building with a baggage section on the right. Inside, usually the locals sat around near the walls, while the tourists, even this late in the season, controlled the center of the room, mingling with one another, making friendships to last for fifteen minutes. Outside, the huge buses waited to take the disembarking passengers to one or another of the tourist towns—Lloret, Tossa, Figueroa.

This morning a little Spanish girl with a pretty white dress sat crying by herself in the corner. She had a bloody nose, which she hadn't been able to stop from running onto the dress. Berta was about to walk up to her when a man of uncertain age bustled past with a piece of cloth that he'd dunked in the water fountain outside, a fountain that had seen cleaner days. The girl's cries seemed to double in volume as her father tried to clean her up, yelling at her the whole time to watch out for her dress. Berta bought her ticket and went outside to avoid the noise. She was only going to Caldetas, about twenty-five kilometers down the line.

When the train arrived, she took a place near the front of the car, happy to have a seat. She took out a full-length comic book and read quietly until the train reached Caldetas, a station rather depressingly like the one in Blanes. Her brother was waiting for her.

Pedro was a small, friendly man who drove a taxi. Saturday was one of the busiest days for him, so he would work until early evening, but he would always be home for dinner. Berta didn't mind being alone in the apartment for the day. Often she would do nothing but sit and watch the television, or go out to the small balcony and take in the sun.

Sometimes she would make a visit to the church in the late afternoon, after it had started to darken and the candles made the only light.

Pedro lived with his best friend, Ramon, a widower who owned a small place in Caldetas. The bar he owned was far from downtown, and frequented almost exclusively by Spaniards. He sold *tinto* for five pesetas the glass, or twenty-five the liter. To the tourists who came in, he charged four times that. He wasn't running a tourist bar. He had nothing against them, but since they would pay four times the price, he saw nothing wrong with charging it. A few years before, a rich and gregarious drunk boy from America had shown him how to make a *Cuba libre,* and he charged thirty pesetas for them. None of his regulars drank them. He would usually work until six, and then his helper would come on and stay until two or three in the morning.

He'd moved in with Pedro seven years before, when his wife had died. It was a peaceful, working household. They were both robust men who liked to laugh, play cards, and eat. They drank lightly, and had never had a serious quarrel. Both were religious, though not like women were, and both believed in Franco.

Pedro dropped Berta off at the apartment with an affectionate kiss on the cheek. With her small bag in her hand, she let herself in through the front door, and rode the elevator to the third floor. The men's apartment took up half the floor. She opened the door and looked around. It was quite dark in the foyer, but she knew her way, past the small Madonna by the door, into the living room, to the curtains. She pulled them apart, letting in the sunlight and the view of the flower-covered porch in front of the sliding windows.

The men did keep a neat house. The walls in the living room held four or five paintings of saints or matadors—almost the same thing—all painted in brightly phosphorescent colors on black velveteen. Down the hall behind her were the two bedrooms and the office with its fold-a-bed on which she slept.

She walked about for a while, whistling to herself, and put on some water for instant coffee. She drank it slowly on the porch. Then she went back to the bathroom and disrobed. She combed her hair out and let it fall freely. It really wasn't that long, but it felt good untied. It did not occur to her to look at herself in the mirror, but if she had, she would have seen a not unattractive body, perhaps getting a little too broad in the hips, and a bit rounded at the shoulders, but still a desirable one. Her stomach had no fat on it, though it curved out nicely. The patch of hair below it was starting to streak with gray. She stood for quite some time, combing out her hair, then stretched languorously on her tiptoes. Fluffing out the tufts of hair under her arms, she chuckled for no reason. Then she turned on the shower and treated herself to a half hour of warm water.

She went to her room and changed into a beige cotton blouse and a yellow skirt which came to the bottoms of her knees. Putting on some sandals, she checked the refrigerator and decided to go to the market and buy food for dinner.

It was pleasant, she thought, to get back to the old rhythms, even if only for a day. Siesta wouldn't be for a couple of hours yet, and she felt grand moving between the booths back behind the town, away from the tourist shops. She almost dropped in to see Ramon, as she passed within a block of his place, but decided it would be better not to. Bars were for the men.

She bought some melons and salt ham for before dinner, and lamb parts and white beans for stew.

Coming back to the apartment, she talked for a while to the woman next door, with whom she'd become friends. They exchanged a couple of recipes, and Berta listened to her complain about her husband's drinking. But it was good-natured complaining. They both knew that men got drunk from time to time. It was only to be expected. She was upset only because he had broken one of her favorite flowerpots on the patio. They talked and wound up laughing about it. What could you do?

Berta went back in and put the beans on a low boil. When she pulled the curtains closed, it might as well have been night. She felt her way back to her room, plugged in the small evening light, a replica of the Virgin, and was asleep in seconds.

When she woke up, the men hadn't come home yet. She finished preparing the stew and then went to sit on the patio and finish her book. Pedro got home first, and Ramon about an hour later. They sat around the kitchen table and shared a bottle of wine, playing cards and waiting for dinner to be ready. Berta slipped off her sandals and rested her foot on Ramon's under the table.

After dinner, they watched television, the two men sitting on either side of her on the couch. When the movie ended, they got up, said their good-nights, and went to their respective rooms.

Berta undressed and put on a long black nightgown. She said a decade of the rosary, then waited until she thought Pedro had gone to sleep.

Ramon's door was already slightly ajar when she came to it. She let herself in and crossed to his bed. Without a word, she took off the nightgown and got into bed beside him. He went very slowly. They were a well-practiced pair of lovers. He kissed her everywhere, pausing where he knew she liked it best, and she felt the beautiful tension rising in her body. Her nipples stood up like hard cherries as he ran his fingers up and down the backs of her legs. She thought she would have to scream, but held herself to a moan as the waves of pleasure ran through her body. He turned her over to her stomach then and took his pleasure in his own way. Then they lay quietly, hugging each other and falling into sleep.

This arrangement had been going on for four years, but it was never spoken about. Berta knew that she still was married in the eyes of the Church, since, so far as she knew, her husband had not died, but it didn't matter to her. She loved Ramon, and he loved her. One day, when he retired, maybe they could afford to live together, or even find out if they could marry. Pedro, of course, knew about them, but he never let on. He knew that people needed to love. He wished his sister and his friend every happiness. He prayed that God someday would make it possible for them to be married, but that he would not punish them for the love they shared.

In the morning, the three of them went to an early Mass, then walked together back to the train station, and the men put Berta on the train to Blanes.

# PART II

*The Sea of Faith*
*Was once, too, at the full, and round earth's shore*
*Lay like the folds of a bright girdle furled.*
                    —MATTHEW ARNOLD,
              "Dover Beach"

# Nine

The ground was warm and wet, and she was glad she had taken off her sandals. The shower after she'd gotten home with Douglas had refreshed her. Now the sun was threatening to come out again. She wasn't thinking, but enjoyed the feel of her legs against the fabric of her pants, her hair falling loose, brushing its wet ends against her neck.

Mike walked beside her, easily, carrying a bottle of chilled white wine in his right hand. His left hand hung casually, barely swinging as he walked. His hair, long and dark, was tied at the back in a pigtail. He wore a blue and orange shirt from India, and frayed jeans. Lea carried his sandals in her hand, along with her own.

They'd met at the café, where they'd had coffee, and Mike had suggested that they go up to the old fort. What with the rain and the late season, it wasn't likely to be crowded.

She followed him along the *ramblas,* watching him walk. When they began to climb up to the fort, they put their sandals back on.

Up within the walls were the old remains of the church. Some of the walls still stood to the height of a foot or so, and the places for the pews were visible. The altar and its nave were intact, though open to the elements.

Pebbles and bits of glass crunched beneath their feet as they walked up what had once been the aisle. When they got to the raised part which held the altar, they sat on it. Out in front of them, they could see the Bay of Tossa, its small boats bobbing in the light, churning water. As they sat, the boat from Lloret entered the bay with its load of tourists. Above them was the old fort, with its lookout posts, the lighthouse, and the gun turrets, all now long out of use. The sky was clearing.

She watched him take a loaf of bread from the sack he carried, then some cheese and a couple of pears. He opened the wine with the corkscrew on a Swiss Army knife, took a sip, and passed it to her.

"Two Americans playing Hemingway," he said.

"Do you feel that?"

"No," he said, laughing. "I've been here too long for that now."

"You should laugh more," she said. "It becomes you."

He cut into the pear. "Drink the wine with this. It's really good." He smiled again. "I'm glad you could come today."

"I wanted to see you."

"Why is that?"

"I don't know."

Another couple walked by. Mike and Lea were silent as they passed. Lea began to feel afraid, as though she were guilty of something. She looked at the boy across from her and shivered, hoping he didn't realize how open she was to him.

"Is something wrong?" he asked.

She gave him a self-conscious little smile, and shook her head. "Not really," she said.

"You can talk to me, you know."

"I know. It's just . . ."

"What?"

She looked down. "I don't quite know where to start. I . . . I find myself wanting to know about you." She continued looking down, and he raised her chin with his hand. He was serious.

"What's there to know?"

She shrugged. "I'm not sure. The other night when you played that song, and a few other times, it's like waves of sorrow come off you. Oh, not that you give the impression that you feel sorry for yourself, but that's just it. All of a sudden, something surfaces, and you seem lost in it. I thought maybe if you brought it out and talked about it once, it might help." She stopped, helpless, staring at him. He looked back at her with no expression. "Forgive me," she said. "I don't know you at all, but . . ."

"That's OK," he said. "Go on."

She trembled slightly. Goose bumps rose on her arms and she pulled them inside her sleeves, as she used to do when she was a child. She hugged her arms to herself.

"There's really nothing more I have to say. Just that I feel you're hiding from something, and maybe it's time you faced it."

He didn't move, and again that trance seemed to be on him. He stared away, up in the direction of the turrets. She took his hand in both of hers, and held it close to her body, under her shirt. It was hot against her stomach.

Finally, he spoke. "I'm going to talk now for a while. I don't want you to interrupt or say a word because I'm not sure I'll finish if you do. But you're right. There is something . . .

"I don't know why I asked you to see me today. Not that I don't find you attractive and all that, but you are married, and—well, but that's not the point either."

He stammered, stopped, began again.

"When I was eighteen, I left Seattle for a summer in Europe. My folks were fairly well off and they gave me enough for a couple of months, and I thought it would be a great time.

"I had a girlfriend then, named Sharon Barrett. We thought it was funny that we both had the same last name, that it was fate or something that we'd wind up together. Anyway, we arranged it so that we'd be here together, and we'd travel and see the world together before starting college.

"We were good kids, too. Virgins when we left, and thought we'd stay that way. Dumb us. We made it two nights without making love. Then the third day it rained and we were stuck in the hotel room all day, and . . . Well, that's not so important.

"So we were lovers and were like new lovers everywhere, I suppose, though it didn't seem like it to us. I guess everybody thinks they're different."

A tear broke from his eye. He spoke evenly, but more tears came, running down his face, spattering onto his jeans.

"We made it down to Marseilles. Then one day we decided to go shopping separately and surprise each other with things for dinner, then meet back near our hotel. So I went to the Marché and she said she was going to the Arab quarter."

He stopped talking, and took a deep breath, then another in an effort to calm himself.

"I never saw her again. She didn't come back to the hotel. I waited until nearly midnight, then went to the police. I described her—tall, blond, American-looking—and the inspector covered his eyes with his hand.

" 'What is it?' I said. 'Tell me.'

"He didn't though, but put me in a back room, and had me wait about a half hour until an American came in. Short, fat man, but very nice to me. I asked him what was going on, if Sharon was dead, but he just talked to me for quite a long time before he finally made me drink a cognac or two and told me about the white slave trade out of Marseilles."

She watched him try to keep talking, but he opened his mouth and no words came. She found herself beginning to cry. She pulled him to her and held him.

The sun broke through. His head was in her lap, and she ran her fingers through his hair, over his back.

Suddenly he got up and walked away, nearly out of the church's enclosure. He stood near the wall for a long time, facing the other way, occasionally bringing his hand to his face. Then he turned back to her and walked again the length of the aisle. He stood over her where she sat.

"I won't have you pity me," he said.

"I don't." She held the bottle up to him. "Have some wine. It's delicious with the pears."

They smiled at each other, and over the rest of the food, he told her of the ensuing months, of his search for her, his failure, his obsession. He had traveled overland to Turkey, into the oil countries of the Near East, around to Egypt. The summer had passed and he hadn't gone home. Instead, working odd jobs whenever he could, stealing when he had to, he had made his fanatical way around to Algiers, where he had been deported for lack of money.

Back in the States, he'd been drafted and sent to Vietnam, where he had tried so hard to die that he'd been cited three times for heroism. After those two years, he'd come back to Europe to drift, to maybe find something. He didn't mention running guns, but to her it made sense.

They sat apart now while he talked, not touching each other.

"But why are you here? What are you doing?"

"Just living."

"And you've never seen her again?"

He shook his head.

She took a mouthful of wine and closed her eyes, the sun beating down on her. She swallowed and took the step.

"Maybe we could find her."

"It's been eight years."

"Douglas and I would help you."

He laughed. "I can't see that."

"So you really think there's no hope? Why did you tell me about it then? I would like to help you, but not if you don't care anymore."

He looked down at the ground, then at her.

"Why do you want to do this?"

Because I am lost, she wanted to say. Because I'm bored. Because I need to feel like I'm doing something that has a meaning.

And thrumming beneath these unexpressible reasons, a current at once more powerful and more dangerous: Because I need an excuse . . . even a foolish, quixotic one . . . to see you again. Because I feel my heart beginning to thaw.

"Lea?"

She couldn't form an answer. No words were adequate. Reaching for his hand, she took it and held it against her breast. Her eyes glistened as though she would cry, but she held back her tears.

With his gaze locked into hers, Michael nodded all but imperceptibly.

He put his hand behind her neck and brought her to him.

It was nearly dusk. They pulled up to the white house in the black Peugeot. Berta got out first. Lea sat for a moment, one arm resting on the windowsill.

She couldn't forget, would not forget that kiss, though it had gone no further than that. They walked back down the hill acting like the strangers they were. He had been exhausted. She, tense and guilt-ridden.

Now, walking into the house, she was afraid. There was a familiar smell in the living room, an odor of old furniture, and today, suddenly, it was repellent.

"Douglas!"

Her husband appeared as if by magic, and as she went to him she took him in. He wore loafers, light blue socks to match his light blue slacks, and a pale yellow, short-sleeved sport shirt. She smiled at him. His face was handsome in a dignified way. He was relaxed, his light hair uncombed.

He kissed her lightly. "Have a nice time?"

His kiss made her nervous. She smiled, and kissed him again.

"If you get me a gin and tonic, I'll tell you all about it."

"Done."

He walked to the kitchen and she sat on the sofa, feeling it give slightly beneath her. She touched her lips with her fingers, and sat not moving. She heard Douglas inside, bantering with Berta, preparing the drinks.

The room darkened quickly. Upstairs, she heard Sean cough. The front door, left ajar, let in the evening breeze. She stretched, and then fastened her eyes on the painting between the kitchen door and the corner. All but invisible now, it was a typical after-the-hunt still life in dark hues—a few pheasants and a hare on a table with a gun. It was an altogether unexceptional work, made interesting only by the gash of red, which Lea knew to be blood running from the rabbit's mouth, out over the table to a pool on the floor.

Douglas came back in, switched on a light, and got the gin from the cupboard. She patted the sofa next to her.

"Come sit by me."

"Should I get the door? You cold?"

"No. Fine."

He sat down and they drank. Gradually, she began to feel better. The drink was good and she told him so. They talked about Sean and his earache, about the letters Douglas had written during the day. He took her hand.

"We were right," she said finally, "about Mike."

"How so?"

"We went up to the Villa Vella today and had lunch, and I asked him . . ." She hesitated. How would she put it in words? "I asked him if there wasn't something hidden about his life. You know, something to account for that feeling, for that song if nothing else."

"And there is?"

"I don't know if you'll believe it."

"Try me."

She began Mike's story, and he listened with a faint smile.

"I'm not sure I believe it."

"If you could've heard him tell it, you'd have no doubts."

"Then why is he here in Tossa?"

"Waiting. Marking time. I don't know."

They sipped their drinks. Kyra came down, followed by Sean, who had a wad of cotton stuck in his right ear. His earache had flared the other night after he'd gone out for a late, drunken walk. Now it was beginning to clear up, but the last time he'd had one, it had left him hard of hearing for two weeks.

Lea whispered quickly to Douglas.

"Between us, huh?"

He nodded and got up. "Sean, how are you feeling?"

"Pain and anguish, the fate of modern man."

"Listen to him," Kyra said.

"Drinks?" Lea was up and moving toward the kitchen. She and Kyra got glasses, tonic, ice, limes.

When they returned, the men were sitting at the dining table, talking. Kyra gave Sean his glass and he patted her on the rear. She sat next to him, resting her hand easily on his leg.

She does love him, Lea thought. She looked at Douglas. And I love him. It might have been a mixture of guilt and pity, but she didn't feel it then. Suddenly, looking at her husband of seven years, she forgot all thoughts of Mike.

She remembered meeting Douglas for the first time, his confident reserve, which went so well with her own style. He'd been so refreshing. Classy. Not a teaser like the one or two other boys she'd gone out with. He'd been surprised that she had not been married before. And their lovemaking . . .

She smiled to herself as the talk continued at the table. This reserved, almost bookish man and she had spent their first three years in bed, it seemed. They had devoured each other. Their friends had thought them antisocial. He'd made her grow up, finally. Not that he'd forced anything with her, but the love, curiosity, and endless lust had worked out its permutations with an ease and variety that had stunned them both. Still, only today . . .

She was aroused, and took his hand under the table, putting it high on her leg.

Berta brought in the dinner. They were all talking now, moving easily from Franco to Nixon to food to a popular record that Kyra had picked up yesterday.

The lentil soup was delicious. A heavy, almost too heavy, dose of rosemary made it distinctive, and Lea thought it was the nicest dinner they'd had yet. Everyone seemed so happy.

Berta joined them at the table, and she, too, was in a good mood. Kyra said something to her in Spanish and they laughed. She had brought in the other courses—a salad, a bowl of lima beans, a tortilla, which was not a pancake like a Mexican tortilla, but an omelette of potatoes and onions, and a lamb roast. Sean cut the tortilla and Doug carved the roast. They drank two bottles of rosé.

After dinner, they'd decided to go to the fun house in Lloret and go bowling. They all piled into the Peugeot and sped along the winding road, singing dirty limericks to the tune of "Cielito Lindo." When they arrived, they discovered that the fun house had been closed for the season, so they walked to a flamenco club nearby where sometimes there were real flamencos. Here they'd been lucky and had stayed for two shows.

"That was fun," Doug said when they were preparing for bed.

"Yes," she said, abstractly.

"Something wrong?" he asked.

"No. I've just been thinking."

"Awful late for that."

"I think we need an event."

"What do you mean?"

"You know, something to look forward to or plan for, or be involved in. I've been thinking about our talk this morning and how we really do seem to be drifting. Not you and me together so much, but in our lives separately. Sometimes I feel that we're only going through motions. Don't you?"

He sat on the bed and didn't answer.

"I'm talking about what our lives should mean, Douglas. Maybe I'm just getting older, but I don't want to think of my life as getting to be an adult, writing some clever ads, then plodding along to senility."

"You're really upset, aren't you?" He sat her down next to him and put his arm around her. "I love your idealism, you know."

She wanted to hit him. "Damn idealism. I'm feeling trapped. Not with you," she hastened to add, "but with this whole way we live." She felt for a moment that she had lied, that it was him, but she kept on. "Isn't that why we're here? Isn't that why we got away? To look at ourselves and see if maybe we're not doing something wrong? And possibly change? I mean really change."

"What do you want to change to?"

"I don't know. I feel almost like I'm sleeping, that nothing touches me." Just then, she began to grow aware that she might be describing him. "That maybe if I'd get involved in something, and not something so artificial as work—something real, that I instinctively feel . . ." She stopped. Then, "Don't you feel that your life is pretty empty, going nowhere? Doesn't it bother you to think that nothing ultimately means anything?"

Kindly, he answered, "It's not that it bothers me or not. That's not the question. I can't really help it if that's what I really believe. You know? Would you have me, or you, believing that events interact, make a difference? No, I used to think that. I used to be religious, too. But I gradually lost faith in all that. It turned out to be meaningless. I didn't want it to be, but there you are. Time went by, and I got used to it."

She lay back on the bed and listened.

"Why do you think I gave up trying to write novels, for Christ's sake? I just, deep down, couldn't buy the fact that events were significant—that anybody could or would give a shit. There was no order, and all this 'artists bringing order to their world' just didn't do it for me. And it does eat me up, Lea. I hate it. It's like a disease, this galloping unfaith in everything . . ."

"And us?" she said.

He was silent for a long time. She aimlessly scratched his back.

"I love you," he said at last.

"But if everything is meaningless . . ."

"What I mean is that, finally, it will never matter that I loved you."

She began to cry. "Why are you so afraid to be hurt?" She didn't know where that had come from. "You're blocking yourself off from me and everybody and everything, just because of some stupid intellectual idea you have that nothing affects anything else. That's not true. I affect you, and you know that. You're just not letting anything near you. This galloping unfaith, as you call it, guarantees that your life is empty and will stay empty."

She quieted down. "I'd like to force you, Douglas, to let yourself feel something."

"I do feel things," he said feebly.

"Name something that really touches you then."

He was silent.

She knew he was wrong. That song of Mike's, that single event, had meant something. It had opened a door for him. In a way, it had exposed everybody. Douglas might have been able to put it out of his mind, but it had been there—a presence, an event. It had flooded her, made her passionate again, and that had affected him. Like this talk now . . .

She wondered if that chance song had changed everything and everyone they knew.

The moonlight angled down through the bedroom window. Outside, the wind was blowing in gusts. She knew Douglas was awake. It was perhaps four in the morning and she hadn't slept at all. He was on his side, turned away from her.

"Douglas." She hugged him from behind. "I'm sorry."

"OK."

She pulled his shoulder so that he rolled onto his back and crossed her leg over his. She whispered to him.

"What did you say?"

"I said I think I want to have a baby."

He breathed heavily. She knew he was angry. "You're too old."

"Then why am I taking these pills?"

"All right, then, we're too old. Let's talk about it in the morning." He turned back on his side.

She was tired and wanted to sleep, but the memory of Mike's kiss kept coming back to her, distracting her, exciting her. She put her hand between her legs, and her fingers finally brought her some relief, at least enough so that she could sleep.

# Ten

The steady drone of the breeze outside was anything but soothing to the man lying, open-eyed, on the couch in the middle of the afternoon. It was the first real hint of colder days to come, and the approach of winter depressed him. For all that, the breeze was only a breeze. It was still warm in the room, a slow Sunday afternoon.

A fly landed on his forehead and he slapped at it with his only hand. He heard footsteps leading down the hall toward his study and in a moment Kyra appeared in the doorway. He closed his eyes.

"Sean?"

"Uh."

"You sleeping?"

"Not hardly."

She came over and sat on the chair by his desk,

picked up the sheaf of papers and hefted them. He swung his feet to the floor and stood up.

"It's coming along," she said.

"Not bad. I had a good day yesterday and this morning was fine, but now I'm pretty dry." He put his hand on her shoulder and shook it gently. "How you doin'? Lea and Doug about?"

"No. Lea got up early and left, and I'm not sure Doug's out of bed yet."

"There's a sack artist for you. What time is it?"

"Around two."

"And he's not up yet. Is he sick?"

She shrugged. "I don't know. They haven't been at their best lately, you know." Suddenly she stood again. "You feel like taking some time off and doing something? I'm going stir-crazy in here."

He looked at the desk and realized he wasn't going to work any more today. Kyra was desirable, as always, wearing white shorts and a blue cotton shirt.

"Sure," he said. "What the hell. What've you got in mind?"

"Maybe Barcelona. Just to get away from here."

"OK." Again he looked her over. "You'll have to change, though."

"Right back." She pecked his cheek.

He sat down at his desk and surveyed the room.

It wasn't large, but it was his favorite room in the house, removed and quiet. Its walls were white stucco, and he'd put a fake Persian rug over the tiled floor. His desk was in the middle of the room, facing the nearly empty bookshelf and the doorway to the hall that led back to the house. The only other furnishing was the couch he'd been lying on.

The room had a strange but natural communication with his bedroom opposite; almost any noise in the one was clearly audible in the other. He often heard Berta cleaning up, and always knew when Kyra was awake. He'd often wondered if the same effect worked with the guest bedroom directly above his office, but he'd never gotten around to checking it. He guessed that it worked only one way, though, since he'd never heard Doug and Lea upstairs.

Still, acoustics could play tricks. He would have to check it someday.

Of course, now with his ear so bad he couldn't hear much anyway, but if Doug and Lea could hear noises from his bedroom, he should know about it. He smiled. Wouldn't that be embarrassing?

He walked down the hall to the front room and stood leaning against the door, waiting for Kyra.

He wondered how he'd gotten so involved with her. A couple of years before, he'd had everything he wanted, less a hand, but even that hadn't been so much of a burden once he'd gotten used to it. He'd immediately loved it in Spain, and this house had suited him perfectly. Then he'd met Tony, and then Kyra. He remembered his first sight of her, looking more or less demure—she could never look really demure—in a pair of slacks and a high-collared blouse. They'd hit it off at once, had talked all night, and she'd essentially raped him in his car in front of Tony's apartment.

Then began what Sean had come to call the Months of Sorrows, when Kyra had alternately screwed around with a near-sublime lack of discrimination, while at the same time she labored to keep Sean on the string, coming to him at all hours, often directly—and obviously—from another man's embrace.

Testing Sean's tolerance, the limits of his capacity to forgive, the depth of his love. She would not give herself completely over to him until she satisfied herself that he would never leave her, no matter how bad her behavior.

And when finally he had convinced her, she had agreed to move in with him, and to be faithful. But simple self-preservation demanded that she not allow him to become complacent, so it was to her advantage always to appear to have one foot out the door, an eye out for the next attractive man to enter their universe.

So Sean, for his part, and as Kyra intended, remained jealous, but his jealous rages took on an odd character. He was more protective of his house than of his heart. Or he thought so. As long as she lived with him, he wouldn't stand for her infidelities. If she were unfaithful to him, it wouldn't so much break his heart as outrage his sense of territory. He was out to protect himself. He knew, or thought he knew, that Kyra had to keep moving, had to keep changing partners, and that her stay with him was fated from the beginning to end with her one day packing off without a word. He'd known that when he'd asked her to move in.

He was a logical man and, except when he was drunk, kept his emotions in firm check. This made him a ponderous drunk, but his friends bore him well. Even his explosions of rage or laughter were once removed from his real feelings. His personality was one logical step removed from his person. All of his acquaintances enjoyed his personality, and no one knew him.

He thought he'd better go in and tell Berta that they wouldn't be home for dinner. She was in the kitchen, sitting at her table, drinking some coffee, and reading.

*"Hola,"* he said. "How's the queen of the kitchen today?"

They spoke together in Spanish, which gave them a bond within the house. Often, at dinners, they would speak to each other and exchange meaningful glances to the amusement of the others at the table. It was another touch of Sean's to keep the atmosphere of the house happy and carefree. He fancied that it worked.

They both enjoyed the ride into Barcelona, passing fields for the first few miles, then catching glimpses of the sea, finally coming through the factories and warehouses and slums into the city itself.

They parked by the Plaza Puerta de la Paz at the end of the *ramblas* and walked holding hands through the old city to the Plaza Berenguer el Grande, where the Roman wall ran near the avenue. It was nearly dark as they took their seats on the plaza.

"Tony should be here today, you know," she said.

"Fomenting revolution?"

She lifted her shoulders. "He is committed."

"I know. I just hope he doesn't get too caught up in it. When Franco dies, if the crusty old fart ever does, things will change fast. You watch."

They leaned back in their chairs and watched the traffic. It was cooler, but they'd brought sweaters, and put them on. Kyra helped Sean like a mother.

"Buttons," he said, smiling. "I don't think I'll ever get good at buttons."

She kissed the top of his head, not bothering now to tease him and feeling ashamed that she ever had, although she felt it had been more Douglas's intrusions than Sean's reactions to her teasing that made her feel that way.

The waiter brought them two cognacs. More people came out for walks. It was, after all, a Sunday. The streetlamps went on.

As they sipped their drinks, they talked first about Tony and the rally being held that day in the city, probably not far from where they sat. She asked him about his book. They talked until it was quite dark, then decided to go to Los Caracoles for dinner. Still they remained seated, not wanting to end the moment.

"You know, Sean," Kyra said suddenly, "I do love you." She kissed him quickly and got up. "Come on. Let's go eat."

He got up and put his arm around her. They began walking across the old city. The streets were ill-lit and smelled bad. Too narrow for cars, they were crammed with people.

As they walked, he held her close to him. She

had never told him she loved him before, and it bothered him. It was as if she'd broken the rules. He found himself unable to say anything, and so they walked in silence. His arm kept her pressed against him. Stopping in a doorway, he kissed her.

The people in the street were beginning to move quickly as Sean and Kyra stepped back down off the curb. Two or three young people went rushing through the crowd, pushing everyone to make way, and a low roar came from behind them.

Somebody said something about the rally getting out of hand.

"What's going on?"

Now there was really something wrong. Behind them people were pushing and screaming. Sean and Kyra were nearly running to keep up with the flow. When they were about two-thirds of the way down the block, a group of fifteen or twenty *guardia* came around the next corner directly in front of them, swinging their nightsticks indiscriminately. By now the noise was deafening behind them, and still they tried to turn and run against the crowd, but it was no use.

Sean stumbled but Kyra held him up. They pressed themselves against the wall, hoping it would pass, but they were almost directly between the *guardia* and the surging mob. Someone from behind threw a rock, and a barrage of rocks followed. They kept trying to squeeze back into the crowd. The police were swinging at everyone. Someone grabbed Kyra and she yelled for Sean. He stepped out and grabbed her, trying to butt everyone out of the way, but he was hit in the head and lost his balance. Kyra screamed his name again as he fell to the street, but then he was hit again, and lost consciousness.

His leg was turned awkwardly under him, and it started to cramp. He tried to straighten it, but there was something in the way. Slowly he came to. The crowd was gone, and he lay in a doorway. Turning to free his leg, he moaned involuntarily. His head felt as though it had been cracked in half. He opened his eyes wide with a great effort. The street was quiet now.

He thought of Kyra and tried to stand, but the effort nauseated him and he was sick into the gutter.

He cursed.

Where was she?

He sat for another minute leaning his head against the wall, trying to orient himself. His neck was cold and damp from his blood, some of which had also dried on his face. He swore again, and stood up.

He knew there was a fountain nearby, and he

had a good idea of exactly where he was. He had to find Kyra, but any search would be useless until he'd cleared his head.

The fountain was three blocks to his left, and the walk to it was eerie. No one was about, as though it were just before dawn, although he felt it was not yet midnight, and probably earlier. Occasionally, through an alley, he could see up toward the *ramblas* where the lights shone as though it were a normal Sunday evening.

At the fountain, he knelt and plunged his head into the water, rubbing with his hand to wash away the crusted blood. He had two lumps on the back of his head, and he realized from the sting as he washed that his face was cut. Still, it wasn't as bad as it might have been.

He struggled out of his sweater and left it on the ground, then got up and made his way toward the lights. His head was remarkably clear. His first instinct had been to rush about calling Kyra's name, but now he realized she must have been arrested, or knocked down, or somehow had made her way back to the car. He contemplated turning then, and going back to the doorway where he'd come to. If she had made it to the car, he could wait for her there. But he really didn't think she had made it to the car.

A small café with five or six old Spaniards at the

bar caught his attention. There was a phone in the back, and he thought he'd call the police to find out if she'd been arrested. They probably wouldn't tell him, but it was worth a try. As he entered the café, though, the proprietor came around the bar, waving him away and shaking his head.

"*Cerrado,*" he kept yelling, pushing Sean toward the door. "*Cerrado.*"

Sean pointed to the phone on the wall. "*Teléfono,*" he yelled just as loudly. "*Solamente teléfono.*"

Some of the men at the bar got up and came toward him, so that he finally gave up and backed out the door.

"Assholes," he said in English. "Pack of bleeding assholes."

They stared after him as he walked away.

There was a police station down near the Plaza de Cataluña, but he wasn't sure he wanted to go in, especially looking like he did.

As he came out of the old city onto the *ramblas,* he was amazed by how normal everything was. The shops were open and people wandered leisurely or sat out eating ice cream or sipping coffee. It was no later than ten thirty. There was no sign of a recent riot. They must have contained it all in the old city. People kept staring at him, and he decided to go to his car and wait there for Kyra.

If she'd been arrested, there was nothing he could do anyway.

But his feet would not carry him there. Kyra kept coming back to him. He walked back into the old city with its dark and narrow streets. He felt in his pockets, and found that he still had his wallet and money. Several people passed him, but he was less conspicuous, and no one paid him any special attention. Finally, a young man about his size passed and he stopped him, offering him two thousand pesetas for his shirt. They made the deal, and in five minutes, Sean had discarded his own blood-stained shirt, and was in another café's bathroom, trying to make himself look presentable. His face in the mirror was scratched and somewhat swollen, but his eyes were clear, and with his hair combed, at least he didn't look drunk. He patted the lumps behind his head with a wet paper towel. The bleeding had stopped.

Coming out of the bathroom, he ordered a coffee and cognac at the bar. He gulped it down, and then walked back out toward the police station, avoiding the *ramblas*.

The building was a solid brick structure, guarded by two policemen with submachine guns. Sean nervously walked up the four steps to the wide door, and they parted to let him in. Inside, the atmosphere was more like an office building than anything else. Uniformed men sat or stood around, and next to the door, a guard sat at a desk in a semi-enclosed booth. Sean went over and questioned him, and was assured that no women had been arrested during the disturbance, although they had taken several men. Was there a chance, the guard asked, that Kyra might have been mistaken for a man in the dark?

"Not even in the dark," Sean answered, smiling.

The guard smiled, too. He had kind eyes, and Sean found himself believing him, though it was against his better judgment. He asked the man if he would take care to watch out for her, and he gave him her name, and his address in Tossa.

"We were just taking a walk," he explained. "We really had nothing to do with it all."

The guard smiled again, and said, "In these times, sometimes it is better not to take walks at night. People think you must be on either side. Have you tried the hospital?"

Sean said no, and the guard gave him the address.

By now he was exhausted, but he made it to the hospital quickly. It was back in the direction of the car anyway.

At the hospital, a nun told him that she knew of no disturbance that night, but checked her rolls to see if Kyra had been admitted. She had not.

He was relieved to find the car where he'd left it, but Kyra was nowhere to be found. He couldn't drive through the old city, but he circled it five or six times, thinking nothing, and feeling completely helpless. Finally he parked the car again near his original place, and waited until very late before he decided that he was accomplishing nothing and should go home.

No lights were on as he pulled into the court-yard. They had said they'd be home late, but he wished as he drove up that someone would be awake. The ride home had been harrowing. Overcome with fatigue, he had twice nearly driven off the road. Once he'd left the highway, it had been easier to stay awake, although the winding road up to the house had seemed endless.

He let himself in quietly and turned on the light, then crossed to the liquor cabinet and poured himself a stiff, neat bourbon. His head ached. He reached back and touched the lumps on it.

He heard footsteps and Doug appeared, wearing his white slacks and buttoning up his shirt. Only his hair gave away that he'd been in bed. He walked to the liquor cabinet.

"I heard you drive up and wasn't sleeping anyway. Want a refresher?"

Sean held out his glass. "Sure."

"It sure turned out to be a late one." He turned. "Where's Kyra? It's been—" For the first time he looked at Sean. "Christ! What happened to you?"

Sean watched Doug pour, and suddenly began to shake. It dawned on him anew that Kyra was in trouble. The drink had cleared his mind as his first drinks so often did. He took a sip.

"There was a riot in Barcelona," he said, "and we got caught in it. I don't know where Kyra is. I thought she might've gotten back here somehow, but . . ." He stopped and sat down again on the couch.

"Maybe she was arrested."

"No. I checked." He recounted his night and got more worried as he talked.

"So what are we going to do now?" asked Doug when he finished.

"I don't know. Wait until morning, I guess. Maybe I should've stayed in the city."

"That would have been crazy. You've got your head bashed open."

"Yeah, but I don't know what to do about finding her. I don't know where she could be. No idea, and it's . . ."

"Why don't you just sit here and I'll get Lea up. Somebody ought to look at your head."

"No." He finished his drink. "No sense in waking her up for that. I think I'll just wash up and

139

go to bed, and try to be up in a couple of hours." He crossed toward the hall that led to his room. "If I were you, I'd try to get some sleep myself. It might be a long couple of days." He left him and went to his room.

Undressing was particularly difficult for him tonight. The cold shower felt good, though. He let the water course down through his hair until there was no trace of the crusted blood. He was becoming more and more lucid, and in turn more worried. Getting out of the shower, he put on his robe and sat at the edge of his bed. For a moment he stared vacantly ahead, his mind empty. Then a noise from outside—Doug putting down his glass and going upstairs—brought him back.

Try as he might, he couldn't be calm. Thoughts of what might now be happening to her kept him on the verge of panic. Where could she be? If she hadn't been arrested or hospitalized, then why hadn't she come back to where he'd been knocked out? Or if she'd run and met someone she knew, why hadn't they eventually come to the car, or back here? She couldn't have simply disappeared.

He was slowing down, but he wanted to stay awake, to decide what to do in the morning, so he got up and paced. Why hadn't he stayed in the city? He should still be there now, looking for her. He had never felt more like a coward.

And what had been this facade he'd put up with her? Tonight she had said that she loved him, and his distrust had been so great that he couldn't believe it, though everything in him had wanted to. Wasn't that carrying the whole thing too far? As long as he never let himself believe her, she could never destroy him, but also they would be nothing more than two drifters pretending to be lovers. Even more, pretending to be living in the rarefied air of risk and danger, but really not living at all. Wasn't his refusal to have faith in her an admission that he was afraid to live? Maybe real death would be preferable. At least it would be real.

He paced. He sat again on the bed, picked up a magazine, opened it, then threw it to the floor. Through the window the sky was lightening. He lay down, turned out the bed light, almost dozed.

Outside he heard a car engine. It must be close, he thought, for me to hear it with this damned ear. Then he jumped out of bed and ran through the living room out to the courtyard. A car was pulling up and in a moment Kyra was out of it and in his arms, crying.

A man got out of the car and stood by awkwardly as they embraced. Sean thought he looked familiar, then recognized him as the guard from the police station. He came over to them.

"We were told to say they hadn't arrested women," he said, "but I know sometimes they don't always tell the truth. So when I got off, I went to the jail with her name and explained, and they let her go out with me. I'm sorry I couldn't tell you earlier but I really didn't know." He hunched his shoulders and smiled. "The whole world is not political, huh?"

Sean put his arm around him. "Thank you. Please come in. Have some breakfast."

"No, thank you," he said. "My wife, she'll be worried enough." And without another word he got back in his car and started it up. By now, he didn't need his headlights. They watched him drive out.

"I don't believe it," said Sean, and they walked inside, hugging each other.

"What happened?"

They were lying, covered and warm, in bed.

"After you were knocked down, I tried to pick you up and get us out of there, but then someone grabbed me and I pushed back and managed to move you off the street anyway. Then I was just sort of swept up into a truck and taken to jail. God, I feel so bad for the men they got. They really beat them badly, first in the truck and then at the jail. It was horrible, but I was so scared I couldn't do anything. I yelled once for a guard to stop kicking the boy next to me, but then he slapped me hard, and I was so afraid. And then I wondered what had happened to you, and hoped I'd moved you far enough away, so maybe you weren't picked up, but then . . ."

She was crying now, holding on to him.

He brushed her face with his hand. "It's OK. We're all right now. Did they hurt you?"

"Not aside from searching me four times." She began crying again, quietly, and kept telling him she loved him over and over. And finally he couldn't stop himself from believing her.

He wanted her to know, then, that he loved her, and that it would all work, but exhaustion was taking its toll, and sleep would wait no longer. And though he thought the words and tried to mumble them to her, somehow they never got out.

# Eleven

It wasn't so much that Lea's absences were getting harder to bear, but her continued obsession with Mike put me in an awkward position. After that first meeting with him, she started talking about this mystery girl he had to find. His whole life, she said, revolved around at least finding out what had happened to her. Weren't we getting bored here? Wasn't it time maybe to do something that meant something? It took her several days to bring it out, but it finally became clear that she wanted us to go with Mike and help him search for the girl. I wanted no part of it.

She went into Tossa several times to meet with him and to try to plan what should be done. I couldn't understand why this had suddenly become such a major problem when for the past several years he'd been content to let it slide into his past.

Now, with Lea's interest, it had again apparently become a priority. Lea told me that it had always been on his mind, but that he'd needed to develop a plan to find her, to make connections with certain people who would or could help him.

"Why does he need you?" I asked. We were in the back courtyard in the late afternoon. A few stray chickens pecked lazily about. She'd been in town during the day, but had come back in a fine mood. She seemed, for the first time in days, genuinely glad to see me.

"He doesn't really, I suppose, but I want to help him." She rested her hand on my arm. "I'm surprised at you, Douglas, that you don't seem to care at all about this. You're the one who's been talking lately about how everything seems meaningless to you. You can't seem to get involved. Well, here's a boy who really needs support. He's so involved. Maybe some of it would rub off on you."

"Look," I said. "It's just that I have a very hard time believing in what he says. Too much of it makes no sense to me. And what would you and I be doing if we came along? Making a diary of the trip to read to our grandchildren? '. . . And here we are in Istanbul seeking a lost waif who's been gone for six or seven years, if she ever existed at all.'"

"Do you really doubt that?"

"I can't believe you don't."

She stood up. "I don't like being called a gullible fool." She started back toward the door.

"Oh, Jesus, Lea, wait a minute. Come back here. I didn't say you were anything of the sort." I got up, went over to her and put my arms around her. "Look, why don't we just drop this whole thing for a day or so? I'm just tired of talking about it all the time, and I'd like to think that you and I have other things to do besides worry about this boy's problem."

She looked at me for a moment with her jaw set and her eyes hard. Then she put one arm on my shoulder and laid her head against me.

"I'm sorry, Doug, but seeing someone care so much about something really affects me. There's an intensity in him that I don't see in anyone else, and I find it stimulating being around him."

"Are you in love with him?"

"Douglas! God, no." Her arms circled my neck and she kissed me, pressing her body up against mine. "It's you I love. Remember?"

"But if you find him so stimulating . . ."

"Not that way." She smiled, at ease. "Why don't we go upstairs and I'll show you who I love?"

Mike was over for dinner the next night. Things had become considerably more mellow between

Sean and Kyra after the riot in Barcelona. She seemed to defer more to him now, and showed less of her bitching nature, at least in public. But that's not quite fair. To be honest, we hadn't heard them fighting in their room for several days.

Except for Lea's excursions into town, I was enjoying the vacation for the first time, spending a couple of hours each day reading or talking to Berta or Sean. I wasn't really worried about Lea's infatuation, and felt sure that it would pass quickly. Still, I wasn't exactly excited to see him come up to dinner.

He was hardly a threat by age alone. Surely, he was no more than twenty-five. I admit that he was darkly handsome, whatever that means. His features were smooth and regular, his limbs long. His hands gave the impression of being strong and dainty at the same time. I wondered if perhaps he were gay. That would be ironic. But, as I said, I wasn't really jealous.

Lea was forty, and while she was a very attractive woman to my eyes, I doubted whether she would be to a boy who should be dating teenagers.

The strangest thing about my attitude through all this was the feeling I had that I was in some play. There was nothing to bring it all to life for me. It wouldn't be quite true to say that I didn't care, but there was none of that sense of urgency that Lea had spoken of.

What would come of it all, anyway? Probably in two or three months Mike would have gone away, and Lea and I would be planning to go back to California and our real work. I felt that all these motions would be gone through, but nothing would make much difference.

Certainly the flow of our lives, which we'd worked to keep even all these years, would continue as before. That wasn't such a depressing thought. I only marveled at how wound up Lea and I seemed to be in what was, I felt sure, merely an interlude.

I had no way to explain, then, the incredible hostility I felt toward Mike when I came down and found him sitting next to Lea on the couch. I suppose I was civil enough, but I was unable to join in their conversation or even to look at them for any period of time. Luckily, Kyra was with Berta in the kitchen, and Sean and I took our drinks and walked out to the front.

It was definitely chilly outside, and getting darker earlier. We stood in silence. Finally, Sean spoke. "I love this country."

And he was right. The trees were thinning out beyond the courtyard wall, and a faint, cool breeze brought on it a trace of the smell of leaves, burning somewhere in one of the vineyards. "But I sure hate the fucking winter." He laughed to himself.

After a minute, he jerked his head toward the house. "What's going on with you two, if you don't mind my asking? The kid?"

"Yeah. I guess so. I just don't understand why she has to spend all her time talking to him."

He nudged me along toward the gate, and we walked together. "He's got a story. Whether it's true or not, I don't know, but it doesn't really matter. He believes it. I know the guy, Doug, and he's not a bad sort. I strongly doubt if he's going through all this rigmarole to put the make on Lea. Christ, I sound like you counseling me the other night."

In the growing darkness I looked at the big man next to me. He was becoming a real friend.

He went on. "Maybe Lea just needs to hear right now that somebody is interested in his own life. You can forgive me or not for saying this, but it sure as hell looks like you guys have not found much to get excited about lately. Sometimes, these endless days off will do it to you. I remember when I first left my job, I got incredibly depressed for the first couple of months until I got the hang of seizing the time I had. Set myself a goal, even though it was arbitrary, and all of a sudden, I wasn't half so depressed. But it seems to me, though, that you and Lea don't have anything really to go back to the States for, and nothing here is that interest-

149

ing for you, so you're both ripe for a little adventure. She's maybe better off than you, being more gullible, but you gotta fool yourself a little. Take some pleasure in small things. It may not mean a whole lot, but it's a start, and blah, blah, blah, here I go again. I'm sorry. I don't mean to be so bombastic."

I shrugged, sipped my drink. "No, it's good to hear you talk. You seem in great spirits, by the way." We were walking back to the house. "One of these days we'll both be in good moods at the same time, and won't know what to do with ourselves."

"Mutual suicide," he said, laughing. "Go out at the peak."

"Or the nadir?"

"Doubt it," he said, still laughing. "Only way to go from there is up. But you're right. Things are really good right now. Of course it might turn around any day, but well, let's just leave it at that."

Again, he turned conspiratorial. "Now, about this mutual suicide . . ."

"Come on," I said, "let's not joke about it. There's nothing worth killing yourself over. It all passes."

He still spoke through his smile, but there was a sober undertone. "Oh, I don't know. I could think of something."

But then Kyra came out the front door and joined us, and the talk turned to lighter things.

At dinner, we were all "on," and consequently it was a pleasant enough evening. Sean was especially perky, and kept us laughing at Berta's expense, talking to her and translating for us what he said were her replies. It was clear, though, that they both enjoyed the game, and Berta understood enough English to get back at him a time or two. My respect for her had grown by bounds.

Kyra sat next to Mike, and it surprised me that that drew no response from Sean. He sat next to Lea and conversed with her, when he wasn't teasing Berta. I was content to sit at the end of the table, saying little.

It wasn't until the coffee arrived that the talk came around to Mike's plans. It had been no secret among us before this, but somehow whenever it had come up, we'd let it drop. Now, with him here, it seemed a good time to clear the air.

Sean began in his usual bantering tone. "So you're looking for some help in this quest of yours, heh?"

Immediately you could feel the tension around the table. Kyra sipped at her coffee, looking down. Lea stared first at Sean, then at me. Berta cleared her throat and got up. Mike put down his cup carefully, and seemed to shrink back into himself.

"I hadn't exactly advertised," he said.

"Well, what is it you need?"

"Do you all know what this is about?" He looked at me and Kyra, seemed to fumble for a minute, then went on. "It's really more a question of deciding to do something now that I've been planning for several years. In fact, I've done more than plan, but it's just that something has kept me from going about it full time. Mostly, I guess, the fact that once I did it all-out and failed, then that would be that. The whole thing would be over. I'd be forced to admit it, and that would be hard. Maybe up until now it wouldn't have been possible at all.

"But lately I've come to realize that I'd be just fooling myself as long as I didn't give it everything I had. Might as well know the truth for sure, even if the truth is that she's dead."

"What makes you think she isn't?"

"Douglas!"

"No, Lea. It's a fair question. Really nothing definite, I guess. She might be." That haunted look came over him. "She might be."

"Well," said Sean, "even supposing that you find her alive and well, I've got two questions: how come she never tried to find you, and what are you going to do about her when you find her?"

"I know," he said. "I know. Maybe the best answer I can give you right now is that it's the best thing for me to do, for myself."

I wanted to ask him, then, why he was involving us so deeply, but checked myself.

"But to answer your questions, number one, I don't think, if we find her, that she'll have been free to look anybody up. In fact, I'm sure of that."

Sean shrugged. "Maybe she just would be embarrassed to have anyone know what she'd gone through."

"Maybe, but I doubt it. I know her, or knew her. Anyway, the other part of the question is the tough one, since I really don't know what we'd do if we saw each other again. For the first couple of years, I just naturally assumed that we'd start up again where we had left off, but now that strikes me as pretty unlikely."

"The whole thing does to me," I said. "How the hell do you intend to go off halfway across the continent and find a girl who's been lost for— what is it?—six or eight years? Jesus! What a way to waste a year or two. Aren't there police you could contact? Somebody's got to have more organization and information than you do."

"I have certain connections that I've built up over the years. I think I've got as good a chance of finding her as anyone else."

"Yes," said Sean, "all that's fine. But even then, what?"

Kyra spoke up. "I really don't see the point at all if there isn't some great personal thing anymore going on. I mean, if you don't plan to take care of her, even marry her, then what's the point?"

"I might do just that."

"Oh, Jesus!" I said. "Someone you haven't seen in all this time? How do you know—"

Suddenly Lea, who'd been quiet, shouted, "Shut up! All of you just shut up! I've listened to all of this for long enough. I've also talked to Mike much more than any of you, and let me tell you one thing. He loves this girl. Maybe it isn't realistic anymore, but it's got more going for it than all of your cynical selves pretending that your reasons for doing things are any better than his. I hope he finds her, and I think if he does, he'll love her, and maybe marry her. What does that matter? Stranger things have happened. And even if it doesn't, what is lost?

"Douglas, you say it's a horrible waste of a year, but it seems a whole lot better than our last few months. At least something's alive. Something's going on and changing. Maybe that's enough impetus right there to do something, quote, stupid." She stopped and glared at us.

"Whoa, Sis," said Sean. "Relax. We're not so

much coming down on Mike as just wanting to know if he's thought out what's gonna happen even if he succeeds."

"Well, it doesn't come across that way."

"I should have never brought it up to anyone else," said Mike. "It's just my affair."

"It's not so much that," said Sean again, "but you have to admit that deciding now to look for her isn't the most predictable thing you could do."

"Her getting kidnapped was predictable."

"And what's so horrible about wanting to help him?" asked Lea.

"I'm all for helping him, my dear," I said, "if I could only figure out what it is we're supposed to do."

But that question never got answered. Kyra stood up and said she'd had enough of this bickering, and why shouldn't we all get up and let Berta clear off the table. Sean announced that he would probably be finishing the first draft of his book within a few weeks, and the talk, rather forcedly, drifted to that.

Afterward, Mike was in some hurry to leave, and we let him go. The four of us then sat together in the front room having some after-dinner brandy. Kyra then got out some cards and we played a desultory hour of bridge.

"You know," Sean said, "I'm sorry I started that

unfortunate talk at the table, but I wanted everybody to be screaming, 'cause with this damn ear I can't hear a goddamn thing." He smiled at us all. "Better when it's out in the open anyway, huh?"

I took Lea's hand on top of the table, and felt her answering pressure. She looked peeved but not really angry. "You've got a banana in your ear," she yelled at her brother.

"What?" he said, grinning. "I can't hear you."

Upstairs, I said, "The main problem is that I don't believe it. The whole bit. The story just doesn't ring true to me. What I think is that he's a mixed-up kid, and I'm surprised and upset to see you so involved with him."

"Would it help any," she asked, "if we found proof that the girl had been kidnapped?"

"Some, maybe."

"Well, what do you want?"

"I want you to be my wife."

She sat next to me on the bed, and rubbed my shoulders. "I am your wife. I'm not his lover. Douglas, he's fifteen years younger than I. That's quite a bit, don't you think?"

"Not really."

"Then you'll just have to believe me." She tousled my hair. "The idea . . ."

When we were in bed and the lights were out, I could tell we were both wide-awake.

"What is it?" I asked.

"Look," she said. "To set your mind at ease, let's go into Barcelona's library and look up the old newspapers and see if there's something in them about Mike or Sharon. That ought to verify things, at least. Besides, we haven't spent a day together in a hell of a long time."

So the next day we drove through a thick fog into Barcelona. Winter was making bolder and bolder inroads along the coast. The reference librarian spoke English perfectly and she informed us that they had back issues of major papers on microfilm on the second floor.

"We'll check the Marseilles papers for July of '69," Lea said. "If we find nothing, I'll drop the whole thing."

I think that was the last time that Lea and I gave ourselves a chance with each other. I somehow knew that if we verified the truth of Mike's story, then she would go with him. How long she might stay, I didn't know, but it was as though she were giving the life she had known with me one last chance before passing it by for another one—a new one of more risk and passion.

Of course, that again was only how I felt. Did

more risk and more passion mean less substance? There were people who contended that those two elements made up that whole part of life worth living. To me they seemed naive and outdated.

For over three hours, we turned the reels and watched the columns of print roll in a green haze before our eyes. I had to stop and look up often because of eye fatigue, but Lea sat immobile, calmly turning the reel and scanning the screen in front of her.

"Here," she said finally. "Look here." And there was the small article that corroborated Mike's story perfectly. A girl of eighteen named Sharon Barrett had disappeared, according to her boyfriend, Michael Barrett. They were both Americans, traveling abroad. There followed her description, and all the rest.

"So it's true," she said. "You see."

I shook my head. "Come on, let's go home."

Halfway back to Tossa, when we hadn't spoken at all, she touched my arm. "You really could help us, Douglas. Don't close yourself off from me."

The lights were on, though it was not yet evening. I drove very slowly through the fog. I realized that I could not close myself off from her.

She was already gone.

# Twelve

It seemed to Mike lately that he was spending all his time either sitting by himself in the bar after it had closed or meeting Lea at a café and walking someplace, saying nothing, united but undeclared, waiting for someone to make the first move toward intimacy or toward Marseilles. What would Douglas do? Would he try to come along? No. It was clear he wasn't wanted, and he was smart enough to see that. It crossed Mike's mind that he might become violent, but violence had never scared him. It was so unnecessary in this case, anyway.

Now he sat in the bar and looked around. He'd tidied it all up. The lights were out, and only some streetlights from outside kept the place from pitch darkness. Occasionally someone would pass, or rather weave by, outside, and sometimes small groups could be heard singing or fighting, but mostly it was quiet. A tall, half-empty glass of gin and tonic sat on the table in front of him. He desperately wanted to talk to someone, someone not from this esoteric world of resort Spain. His resolution to act on what he'd thought had been the driving force of his life had come for all the wrong reasons. But even that wasn't clear to him. At least he was moving in some direction now, not drifting.

He downed his drink and stood up. His mind was clear. He normally drank lightly, and the one he'd just finished had been only his second or third drink since he'd come on. Walking behind the bar, he took a gin bottle and three smaller bottles of tonic, put them in a carry sack, checked around to make sure that the bar was well locked up, and walked out to the street.

Back in his apartment, he turned on the small light next to his bed and poured himself a glassful. The window in the room, which had been open continually since he had moved in, now suddenly let in too much of the cold. He got out of bed and went to close it, but the shutter was jammed. Figures, he thought. Just what I need tonight. He had a fur-lined leather jacket in his closet, and after giving up on the window, he got it and draped it over his shoulders when he got back into bed. He'd been in the middle of studying some chess problems in a book Tony had given him, but after a minute of looking at them, he knew that chess was the farthest thing from his mind.

God, it was cold! These *pensións* weren't equipped for the winter. There was no heat, and he hadn't had the foresight to get an electric heater, although with the window stuck open it wouldn't have done much good anyway. He thought of getting up and going to see Victor. Even if it was four in the morning, he knew the singer would be up. He wondered why Victor stayed around so long. They'd stopped paying him after the season ended, but he still played every night, like it said in the song, for drinks and tips. But he didn't really feel like talking to Victor. They weren't friends that way. Didn't really talk about anything. When you got down to it, they only passed the time. Seems that's what everybody does here, he thought. Except me and Lea, maybe.

He lit a cigarette and poured more gin into his glass. It was that goddamn mood that had gotten him into all this. Playing his song that night up at Sean's, and then Lea coming around the next day. It was funny, he thought. All this time he'd lived on his own, not really bothered by how everybody else was. He was used to things being how they were with Victor, or with Tony, or Sean, or anybody else for that matter. Hold things in. That was fine. It was the way it ought to be. But maybe not. There was that night after he'd quit the gun business, and something had wanted to get out. He had had to get something out, and there had been nobody there but himself. He shook his head.

Ought to slow down on this gin, he thought. Then he smiled and poured some more.

And what had happened up there at the fort? Here's this woman I don't know at all and suddenly I'm out of control.

He really needed to sort things out. They might at least have another blanket in the room somewhere. He looked at the glass in his hand, and put it down by the bed table. Enough. Getting out of bed, he grabbed his pants and put them back on. In a minute he was dressed, sitting on the side of his bed, looking out through the open window. He remembered back to high school, of all things. Hadn't he had some friends then? People to talk about things with? At least it had seemed so. Fleming and he had been friends. Thinking back, he realized that mostly they'd talked about girls and football, but there had been other times. That time when Fleming's parents were getting divorced and he'd stayed over with Mike for two weeks. They'd talked a lot then. And, now that he thought of it, there'd been lots of nights with Sharon, sitting up and bullshitting about things they cared about.

He knew he could reach Fleming by mail. He was sure his mom still lived in the big house in Bellevue. He could write to him there in care of her. Maybe that would help. He had lots of paper, and maybe it would clear things up for him, too. He felt a little dizzy, but poured himself a short one anyway, then sat down on the bed with the pad on his knees, his back propped against the wall, and began to write.

Dear Flem,

This may be the most unexpected letter you ever got, but still it's one I've got to write, and I can't think of anybody else who ought to listen. I'm writing it care of your mom, as you can see, and hope that she gets it to you before too long. I suppose, really, that it's stupid to write, and I don't expect you to write back. Hell, I don't even know if you're still alive, or if you're married and have three kids, or what. Still, it's not exactly that times are hard with me right now. Fact is, I'm working steady and have lots of money and free time and plenty to eat and drink. But I'm in a pretty bad state of confusion and think maybe that just setting things down will help clarify things. So if you're hassled with your own life, or whatever, you don't even have to read this. I just have to write it.

I'm living, as I guess you can tell by the stamp, in Spain, and right at this minute it's not the sunny place it's hyped up to be. I'm sitting on my bed having a drink and it's the middle of the night, when I should be asleep. For the last—let's see, how long now?—I don't know, I've been here awhile, working tending bar and a few assorted other things to keep me busy. Since I don't know if there are censors reading mail here, I won't go into whatever they were, but it's been interesting.

Probably you heard from my folks when I didn't come home that summer all about the story with Sharon and me. It also probably sounded like it couldn't happen, but it did, and since then, I've been more or less trying to get it together enough to find her, but it takes connections and money. Also, there's the point that I don't even have a clue as to where she is or what she's been through. I assume she was sold into slavery—God, it still sounds unbelievable to me after all this time— since that's what the cops in France seemed to believe. At least her body never turned up. For a while, the main thing the frog cops wanted to know was whether we dealt heroin, and how do you go about proving you don't? Anyway, they treated me pretty well, but they pretty much gave up on Sharon. For a while, I suppose I went crazy, but after traveling and the Nam, kind of mellowed out enough to get a plan going.

Well, all that's really neither here nor there. I finally arrived here in Tossa, and went to work, and got used to living again. I mean living without this guilt and sense of loss. I don't know if time just made it all seem, after all, hopeless, or if I really stopped caring about finding her, or what. What would we do together now? Where the hell do they even take white slaves? Half of me—no, more than half—came to believe that she was killed and somehow just buried and never found, or dumped out at sea, or any of a number of things. Gradually, she just receded.

But the thing was, I'd set myself on a way of acting that was based on this need to find her. I should also say that while I might write this as though I saw the light in a matter of weeks, what we're talking about here is years. And by the time it had really ceased to matter, I'd become obsessed with this image of myself as a seeker, as someone who had to find something, and even though now that something didn't make much sense, there was this backlog of five years of actions that seemed to reinforce it, at least for me. Needless to say, all of that made it harder to admit, even to myself, what I had really come to believe, which was that there was nothing to look for.

I say to myself, "I'm only twenty-five. That's not old. Why don't I start living, and forget Sharon?" But something in me just wouldn't go along with it. I still remember her so well it's scary. Finally, I came to *know* that she was gone, and gone for good, but still the old feelings wouldn't let me go. I was really more possessed than obsessed, and maybe what I needed was to get exorcised.

But I'd developed this new way about me. I don't . . . Well, what brought it on was this feeling that I was completely on my own, and didn't want to depend on anybody again for anything. I don't know if you remember me as being exactly gregarious, but it seems to me that I was friendly enough when I was younger. Well, that pretty much stopped, and it was funny to notice it, because I didn't feel any different. I just acted harder, and became quiet. I just stopped talking. I don't know why, really. Felt I was safer, maybe. I *was* dealing with some real assholes there in Vietnam for long stretches of time, let me tell you. I didn't trust anybody, though always, to myself, I thought I was the same.

All that acting tough, though, eventually got internalized, I suppose, because I noticed that people stopped being friendly to me, and, in fairness, I have to say I never cared that much. I just did my work, and kept to myself, and nobody seemed to give much of a shit, so I didn't either.

But see, the whole thing was building on itself, and didn't have much to do with me. I mean, sure, it was me all along, but not really. Does that make any sense? The "real" me was still old Mike Barrett who liked to sing and goof around and who fell so completely in love with Sharon. I mean, it didn't make sense to me that I could love somebody that much and then turn around and become such an unfeeling son of a bitch. But

I stuck with acting that way. It was, after all, the way I was.

Then a while ago, I quit working with some people, and it was like all of a sudden the "real" me had had enough. I wanted to talk to people and have some fun. You know, just not take everything so damn seriously. But still there was this Sharon thing inside me, and I'd gotten so used to being quiet, almost sullen, that it just didn't seem to be working. I was, in fact, getting to be almost happy all the time, but never acted like it, and I felt like a phony in spades. I just didn't know how to act carefree. Still don't, I suppose. And there was all the feeling about Sharon I couldn't ignore. You want to know the truth? This is the first time, and I mean right now, that I've been able to say she's dead, or at least gone. Maybe this letter was the right thing to do after all. It's good to have some idea where you're coming from.

So here I was, not even able to admit that I wasn't feeling so bad, and man, I'm telling you, dying of loneliness. And now we come to this exorcism and all that it's led to.

He put down the pen and shook his head to clear it. Fleming would think he was an idiot, but then what did he care what Fleming thought? He'd probably never see him again in his life. He got up to pee, taking his drink with him. He was getting drunk, but the kind of drunk where he felt exceptionally lucid. No longer was he concerned with how many times he'd reached for the gin. Now he only wanted to finish the letter. He felt that at last he was getting somewhere. It was a start, this writing, getting at how he felt.

He came back to the bed and arranged his coat again over his shoulders, yawning. His breath hung in the air in an opaque cloud for a second. Must be the coldest night since I've been in Spain, he thought. He shivered, brought the bottle to his lips, and took a short sip.

I've always hated the word romantic, probably mostly because of your definition of what a romantic person was—not somebody who cried alone, but somebody who wanted to be seen crying alone. I never thought I had any of that in me, but I should have known how wrong I was by how violently I reacted against that. When I heard it, it must have fit me to a T. Anyway, I sure as hell fought against it long enough. I bet I didn't cry once for five or six years. Fuck that pity, I thought. You've got a job to do. But, as I said, I just got to feeling more and more that I had to let loose, let this burden ease up for a time. Then this guy, actually a pretty good friend of mine on the level I've been talking about, was up to the bar, and we got asked up to a dinner at this palace outside of town. Not really a palace, but a damn nice house. We had a great dinner, and drank a lot, and then afterward we all sat around and drank some more and I played some guitar.

There was a lady there named Lea, and all I can tell you is that she just killed me. I don't even know if she's that pretty, but there was something about her that . . . Well, you know. The trouble was she was married, and her husband was there, of course. So while I'm sitting there playing guitar, all of these feelings of having to communicate with someone become almost too much to take, and I start playing this song I wrote which I don't play that often, even to myself. Suddenly it was all quiet and I felt as though I'd reached someone with it. But then again, almost immediately, I felt guilty, as though—you'll probably think I'm crazed—as though Sharon were watching me. So I stopped, I felt I had to leave, but just as strongly I wanted to get to know this woman.

When I got home, I felt pretty shitty, as though I'd betrayed myself, and I didn't want to get involved with anybody who was already married and had her own life. But it was the first time in my memory since Sharon that I'd been attracted to anybody else.

Well, the next day I saw her. We just went up to a hill and had some wine, and talked, and before I knew it, this whole thing with Sharon came pouring out, and I was crying like a baby. And the crazy thing is that even as I was crying, even as all this hell of wanting Sharon for all this time came back to me, I knew that in a sense I was finally

getting rid of her memory. I sat there and held on
to Lea for all I was worth, and knew that the thing
with Sharon was over and done. And still I held
her. I hated myself, but couldn't stop. I held her
to be holding her. Not for comfort, but because
I wanted her. And all the while here she is believing, as she should, that I'm wrecked over the past,
and as we talk I become more and more unable
to imagine not having her, even if it means lying
to her about what Sharon means. Because I sense
that she'll stay with me. Maybe out of pity, at first,
but I don't even care about that. Let her think
I'm a lonely bastard who needs somebody to talk
to. She'd be right. But now she wants to help me
find Sharon. God! This is ridiculous. She wants
to help me find Sharon, and I don't want to find
her anymore. There! It's out. But if the search for
Sharon will keep Lea with me, I'll do it.

And still, you know, I don't feel it's wrong. I
can talk to her. I haven't even gone to bed with
her. I only kissed her once, but felt that here I was
alive again. So what am I doing? Moving from
one impossible love to another? I don't think so.
I think we'll work this thing out. She's bored with
her husband. I know that. Not that she's told me,
but he's one of these guys who seems to have bot-
tomed out. No spark.

She's infatuated with me, but won't touch me,
and I won't even try. I want to take my time, and
have her get to know me. Maybe what she likes in
me is the passion she saw that I had for Sharon.

I don't know. Like I said, I'm confused. Nothing really seems like I'm going about things the right way, but at least I'm seeing her, and I—and seeing her is the most important thing right now. Still, I can't tell her that. Maybe it'll take a few months of looking together for a trace of Sharon, but by then we'll be together, and she can believe that I've slowly come around to loving her.

Shit, he thought. Do I really believe this? Can I really be that cold a bastard? His eyes burned as though the lids had been branded as he struggled to keep them open to read over what he'd written. The gin bottle was a good two-thirds gone, and out his window the sky over the Mediterranean was lightening. He lit a cigarette, and got up, pacing around the room. It all must be bullshit, he thought. If I found Sharon, I would take her. What's all this talk of exorcism? What have I been living for all this time if not finding her?

But then his thoughts turned to Lea cradling his head against her breasts as she let him cry himself dry. He should leave her alone. He knew that she was falling in love with him. No, not in love. Infatuated, and for all the wrong reasons. It couldn't work. But it had to. God damn, he'd had enough of being alone.

He lay down on his stomach on the bed, and took up the pad again.

So, Flem. What am I trying to say? That I'm confused, I suppose. I might be dead wrong in what I'm doing, but I've got to do it. It's a cold world. Somebody's got to lose, I guess, and I'm tired of it being me. Write if you want, but you don't have to, obviously. I hope you're happy.

He woke up facedown on the bed. When he tried to swallow, the sides of his throat were so dry they stuck together. He coughed, and turned his aching head toward the window. The sky was a clear blue. It must be afternoon, since the sun had passed over the window. The papers of his letter lay spread out over the bed. A few had fluttered to the floor.

Slowly he pulled himself up. He let the clothes he'd slept in lie where they fell, went into the bathroom and quickly got into the shower. The cold water hurt, but it brought him around slightly. He was, at least, awake. He took four aspirins, and walked, not quite dry, back to the bed, where he gathered up the papers and began reading.

Before he'd finished he realized that he must have been crazy drunk to have written all that. He didn't know what he was talking about, all that crap about not loving Sharon and wanting Lea. It all read like a soap opera. Besides, what would Fleming care? Putting all the pages together, he tore the letter into strips and then into little pieces, which he dropped into the wastebasket under the sink in the bathroom.

He'd have to watch what he did when he drank like that, he thought. Luckily it wasn't often.

He got dressed and went outside. It was a bright, sunny day. Some high, white, fluffy clouds occasionally blocked the sun, but they passed quickly. It was late afternoon, probably close to four. There was no trace of the chill of last night, though it wasn't hot. He stopped in at the Aster, a hotel he felt comfortable in, for some badly needed coffee. A friend of his was there, reading.

"What's the book?"

The friend looked up. "Schoolwork. Philosophy. Good for the soul."

"I need something good for my soul. You think they'd take me in school?" He smiled, and signaled the waiter to bring the coffee.

"Rough night?"

"Look like it?"

"You have looked better." The friend went back to his reading when Mike's coffee arrived. He drank it in silence. When he finished, he clanked his cup down a bit too hard, and stared stonily ahead.

"Anything wrong?"

Mike dug his thumb and forefinger into his eyes in an effort to clear his mind. "No," he said

quietly, "not really. I guess I'm just hungover."
Again he rubbed his eyes. "You know, I guess I
don't want to talk about it."

He got up, patted him on the shoulder, and
walked outside, blinking against the afternoon sun.

# Thirteen

Lea kicked the blankets, which had become tangled in her legs. Doug was gone again. It must now be nearly two weeks since they'd gotten up together. Still, it wasn't bad. She was finding less and less to say to him, and the times they'd gone up to bed together had been disastrous. She thought of the last time, when he'd finished before she'd been ready to start. Then he'd gone downstairs to read, leaving her tensed, curled up in the cold bed until she'd slept. When had that been? Four days ago? Maybe five?

He was acting like a child. She couldn't understand it. It seemed to her that ever since they'd arrived, he'd been bored, anxious to—no, *desperate* to believe in anything, something that would end his spiraling despair. And now here was the opportunity, and he saw in it only a threat. After all these years they'd been together, how could there be a threat? But she had to admit that she enjoyed Mike's company more than her husband's. It might be that Doug's lack of interest across the board had finally affected her and made her realize that he had stopped living, and she wasn't ready for that. Not for a long time. She felt younger than she had in years.

Let him brood, she thought. If he doesn't come around, why should I give it a thought? He doesn't care himself. He was probably out drinking now, even this early in the morning. Drinking, with no plans, and no future. For a fraction of a second, she wished that they had no money, and that they would need to go back to work again, but that wish quickly passed. They had saved for this, earned it, and she would take it. Besides, it was more all-embracing for him than simple lack of work, although she supposed that that was what had brought it on.

Then all at once it came to her that he no longer loved her. That would explain it all, wouldn't it? The boredom, the feeling of going through motions socially, the perfunctory sex?

The sheets and blankets still held her legs captive, and she twisted to get herself out. The room was cold. The electric heater didn't do much good. She went in and stepped into the shower only long enough to get wet. Looking in the mirror, she surprised herself smiling, and stared at her face. Her looks pleased her. She pinched one of her nipples, and smiled again as it hardened under her touch. Too old, huh?

She was only now coming into her own. All this time of being a wife and a working woman and following all the proper steps to what? To happiness? Only now was she even becoming aware of what she wanted.

And what she wanted was to live, and not in her staid, old, predictable way. But she didn't even say that to herself yet. Instead, she felt that she would have to make a fool of herself a few times. It wasn't clear how, and she didn't try to reason it out. She felt it as a tension.

She'd never done anything foolish. Her life had always been reasoned and correct. Now was she making a fool of herself with a boy fifteen years younger? She didn't think so, but only because she really didn't think she could yet act foolishly. She only knew, somewhere beyond her thinking, that she would have to make mistakes, and afterward she would know that they had been errors all along, and that she had known it. She sat down on the toilet, and felt the beginning of a menstrual cramp. Too old, too old, too old.

Coming back to the bedroom, she began putting on her clothes in a lighthearted mood. Suddenly she felt an overwhelming excitement, and simultaneously a curious indifference to whatever might happen in this house, particularly with her husband. Though she would never have admitted it to herself, she had in fact passed into something beyond indifference. Had she been more in touch with herself, she might have looked into the dressing mirror, smiled at the reflection, and said, "Then fuck him."

On the floor in the hall outside her room was a note from her brother, asking her to come out at her convenience and meet him on the roof. She'd gone up there several times before to enjoy the solitude, and knew that it was also one of his favorite places. The note actually said: "Get yo' skinny ass up on the roof here 'fore noon, and mebbe we kin git some words in together 'fore you leave."

She smiled and walked downstairs. The house was deserted except for Berta in the kitchen, and she wondered where Doug and Kyra had gone. It was still early. She took her coffee and hot milk in a handled bowl and walked out through Sean's office, across the back courtyard to the stairs that led up to the roof.

Sean sat out on the beam that extended from

the house, straddling it. Smoke from a thick cigar rose evenly over his head in the still morning air. He chomped at its end as though it were a piece of gum. His coffee cup sat in front of him on the beam.

She looked at him with interest. There, she thought, is a happy man.

"Hey," she said, mounting the stairs, "what makes you think I'm leaving?" She handed him the note. "Says here, 'before you leave.'"

He looked down at her. "Come on to this side of me, will you? I can't hear a damn thing out of this ear. And give me some of your coffee, sill voos plate."

He held out his cup, and she poured half of hers into it. He looked at it critically. "All that milk make your shit white?"

They laughed. "You are gross."

"I'll not deny it."

She sat down on the ledge that circled the roof, and he backed off the beam, and turned to face her. He sipped at the coffee. "I love it up here. Just look down there at Tossa. Even with the trees mostly bare now, it's a great sight. And with the fort there, you can imagine anything happening."

"That's never been a problem for you, has it? I mean imagining?"

"No, I guess not. But here is something special. 'Course I suppose that's why I decided to stay here. It's a good place."

Out beyond the town, right on the horizon, a ship moved slowly over the water, leaving behind it a spume of black smoke. They watched it in silence as it crossed their vision, keeping their own thoughts. When it moved behind the fort, Sean seemed to come to a decision. He took his cigar from his mouth and threw it down to the ground below, then polished off the coffee.

"Seems to me, Sis, and you can correct me if I'm wrong, that we've been doing a pretty good job of avoiding each other this past month or two, and it's on my mind a lot now. It'd be a shame to never get to know you in person after the reams of paper we've sent to each other. Is there maybe something getting in your way around me? I know your husband a lot better than I know you, and there's nothing wrong with that, but you've always been, well, at least you've always had a special place in my mind, like we were the ones who should be close, and somehow, now you're here, I feel farther from you than I ever have, except for right after the war when you were just a kid."

She studied his earnest face. "It always seemed like you were avoiding me," she said. "I've always thought it should be you that takes the first step, like you'd consider me intruding."

He smiled, shaking his head. "Man. That son-of-a-bitch act I do must really work well."

"Oh, it's not so much that . . ."

"Then what?"

"I mean, it's not that you act cold. You're friendly enough. It's just like you don't want to be any more friendly."

"And you don't call that being cold?"

"Well, maybe."

He laughed. "Maybe. Damn sure. What else would it be? And probably I'd go on being that way, except that lately it seems as though things with you and Doug have pretty much gone beaver, as they say. And I don't like to see it happen. I care a lot about you both. And maybe also for the first time in my life, I'm beginning to realize how nice it is to let yourself care. It's a good thing."

"Well, it's what's wrong with Doug and me."

"Yeah, it seems like it."

She cupped her hands around her coffee, and stared again over the trees toward Tossa. "I guess I'm just tired of—" She stopped herself. "I don't know. Doug has always had a way about him. Kind of an enthusiasm. And since we've got here, I'm beginning to think that it's always been a superficial thing. No, that's not it exactly. But it was for some outside interest. Always. I mean, he'd get excited about a piece he was doing, or about a new room we'd want to put in our house, or about almost anything he was doing, but always it was on that level. I think when we got here, and there wasn't anything to do, he tried to internalize all that gusto and found there wasn't much there to get enthusiastic about."

"You've tried to help him?"

"Come on. Sean, I'm not such a callous beast as that. Of course I tried, but somehow I was part of all he didn't care about."

"And how did that grab you?"

"What do you mean by that?"

"What I mean is, were you upset or mad or anything else that you'd seemed to have lost your place in his affections? Something that major going on with your husband of some years, and I should think you'd fight for your position a little more."

"Instead of what?"

"What do you think?"

She swallowed down the last of her coffee. The grounds nearly gagged her, and she made a face, then smiled at her brother.

"You think I'm having an affair with Mike."

"No. But I'm probably the only one who doesn't."

"Well, I'm not."

He shrugged. "It's not important. Doug thinks you are and that's important. That he doesn't let on that he cares is the real problem, Sis. Don't you talk to each other anymore?"

She shook her head.

"Because maybe what he needs is a little jolt from you. Something to make him realize that . . ." He stopped. "You know all I'm trying to say, I guess. Unless you've kissed him off, you ought to help him."

"I haven't kissed him off, as you put it."

"Prove it." He crossed his eyes and stuck out his tongue at her. They both laughed. "It doesn't matter much to me, you understand, but I'm looking at it from your perspective as somebody who doesn't want their marriage to be over."

She was quiet for a minute, and then said, "To tell you the truth, Sean, I'm not really sure. I don't know if you've ever lived with someone when the spark just went out. It's like there's a vacuum and if you get too close, you get sucked into it. Doug's given up on living, as far as I can tell, and I'm just starting to come alive."

"But don't you ask yourself why?"

"Sure. I think it's got to do with us both having the time to examine what we're doing, and while I've come to the conclusion that I've been wasting time and should do something about it, Doug is at the opposite pole. He never thought before that he was wasting his time, and now he thinks he's come to realize that everything is a waste of time. Up until we stopped talking, whenever that was, he kept going on and on about how nothing had any meaning for him. He'd say that if he could just find a small thing that touched him, he'd use it as a base to build on, but he's gotten so morbid. 'We're going to die in the end, anyway.' Or 'What will it all matter in a hundred years?' I tell you, it drives me crazy. It's not how I feel at all, and I also feel powerless to touch him, or bring him back. He's going to need some shock, or something, and maybe that won't even make a difference."

"Is that why you're seeing so much of Mike?"

"No." She paused, then came out with it. "I'm fascinated by him."

The big man stood up and, putting his hand on the ledge, vaulted over it to the flat roof. He walked across it to the outer edge, and took another cigar from his shirt pocket. Biting off the tip, he struck a wooden match against the stucco, and stood puffing for a moment before he turned back to face his sister.

"Well," he said, "at least we're talking."

"What do you think I ought to do?"

He sat back down. "Shit and Shinola. Damned if I know. It's hard, though, isn't it?"

She looked at his rugged face and, for the first time since she'd arrived, saw the brother she'd known as a child. His face must look like that when he sleeps, she thought. She reached out and touched his hair. He stared at the ground below, and sighed.

What went on with him? she wondered. This was so rare for him—letting anyone see him without his face being animated. She didn't really know what his natural look was. Whenever he talked, or appeared in a room, his eyebrows arched, his step quickened, and he was alive. He rarely showed himself as tired or dejected, and when he did, it was always with an intensity that made them almost positive ways to feel. Now, though, he was simply relaxed. His shoulders hung easily, not in a tired way, and his eyes looked neither left nor right. He chewed absently on the cigar. Even as she watched him, it stopped smoking, and still he chomped away, by all signs unaware that he was not alone. She stroked his hair as though she were petting a dog. The intimidation she'd always felt around him had eased, and suddenly she felt at home with him again.

"How are you, really?" she asked, almost whispering.

He took in a deep breath, let it out slowly, then shook his head. "Well, I'd say offhand I'm coming out of the other end of the tunnel that Doug's going in." It was strange to hear him talk with that vacant look on his face. His mouth moved and he seemed to mean what he said, but he didn't emphasize. "Most of the time now, I find myself slipping into something like awe over the simplest, smallest things. For the longest time before, I wouldn't let anything get near me, as I guess has been obvious to you, and pretty much passed through things with a cynical eye, if you want to call it that. Not that I felt just like I suppose Doug does. I always knew things could reach me, or hurt me, or whatever, but in a way that knowledge protected me. I knew I was playing with fire." He chuckled without changing expression. "Learned that early enough, I guess. Anyway, now I think I'm starting to believe that you ought to live out on the edge, and frankly, Sis"—here he seemed to come again to life, and began feeling for a match—"it scares me."

"Because of Kyra, you think?"

"Yeah." He puffed on the cigar, deep in thought. "Yeah, because of Kyra."

"What happened?"

"Why the change, you mean? I don't know. I'm

getting old, maybe, is all, and I see her as my last chance."

"For what?"

"Same as you. To live. I'm scared all the time now, I tell you, but it's new. When I lost her that night in Barcelona, I thought I couldn't stand it, and thought about what it would be like if she were gone, or lost, or whatever, and it came to me that, like it or not, she was far and away the most important thing in my life. Then I also knew, like a bolt out of the blue, that she loved me too." He wagged his head from side to side, his eyes dancing. "Nice poem, that." Anyway, I guess you'd say I've opened up, at least to letting myself feel things. And on one level, I'm a wreck. I lie awake now at night and think how lucky I am, and when I come up here, I see all this around me, and I'm like a kid again. I mean it all gives me so much joy." He shrugged. "I know it sounds silly to talk about it."

"No, it doesn't."

"Well. It kind of reminds me of the first time I went up in a glider. I remember that first drop to clear from the pilot plane, and how I really thought we were gonna die. In fact, the whole time up there I was scared to death, but I don't think I ever enjoyed anything more. I thought of that the other night, and I wished I'd have applied that analogy a little sooner, instead of just having tried to make it through however many years it has been. Of course maybe I am a fool. I know in my mind that everybody watches out for themselves, but it's different with Kyra. We both feel kind of like you do, as though we're coming out of something together. And now things fit together, and I couldn't go back, not even if I tried, and I don't know why in the world I would ever want to try."

She came down after a few more minutes. He said he wanted to stay up for a while. Her cramps were getting painful, and she decided to go back upstairs and lie down. Sean had said that Kyra and Doug had gone into town to buy mussels. "They're both stir-crazy anyway, though I guess their reasons are different enough."

She changed to her robe in the bedroom, then stuck her head out the window and yelled up toward the roof.

"Isn't there any damn hot water, Sean?"

Presently her brother's face appeared over the edge of the roof, smiling down at her. "Pardon?"

"Can't we get some hot water?"

"I'll have Berta draw you a bath downstairs," he said, and she heard his footsteps crossing back overhead.

She lay on the bed with her eyes closed, and almost immediately, it seemed, though it must have been nearly a quarter of an hour, Berta knocked at the door.

"The bath is ready."

She opened her eyes and followed her down to Sean's bathroom, where the mirrors were already steamed from the hot tub.

While she soaked, Berta came in twice. She brought her a cup of hot tea with lemon peel, and some fresh white towels. Lea found herself wanting to talk to her, but in the end was content to lie silently in the hot, soapy water. What could she say? Her Spanish was poor. The woman certainly was a jewel, but really, what did they have in common? Maybe when Kyra got back, she would talk to her. Or maybe she'd go on into town. The hot water felt wonderful.

Sean was right. When Doug got back, she'd talk to him. But God, she was getting sick of talking. A shiver ran through her. She turned the hot water on with her toes. At least they wouldn't be home for a couple of hours. In all that time, she might think of something to say.

# Fourteen

At first, I wasn't at all pleased that Kyra had decided to come down to Tossa with me, and for a moment, I was tempted to pretend I didn't see her and roar with squealing tires and spewing gravel stones from the courtyard as she ran waving at me from the house. But on reflection, even before I reached the main road, I was glad of her company.

We'd never really gotten along well, to say the least, and since I was now seriously contemplating moving on, it seemed a good time, or at least an opportune one, to find out what she was like. I admit that I'd been unfair. She was no more nor less than a remarkably well-built woman of twenty-five, probably no more conniving than others, whom I had taken it into my mind to dislike. True, there had always been a stridency in her voice that I had instinctively hated, but as we drove on down toward Tossa, her voice, in its quieter reaches, sounded like Lea's.

I had a bottle of *tinto* cradled between my legs, and from time to time would take a drink. Drinking in the morning wasn't the great evil it was cracked up to be.

"What are you going into town for?" I asked, offering her the bottle, which she refused.

"Sean's going to write. I like to get out when he's busy."

"Well, we'll find ourselves some mussels and have a hell of a dinner."

It didn't really much matter to me if we actually found our dinner in town. It had grown next to impossible for me to be around Lea, and any excuse to leave was good enough. The morning was exceptionally clear, and we drove slowly, watching the passing scenery, the lifting mist, the occasional white house with smoke rising from the chimney.

When we got into town, I parked just off the main road, and we walked together to the market, a group of stalls set around a square on the water side of town. There were a few permanent buildings with their faces open to the square, but the majority of the marketing was done in the little stalls, most of which closed for the day by siesta time. It was not crowded in the square, but a few people were up and about. We saw the fish booth we wanted, and crossed to it.

A small, fat man with an enormous mustache was filleting some white fish for display. His wife toiled over a sink behind him. The counter was piled high with fish, and on the right was a pile of the black mollusks we'd come for. The man seemed in no hurry to wait on us, and we stood and talked while I drank more of the wine. Finally, smiling patiently, I caught the man's attention and offered him a drink from the bottle. Kyra spoke to the wife, while he joined me with the wine, and in a moment we had our plastic bag filled with a kilo or two, while the woman opened a few dozen and laid them on the counter. They ate them with vinegar and black pepper, and I saw no reason not to do likewise. When we'd paid and eaten quite a few each, I left him the bottle, and we walked back to the center of town.

There wasn't really much to do so early in the morning, so we decided to stop in at a *tapas* bar for more to eat. I hadn't had breakfast, and the mussels had whetted my appetite. Kyra said she'd just watch, but didn't mind accompanying me. I ordered a tortilla and a beer, and we settled down at a booth across from each other.

"Jesus, this is a degenerate life."

"I don't think it has to be."

"Is that directed at me?"

"Take it as you will."

I finished the tortilla without speaking. Neither did I look up at her, though I sensed her eyes on me. I went to pick up my plate, but she put her hand, rather roughly, I thought, over mine.

"Just what is it," she said, "that you don't like about me?" When I started to protest, she went on, stopping me. "I don't ask because I think about it often, or because I have any strong feelings for you either way, but it's just a little weird. I've never had much trouble getting along with men. Is it that you can't have me?"

"Well, aren't we presumptuous?"

"Answer me, then."

She had immediately taken her hand away from mine, but I found myself wishing that she hadn't.

"You're conceited," I said. "Or maybe it's Sean. I don't know."

"What about Sean?"

"You're not good for him."

"And what makes you the grand arbiter anyway? What's he to you?"

"A friend, *comprendo*?"

"You know, you're a nasty and vindictive little man. You've got some nerve telling me—"

I got up. "I don't have to listen to this."

She nearly screamed. "Yes, you do. Sit down, would you? Now, let me tell you a thing or two about Sean. And about being conceited, while we're at it. Men find me attractive. What am I supposed to do about that? Act like I don't know it? Since I've been a child, I've had men trying to fondle me, get close to me, talk to me. I'd be an idiot if I didn't act like I knew it. Sure, I come on. It scares a lot of men off, and that's a relief to me. Who needs it? But Sean—I don't—I won't have you thinking that I'm no good for him. I am what he needs, and though you may find it impossible to believe, I need him. Not just feel good about him, or want him to be my sugar daddy. There's more going on inside him than in any ten men I've known before. Now you, with Lea acting her docile self in front of you—don't you get up; I'm not done—you don't have any idea of anything besides that stereotyped idea of a woman supporting her man. You know—and this isn't the first time I've thought it—it occurs to me that that's the whole problem with you two: there's no way she can get to you without completely breaking away. There's nothing else. She's either with you in calm waters, always ready to support you, be the dutiful wife she has been, or she's against you, and if you ask me, she's gone over now. But Sean and I—well, we're not like you. We fight, maybe too much. We try to stop. We've even succeeded to some degree since—since that Barcelona night. But you know, we feel things. Don't you tell me I'm no good for him. You don't go to bed with him. You don't see the man I know. Sure he complains to you. What the hell can he do? Your whole frame of reference is master-slave, and maybe his used to be. That, and he's been afraid, almost as afraid as I am, and that's hard to overcome, but, believe me, we will overcome it. I'm not against him, but there's a person inside me that counts. Maybe you should give your wife the same credit."

I wanted to get up and run. I wanted to get up, hit her in the face, and run. She stopped for a moment, then went on.

"I've got a theory, you know?"

"Do you want me to ask about it?"

She paused. "You really are a small man."

"Thank you."

"And it's funny, 'cause you're not a bad man, I don't think. I wonder if it's just defenses."

"Oh, I'm sure it is."

She seemed to soften, staring at me. "Give me your hand." I put my hand on the table and she took it in hers, kneading my palm softly. In spite of myself, I relaxed.

"Let me tell you my theory. I think I represent

something that you envy. No, now don't pull away. I'm not seducing you, and you know it. Let's be calm now. I want you to understand."

Her hand was closed now around mine, and the small physical contact took the tension away. I no longer wanted to run.

"See, Sean and I, we're taking a chance, and we know it. And I think it's pretty obvious to you, and maybe to Lea. You've been around us enough. And sometimes—no, all the time lately—I get the feeling you'd almost rather have Lea go away, or leave yourself, or at least have something change, but you don't think it would really matter. So you do nothing. And you see us, fighting and being too loud, and laughing, and even getting beat up, and it all seems to make a difference, and you say to yourself, 'Those children, isn't that cute,' but the other half of you thinks Sean is a fool, and resents me for being part of it, for bringing it out in him. And I'm glad I do, Douglas. He's alive now. I know he's happy."

I knew she was right. And she did love him. I couldn't keep myself from feeling that they were fooling themselves, but now I felt it, or was beginning to, with a certain sympathy.

About Lea and me, I didn't know. The whole fabric of my life had been woven into a suit that maybe had become out-of-date. And part of that suit—maybe the left front pocket, ha-ha—demanded that externals be unruffled. Keeping that exterior up has taken its toll. Even if something did touch me, hurt me, reach me, would I admit it? Would I let it in?

Kyra sat across from me, holding my hand, earnest, and even as I took pleasure in her touch, I was amused by her sincerity. But kindly, now, kindly.

Let her love Sean. It would run its course. Lea had loved me, and it should matter more. So what was I? A victim of the age, an age that couldn't produce tragedy? God, I really was out of date. Did I want to believe that it all related? That some cosmic order would be restored? Ha! A little personal order would do well enough.

But I saw then what I needed, and didn't give it much hope. I needed to see some connection, some way that I could believe that everyday life counted for something, and like circles growing out from a rock hitting a pond, little events, perhaps meaningless in themselves, would take on some significance beyond themselves, if only to make us feel more in it all together.

But I looked across at her, intense and protective, angry that I felt the cold passage of the years in her warm hand, and saw her retreating back, further and further, surviving, until she was alone, too.

I smiled and squeezed her hand. "Can I meet you back at the car at around three? I want to do some thinking."

"Sure," she said. "I'm happy in town."

I stood. "Thanks for trying."

# Fifteen

Sean wasn't in the mood to talk. He had things to do, and he was annoyed that he'd given the car to Doug and Kyra. Besides, his head hurt, as it had since he'd been beaten, and he was seriously worried that he was going deaf.

He sat huddled in the backseat of the cab, buried under his jacket. He hadn't taken many cabs since he'd moved here, and these men drove like maniacs. Worse, he was convinced they actually were maniacs.

How could he be so stupid as to forget his appointments today? You'd think the ear alone would have kept it on his mind. In spite of himself, he smiled. Nice to be disorganized for a change. But he shook his head to clear that thought away, and it throbbed anew. Not today. Today was for getting things done.

The cabbie took a corner too fast, and the car skidded, then left the road and slid for several yards, half fishtailing on the roadside. They bounced to a stop and the driver turned around with a ridiculous grin. Sean frowned at him.

"Slower, eh?" he said in Spanish.

The man shrugged his shoulders as though what had happened had been completely beyond his control. Then they began rolling again.

First he had to see the doctor in Blanes. Then he was meeting Tony and Marianne for lunch. And finally he'd made an appointment with his lawyer to check over his tax situation, his will, and his resident status, which seemed to change with the seasons, though he'd taken all the proper steps months before.

As soon as the cab reached Blanes, Sean stopped the driver and paid him off. Even if it meant a long walk, it was preferable to negotiating the streets in a taxi. Besides, he liked the city. It wasn't only a resort town, although the hordes coming in daily from the beaches during the season gave it some of that character. It had its own downtown, and seemed to struggle successfully against the tourists. Here there were, to Sean's mind, "real" *tapas* bars filled with genuine Spanish businessmen who felt the link between their work and their homeland, whose lives had changed little since the late '50s, when the Costa Brava had "caught on."

Of course, the air here wasn't as clear. From time to time, when the wind was right, the whole city choked under a sulfur cloud from the factory by the train station. Today, he didn't much care. Whenever he started smoking cigars in the morning, he would normally continue all day, and now he smoked as he walked, inhaling sometimes, and coughing.

Dr. Caldez was a man of about Sean's age, with snow-white hair and a wispy mustache stained brown on one side from tobacco. He spoke in whispers only, and didn't appear to have many patients. Sean always got right in to see him, and went back to him because he liked his style. He cared about medicine when he had a patient, and when he didn't, it was the last thing on his mind. They'd gone out drinking together after one of Sean's visits, which were infrequent, and the doctor had confessed that he liked his free time too much to have a really successful practice. Oh, when he'd been young, it had been different, but now he'd rather not work much. He preferred to sit in a park and observe things. He was an avid bird-watcher. In a couple of years, he planned to retire, and move to Madrid with his wife. Or maybe he'd go to Seville. It didn't really matter. The change was the thing.

As usual, the office today was empty of patients. It was on the third floor of a six-story building that fronted the river, now dry, which, in season, ran through the town. Sean took the steps two at a time and greeted the elderly secretary courteously. The doctor, she explained, had only just arrived for his appointment, and would see him immediately.

They shook hands and talked for a while before Sean got down to his troubles. He sat deliberately close to the doctor so he could hear him.

"Really," he explained, "it's only the right ear that seems to have gone, although I'm not sure about that. The balance is wrong, you see."

The doctor took out his instrument and looked in the ear.

"Ai."

"Look bad?"

"Pretty badly infected. Does it still hurt?"

"I guess I'm pretty used to it."

Caldez patted him on the shoulder. "That doesn't make it better, now, does it? What are all these other bumps on your head?"

Sean explained about the beating he'd taken in Barcelona, making light of the episode as much as possible. The lumps had gone down significantly, though his head still hurt.

"Do you hear ringing? Do you black out?"

"Nope."

"Any change in the ear after the beating?"

"No."

The doctor sat down and lit a cigarette. He shook his head. "I'll prescribe something for the infection, and it should clear up in a week or so. You should be more careful, you know."

"I think the beating was just a fluke."

"Not just that. Your ear has been bad for a while now, and you should have come to see me the day after the beating."

"You wouldn't have been here," said Sean, smiling. "You know you need a few days' notice."

"No, seriously, you should take better care of yourself. You're not so young, you know."

"No older than you."

"But I," whispered the doctor, "I take care of myself. I don't think I am so young."

"Well, I guess I do." He took out another cigar and bit off the end, spitting it into an ashtray. "I don't remember when I've ever felt younger or better or stronger, though I admit my head has felt better."

"You could've had a concussion."

"I guess I would've noticed something that bad."

"Well, take my advice. Start noticing your body a bit more. It starts to make a difference at our age. Some little thing, that wouldn't have mattered twenty years ago, can go untreated and become a big problem. How would you like to be deaf, from just getting used to an earache?"

"Okay," Sean said, patting the doctor's knee and puffing his cigar, "you win. You've got a point there. I'll watch things a bit."

"Good. You're not as flexible now, you know. Things break down more easily, and get harder to fix up."

"OK. *Basta*. I'll be a good boy."

"All right. Now sit here while I write you the prescription. And open the window, will you? That cigar stinks."

Tony was waiting at an outside table when Sean walked up, but they decided to move inside. The place was serviceable and pleasant. A jukebox played Spanish songs, and the bar along the right wall was loaded with calamari, mushrooms, anchovies, snails, chicken—all the standard *tapas*. They walked through to the back room, where tables had been set for lunch. The room had a large window high on the back wall that provided the only light. The lights were turned off until evening. They sat at a table covered with a starched, plain white tablecloth and a spray of flowers in the center. The waiter came and took their orders, remov-

ing the extra utensils as he left, and they had a beer
while waiting for the food.

"So where's Marianne?"

"Left, shipped out, gone home."

"How come?"

"Homesick, she says. I don't know. I think she
was just scared, myself. People don't get homesick
that badly anymore, do they?"

"I don't know. What was she scared of?"

Tony laughed, showing his white teeth. He
drank some beer. "You kill me," he said. "You ask
me why she's scared after you almost got yourself
killed last week."

"You mean the political thing?"

He nodded. "She really tried to be aware po-
litically, I think, but she just never got to feeling
at home here. She didn't know what to think,
except that when Franco dies, if he ever does, it
will be a dangerous time. So she wanted to get
away before that."

"Is that what she told you?"

"No. She told me she was homesick."

They finished their beers and ordered two
more.

"Do you miss her?" Sean asked.

"That's a funny question, coming from you."

"Why's that?"

"I don't know," he said, smiling. "It betrays a certain softening."

"Well, let's pass that. Do you?"

"What?"

"Miss her?"

"Yeah. I think I do, though it's funny. I didn't have much going with her. But you know sometimes when you get a feeling that things are going to be much better, if you just give them some time? Well, that's the feeling I had. Not that things had been bad. I just felt hopeful. I felt as though we could talk to each other." He brushed his hand against the tablecloth, as though wiping something away. "I guess it was just me, though. Evidently she didn't think much about it."

"That's too bad."

He shrugged. "Well, better to find out sooner."

The lunch arrived, along with a bottle of *tinto*. They were both having *entrecôte*. Sean looked down at the skinny piece of meat, and doubted very much whether it was *entrecôte*, but it tasted delicious, though it was tough. Everything tasted good to him lately. These Spanish cooks knew what they were doing.

Tony, as he so often did, brought the conversation around to politics, asking what had happened at the riot.

"You weren't there?"

"Other side of town," he said. "No trouble there. I miss all the fun."

"Yeah, it was a good time." Sean rubbed his head for effect, and smiled. "I don't really know what happened. Of course, I read in the papers the next day, but they didn't say anything, as usual. I don't really know what brought it about."

"Going into the old city brought it about."

"What do you mean?"

"Narrow streets. Bad lighting. If you wanted to beat up some radicals and hush it up, where would you do it?"

"But why hush it up? You'd think they'd want it publicized as an example or whatever."

"Yeah, but these are funny times, as we've said again and again. No one knows for sure what will happen when Franco dies. There are even people who believe there will be no violent change, though I think they delude themselves."

"So you think . . ."

"I think, to use an Americanism of yours, that all hell will break loose." Tony finished his wine and signaled for another bottle. "Looks like we might drink too much again. You're bad for me."

"*¡Salud!*" Sean drained his glass.

"But see," Tony went on, "the officials are in a bad position. They know the wind is blowing, but not in which direction. Many of the police are

Basques first—no, it's true; I know it—and if there is revolution, they will fight with us. They will remember, then, who stood strong with Franco, who ordered that he wanted to see radical blood. And the officials, at least many of them, are reluctant to do anything. They must stop the rallies, or Franco's government will be on them, but if they are too forceful, or visible—well, you see. It's a terrorist's time."

The wine was having its effect. Sean gave up trying to cut the beef and, picking up the steak, discreetly brought it to his mouth for a bite.

"Excuse me," he said to Tony, "for my abominable manners, but I'm getting impatient to eat this stuff." He took another bite.

Tony, amused, was also impressed. His elder friend here was undoubtedly the only man he knew who could pull off such behavior with élan. He poured them both more wine. "You don't seem," he said, "any the worse for having been there."

"No. But talk to my doctor. Actually, I think, all in all, it was a good thing for me, not that I'd relish doing it again."

"What was good about it?"

"Kyra," he said. "It turned things around somehow. Since then, all the bullshit has—well, that's not quite true—but most of the craziness between us has let up. I think the main difference now is that we believe each other. No, even more than that, we believe in each other. And really it was that night, when we both thought we might be dead or in jail or beaten to a pulp. All of a sudden I realized that I'd been approaching it all wrong, that maybe the secret was to just say 'Damn the consequences. It's about time you let things out.' It was that feeling of loss, but more than that, the feeling that if she'd been killed, or would be gone for a long time, she'd never have known how I felt about her. How could she have? And as soon as I recognized that, I changed. I can't explain it better than that. The defenses dropped, and I felt young again. I don't know. Maybe she picked up on that, or maybe she felt the same things, but since then things have been as close to perfect as I've ever had."

"You're not jealous?"

Sean's face clouded and then cleared. "I don't much think it applies anymore."

But Tony didn't miss the brief change of expression, and he didn't pursue the subject.

Over orange flan and coffee for dessert, Sean asked Tony if he'd meet him in two hours and drive him home. He didn't expect his lawyer to detain him for long, and besides, he was high enough on the wine that he couldn't envision concentrating more than two hours on anything.

Sean decided to walk from the restaurant. He wasn't yet drunk, but he felt good. His mind was at ease. Things were going well. It was midafternoon, and the streets and sidewalks were comfortably free of masses of people. Siesta time, a glorious tradition: It was at this time that Sean felt most acutely the difference between Blanes and the resort towns.

He walked along, buoyed by drink, and took pleasure in the closed-up businesses and shops. Not that places didn't close in Tossa, for instance, but there never seemed to be the accompanying slowdown. He thought that the midafternoon slump was the most natural thing in the world, and that it had been genius to institutionalize it. He felt here that the very streets reflected that full-bellied, wine-soaked lethargy.

And yet today he wasn't tired. He whistled tunelessly as he walked, and he walked steadily, though slowly. He stopped and asked directions from a toothless old man who was sweeping the gutters with a broom made from a bundle of tied sticks. Then he tipped him a hundred pesetas. He already had a good idea of where he was. He'd just liked the looks of the man, and wanted to speak with him.

Carlos Bertran was the first man Sean had met in Spain. He was about five feet, two inches tall, and weighed at least two hundred pounds. He had known of Sean's arrival from a mutual friend, a lawyer in New York, and had been at the plane to meet him. Sean had stayed at his house while he'd toured the coast, but they had never become friends. Sean, instinctively, had never liked obese people, nor had he particularly enjoyed the company of nondrinkers. Bertran, for his part, had not pursued him as a friend, but as a client, and in this he'd been successful. It couldn't hurt, he'd explained, to have a representative in a foreign country, and for someone with money who was planning to settle, it was imperative, lest the various licenses, visa problems, and graft take more than was absolutely necessary.

Bertran didn't take a siesta. He didn't drink at lunch, and so rarely returned from it heavy-lidded. Sean wondered how he'd gotten so fat when he didn't drink. Maybe he had when he was younger.

His office was nearly a mile from downtown, set back from a quiet, shaded road. He worked in the back half of a square, white, one-story house. In the heat of summer, he would often take clients outside to the patio behind his office, which was covered with a bamboo-slatted awning. Now, though, he sat behind his large desk, offered one of the comfortable red leather chairs to Sean, and proffered a Havana cigar.

*"Gracias."*

Bertran lit it for him.

Sean blew out the thick, blue smoke, and settled back in the chair, starting to feel drowsy. "I almost forgot our appointment today."

The lawyer turned his palms up and smiled. "Tomorrow would have done as well."

"Ah, but the timing, the timing. So much is the timing."

They didn't feel comfortable with each other, and so often spent half of their meetings in an effort to ease things a bit.

Bertran laughed politely, bobbing his head up and down. His face, surprisingly, was good-looking. It had none of the fleshiness of the rest of him. His eyes were maybe a little too dark, a little too piercing, but they didn't squint. His cheeks were full but not flabby. Always clean-shaven, he looked nearly aristocratic above the neck. Again he chuckled.

"I have a story that will amuse you," he said. "I have a client, a woman, who owns a house near Barcelona, just outside the city, inland, where the forest begins. I should say she used to own a house there. It has since burned down, and she is suing the department of roads. That is strange, you say. Why the department of roads? You know the toll booths they have erected on the autoroute? Yes?

Well, there was a fire in the hills near this woman's house, and she called the Barcelona fire department, which immediately set out. I see by your smile you can guess, and it is true. The men on the fire trucks, in their uniforms, carried no money, and the toll taker wouldn't let them through. They had to beg from the people in cars backed up behind them. In the meantime, the woman's house burned down."

Sean stared at the ceiling, shaking his head. "That's a good story. God bless the bureaucrats."

"I remember reading about the fire and this incident in the papers, little thinking I'd become involved in it. What must go through the mind of that toll taker?"

"I suppose that's what happens when you're trained your whole life not to question orders. Someone had ordered him to let no one through without paying. I'll bet he still thinks he did the right thing."

"God help us."

They were relaxing now, and gradually got down to business. A window in the room was open, and occasionally Sean would stare at it to wake himself up. Still, business matters bored him, and it soon became all he could do to keep from dozing.

Slowly, in a monotone, Bertran went over some new regulations concerning money brought into the country. Sean still was having most of his money sent to him from his broker in the States, and Bertran suggested that he might consider keeping a larger portion of it on hand in Spain.

"It might make things more stable," he said.

"Here?"

"Yes? Why not?"

"And if Franco dies?"

Again he turned his palms up. "Yes? What of that?"

"Things will be stable then?"

The lawyer smiled. "Of course. You don't think all of this unrest will lead to anything, do you? The transition is secure. Juan Carlos is stronger, personally, than is generally believed. You wait. It will be business as usual."

Sean replied that he would wait until that was certain.

After an interminable forty-five minutes, they had nearly finished. Sean's eyes felt as if they had salt in them. Outside, the breeze had picked up, and he saw a few white clouds pass across the window. Bertran was saying something now about his will, which he'd rewritten a year before. At that time, he'd left his entire estate to Berta, since there'd been no one else around. He'd thought it would be a nice surprise for her. The only personal stipulation he'd given was that he be buried on his land. Now he was in that same lackadaisical mood he'd been in when he'd named Berta his beneficiary. All he wanted was to get out of this stifling office and into the air again. Suddenly he perked up and chewed ruminatively on his cigar butt. He stood up.

"Carlos," he said, "I've got to go. Everything sounds fine. I want you, though, to include a clause in that thing, giving ten thousand dollars to Denise Hanford, at my address. And hurry up. Let me sign the addition."

He paced the room while the lawyer penned in the clause. It was only a gesture, he knew, but he felt good about it. He could always undo it. When he'd signed it, he asked for another cigar, got it lit, said good-bye, and walked outside.

It had clouded over, and walking back to meet Tony revived him. He enjoyed the new heaviness in the air, the slight chill. At a café that had just reopened, he stepped inside and ordered a brandy, which he downed in two swallows. The cigar was delicious, much better than the one he'd had in the office, though he knew it was the same kind.

When he stepped back onto the sidewalk, it was raining in large drops. One of the drops hit the tip of the cigar and knocked off the ash with a sizzling noise. He stopped and looked at his face in a window, grinning.

# Sixteen

We all had breakfast together for a change. Time seemed to have crept by, with Sean and Kyra forever growing closer, and Lea and I coming apart like an old paperback when the binding has gone brittle. I knew I would be leaving soon, and Lea hadn't committed herself, though I suspected she would stay on, if not here, then on her crusade with Mike.

At breakfast, Berta rather mysteriously asked for the day off, which Sean, of course, gave her. Lea was going into town, and Kyra offered to drive her, since she was going out to shop anyway. I announced that I would be going into Blanes with Sean to keep him company. Though it hadn't yet been two weeks since he'd been there to see the doctor, his ear continued to be bad, and he'd decided to go back and get something done about it.

We let the girls have the car, since Kyra had been planning on having it for several days, and we decided to take a cab down to Blanes with Berta. We were still waiting for its arrival when Kyra and Lea left, and just afterward, Sean changed his mind and decided to stay at the house and try to write.

"I don't want to get hysterical about this ear thing," he said. "Give it another week maybe, and it'll be fine. Besides, at least it doesn't hurt anymore."

So when the cab came, we packed off Berta, and Sean went back to his office to write. I was not unhappy to stay home. It was a blustery and overcast day, and I thought I'd go up to my room and spend the day in bed, reading.

But when Lea had gone, she'd had the impression that the house would be completely empty all day long.

# Seventeen

The white stucco of the house glared dully by contrast against the slate gray sky. The silence was complete. Not a bird chirped. Even the chickens had settled to roost. The air hung heavy with unreleased rain, charged with static electricity. It smelled metallic outside. Here and there the house was streaked with a murky blue where the stucco had run from the previous rains—a bruised, wet blue turning to gray at the edges, painted with the same brush as the sky. Where the stucco held, the white was a glaring, garish, almost neon white.

Inside, there was no noise. Upstairs, a man lay stretched out on his bed, his head propped up by a pillow. He held a book in both hands, though he wasn't reading. The book was open, pages down, upon his chest. From time to time, he would force his eyes open and wade through a paragraph, but it was an effort. Downstairs, another man sat quietly at his desk. Beside him was a bottle of whiskey, from which he would occasionally sip. He was trying to write with no greater success than the man above trying to read. He'd write a word, then stop, staring with increasingly blurred vision at the clouds outside the open door. He'd take a drink, then look down and cross out the word.

Lea sat with her palms spread out on her legs. The smooth, thick gray wool of her slacks felt good against her hands. Watching the road, Mike gripped the wheel too hard. They were both nervous. In spite of what everyone believed, they were not lovers. They had not even kissed since that first day at the fort. This morning, Lea had met him at a café, as usual, and they'd begun talking of their plans to find Sharon. After a while, Lea asked him if he'd drive her up to the house before the rain came. The road, she said, terrified her when it was wet. They could talk up there. Maybe he could stay for dinner.

Lea never asked herself what she would do if they found Sharon. She never asked Mike. She had cast aside her logic as irrelevant. It simply didn't matter here. She knew that in her bones. She had never decided to be consciously illogical, but if she were to be with Mike, that had to be one of the conditions. She still believed in her rational mind that she could work things out with Douglas. After all, she had not been unfaithful to him. She even told herself that she wanted to work it out. She had invited Mike up to the house to talk. She had not consciously remembered that no one would be there. She didn't really have enough strength to hurt someone knowingly, to admit she was acting in her own interests. She preferred it to appear that she was being carried away by events over which she had no control, and perhaps it was true. An earlier Lea might have been able to stop herself, to back off and appraise things, but now she had been sucked too far into the maelstrom.

She shivered as the car took a curve. Mike looked over at her, asked if she were cold, and put one of his hands over hers. It was like ice, resting there on her thigh. He went back to driving, taking his hand away. Now she did feel cold. His touch had been like a current through her body. She pulled her feet up under her and crossed her arms hard against her to warm her hands. She turned herself in the seat so she could be looking at him, at his face now set so hard in concentration. She wanted to talk and break this tension, but she couldn't control her breathing. It came in gasps she could barely keep down. She wanted to remain calm, and so said nothing.

The white Citröen pulled slowly into the courtyard and rolled to a stop just outside the front door. They got out into the oppressive silence. When they closed the car doors, the noise was a shock, though it was quickly swallowed up. Mike squinted against the whiteness of the house and followed Lea to the front door. She stood for a moment on the stoop, trying to get her breathing under control.

Inside, she closed the door quietly. It was barely light in the room. She crossed to the window and, looking out at the clouds, shivered again.

Only now did she remember that the house was empty. It was early afternoon. People in Blanes and Barcelona were just finishing lunch, preparing for their siestas. Mike stood by the door, looking at her. They hadn't said ten words to each other since leaving Tossa. Lea decided to take a tranquilizer. Maybe it would help. They were in the medicine chest in Sean's bedroom.

Mike gazed around the room in the semidarkness. . "It's awfully quiet," he said. "Is no one home?"

"No." She still looked into the courtyard. She wished the rain would begin. "I'll be right back." She turned and walked into the hall leading to Sean's room. Mike followed her.

In the bedroom, she switched on the light and walked quickly to the bathroom door, then opened the medicine cabinet and took down the bottle.

"What are you doing?"

The voice startled her. She looked at Mike's figure, framed in the doorway, and put the bottle down.

"Are you sick?"

She smiled feebly. "I don't know," she said. "I don't feel well."

"Well, here. Come out of there. Lie down on the bed."

She obeyed him, brushing him as she passed through the doorway.

"Would you please turn out the light?" she asked. "It's too glaring."

She watched him cross the room, then stretched out on the bed, moving over to give him room to sit beside her.

"What's wrong?"

"I don't . . ." She stopped. "I can't seem to get my breath."

"Do those pills help? I'll get them."

"No. They're just tranquilizers."

His hand felt her forehead, then caressed her face, her neck.

"You don't have a fever."

"No. I'm cold."

"What do you need the tranquilizers for?"

She hunched her shoulders up, girlish, but her eyes never left him. Her face was set.

"I'm nervous," she said. "I can't seem to get a deep breath."

Again he touched her face, but she took his hand away, and held it.

"I feel like my heart is going to beat through my ribs. It's shaking my whole body." She took his hand and put it under her sweater. "Feel it," she said, guiding his hand. She wore no bra, and as his hand closed over her breast, he stared at her for a second, then leaned down and kissed her, open-mouthed.

She came up to meet him, folding her arms around him. He took her sweater into his hands and lifted it over her head, catching some of her hair with it, and they laughed nervously. She could feel his hands shaking and her eyes, to him, looked filled with a mixture of fear and passion. She began to say something, but he quieted her with a kiss. He began to kiss her body, moving his tongue over her nipples and her stomach. Her staccato breathing became marked with little sighs, and she reached for him.

He stood and let her take down his pants, and watched her take him in her hands and her mouth. Their breathing came hard and they looked at each other with glazed eyes, hungrily.

He lay down and pulled her over on top of him. Impatient now, moaning, she wiggled her woolen slacks down to below her knees and straddled him. When he pushed himself into her, she cried out and then they were rocking back and forth. She saw his face tighten and thought it would be too soon, but suddenly, as she felt him starting, she lost control herself, so that they cried out as they came together.

She fell upon him on the bed, but their cries had already cut a wound into the dead silence outside. In another moment, the day returned to its dull, utter soundlessness.


Upstairs, Doug heard the car drive up through a fog of half-sleep, and roused himself to see who it was. He walked to the front window and, looking out, saw Lea and Mike getting out of the car. He pulled back quickly, not wanting them to see him, and not wanting to see them. How could Lea be so insensitive? The last time Mike had been to dinner had been horrible, and now she had asked him up again.

He looked at his watch, surprised at how late it was. Then he remembered that she must have thought that the house was empty. What was Sean doing downstairs? Maybe he should go down and see them. But he simply didn't feel up to it. Sean would take care of them. There'd be plenty of time later on in the day.

He sat on the edge of the bed, now wide-awake. How had all this gone so far? He was actually afraid of going down now, afraid of what he might find, afraid of his reception. At that moment, he made up his mind to leave as soon as he could arrange it. He'd checked around at the travel agencies in town, and knew that he could be gone in a matter of days. Still, oddly, he knew that he had no intention of going back to work in the States. Maybe Africa, he thought. Maybe just work my way around a bit until something starts to make sense.

He lay down on the bed and folded his arms underneath his head, planning. He didn't have much money left, maybe enough for two or three months of traveling, and that would leave him completely broke, something he hadn't been for many years. He realized, then, that he was thinking in terms of his own money, and not his and Lea's. Of course, they had some stocks. In fact, they were rather well off, but he didn't like to think of taking that money. But he was thinking of leaving without her. Why not take advantage of the situation?

Was he not, though, being unfair? He'd never even accused Lea of being unfaithful, and had no proof that she had been. And after all, he thought, would that be so bad? Many women her age had affairs. It didn't necessarily mean that they wanted to leave their husbands. Perhaps he should have had a few dalliances himself. But it really didn't suit him. He wasn't attracted to other women. Occasionally he'd get a crush on someone, but it was more a schoolboy thing or a fatherly feeling, as with Marianne.

Then he thought of the things about Lea that he didn't like, little things that over the years he'd come to accept as those flaws in a person that one must learn to live with. In their first year or two together, he'd thought her calm exterior would drive him crazy, but he'd adjusted.

Suddenly, all the idiosyncrasies that he'd come to regard almost as his own fell into their perspective. He remembered that long ago he used to sing in the shower, and Lea had asked him to stop, and it had been a small thing, so he had. And he used to dog-ear pages until Lea had scolded him jokingly about it. He also used to wipe his mouth with a dish towel, and drink milk directly from the bottle, and use too much mayonnaise on ham sandwiches, and stack more than one record at a time on the record player. But all that had stopped, and now he realized that it had been Lea and her influence that had changed him. Had it been for the good? He doubted it. It really didn't make much difference, other than that the accumulated weight of all those trivialities sometimes made him feel trapped.

Wouldn't it serve her right if he left her? He was already starting to think of himself as free of her, as though she had been a burden to him all these years, which was not true. He was simply faced with the phenomenon of himself as his own man, responsible to no one else, and the thought didn't frighten him. After all, he was well into middle age. It was a purifying thought.

Now, lying back, he thought of the other changes he'd made. He'd had to keep working all the time bringing in a paycheck, even though Lea's job had provided plenty of money. Still, he admitted, he had enjoyed his work. It had given him enough, but not too much, free time. But what about that novel that he'd talked himself out of being interested in? Hadn't that gone by the boards because of Lea's insinuations that he could spend his time more profitably? In other words, getting paid.

Then, in the dead, still quiet of the room, he became conscious of some noises. They had that same muted quality he'd come to recognize as coming from Sean's room. He got up and walked to the window. Yes, it was clearer now. There were voices—Lea's and Mike's, unmistakably. The light was on. A shadow passed in front of the shutter, and then the room went dark. The wind outside freshened for a minute, then calmed again. He heard more voices—whispered voices. Then it was quiet. He stood at the window, looking down on the courtyard, not really thinking. He thought of yelling out, announcing his presence. But he couldn't make a sound. Where was Sean? Had he gone out?

The clouds above were lead black, like wet slate, and they wouldn't break. He leaned one hand against the sill and with the other rubbed his eyes. He was sweating. His scalp itched. He heard Lea cry out, a cry he knew well, followed almost instantly by a similar cry from Mike. Leaning heavily against the sill, he closed his eyes, wondering how he could leave the house without being seen.

Sean looked up through bleary eyes at the door to his office. He'd heard something outside, something like a car driving up. He tried to get his head clear, then reached for the bottle beside him on the desk. That would be Kyra getting home, he thought. What time was it? It was getting dark out, but he didn't feel as though he'd been asleep that long. He took a sip and cleared his throat, still sitting. He thought he might get up and greet her, but realized he was too groggy to pull it off with any élan whatever, and so decided to stay until she came in to see him. He looked down at the page in front of him, and swore to himself. Some day's work.

He didn't hear the front door open, but he heard, or rather felt, the soft impact of it closing. Kyra would be in in a second, and would laugh at his besotted state. He knew what she would say, that she couldn't leave him alone even for a day with a bottle nearby without him getting drunk. And he would say, truthfully, that he found it impossible to concentrate when she wasn't around, and missing her made him drink. Then she would muss his hair and kiss him, and he would pat her gently on the rear with his good hand. Then maybe he would take her over to the couch.

But she didn't come in, and he thought he heard a male voice coming down the hall. Would that be Tony? Did she think no one was home? She'd said there was a chance she would see him and bring him back up to the house. Well, that would be good, he thought. He hadn't seen Tony since that day in Blanes, and he always enjoyed his company.

He quietly pushed his chair back, stumbling slightly as he did so, but he was barefoot, and didn't intrude on the stillness of the house. What the hell was Kyra doing? Why didn't she come and see him? He stood at the doorway out to the courtyard, and saw the light in his room go on. Ah. She thought he was in there sleeping.

But then he heard Tony's voice also coming from the room. There was whispering, and then the light went off. Still, the voices continued. He strained to hear, but could make out no words.

Kyra and Tony. He wanted to call out, to scream out her name and ask her why, but he couldn't.

Already he'd drunk so much that he couldn't focus his eyes, but he crossed back to his desk and took a long drink from the bottle. Then he went again and stood in the doorway. His legs didn't want to work, so he locked his knees to keep himself standing. By now he could hear them again, though the sounds were muffled through the shutters. It was clear what they were doing.

He had no idea how long he stood there, but he didn't move. Breathing heavily, he leaned against the doorpost with the bottle in his hand, and bit down on his tongue. It was numb. Finally, he heard Kyra whimper with pleasure, and then they both cried out, and he sank to the ground.

In his blurred state, he felt lost. He'd always said that he'd kill himself if Kyra betrayed him. And now here it was. He almost smiled. So this is how death comes, he thought. Unexpected and uninvited.

Tears came and overflowed his eyes. There

was no doubt what he would have to do. He just hadn't even considered that it would be today. It had always been in the future.

He pulled himself up and walked, staggering, out into the courtyard. Standing in the center of it, he looked up at the sky with its burden of rain. He didn't sob, but tears ran down his cheeks, covering his face, and he didn't wipe them away.

Behind him, the room was now silent.

Out in the back by the fence was the old shed where he stored his tools. He walked back to it, his index finger jammed into the neck of the bottle to keep it with him. After falling up against the door, he got inside and felt around in the dark until he found the large coil of rope that the painters had used with the scaffolding. His bare foot landed on a cockroach and it squashed underneath, but he barely noticed. It didn't matter now, anyway.

Looping the coil of rope up around his shoulder, he picked up the bottle again and walked to the stairs leading to the roof. He wiped the back of his hand over his eyes so that he could see the steps, and walked up to where the beam protruded. Sitting on the ledge, he put the bottle down and took the coil from his shoulder. He sat on one end of the rope, and holding it against him with his stump, he managed to tie a loop knot in the end. Then he made a lasso and threw it out over the

end of the beam, catching it on the second try.
He took the end he held in his hand and made
another knot, pulling the rope back through it so
that it made a noose, which he put over his head
and made tight.

The rope was ten feet long. Just about right.
Inching his way out onto the beam, he grabbed
the bottle and kept it beside him. He could see
Tossa down in the distance, above the bare trees
and under the blanket of cloud. He took a long
drink. It was beautiful, he thought.

What was he doing up here?

Suddenly he realized how drunk he was, and
how bad his hearing had gotten. Was he willing
to die for the evidence his ears had given him?
He laughed at himself, at his ludicrous position.
Surely, this was the silliest he'd been. There must
be other explanations. It might not be Kyra, even.
There were two other women in the house. He
would have to confront it. If he believed in Kyra,
here was his first test.

And then there was the nonsense of having told
everybody that he would kill himself if Kyra was
unfaithful. Even he'd come to believe it. Yes, he'd
said it enough times, but that was the kind of statement that people shouldn't hold you to. There
were too many questions yet, and he didn't feel

like dying just now as he looked down at Tossa. He regretted that he'd made such a big deal out of the suicide thing. His friends would take him less seriously in the future, perhaps. But at least there'd be a future.

The more he thought, the more he became convinced that it hadn't even been Kyra and Tony. His ears really were bad. He had just been drunk and groggy, and now he was beginning to feel tremendously relieved. Not only had it not been Kyra, but he could live, and suddenly he wanted to do that very much.

So he began to inch his way back to the ledge, but his dizziness began to control him. He looked with longing at the house, only a couple of feet away, and almost lost his balance. Righting himself, he took a couple of deep breaths, and then made the mistake of looking straight down. Again, the dizziness came in a wave. Suddenly he remembered the noose around his neck. He had to get that off—at least then if he fell, maybe he'd only break a leg. He reached up with his hand and started to loosen it, but he couldn't open it enough to clear his chin, and he got impatient and gave it a little jerk. That made him lose his balance and he reached out to grab for something, but his stump only smacked painfully against the beam.

He knew he was falling, and tried again to wrench the rope from around his neck, but it was still in place as he fell out into the air.

The Basques drank a lot of champagne on that and the following day. Franco finally died in Madrid, and there was freedom in the air.

# PART III

*Two minutes and a quarter from now
Nikolaus will wake out of his sleep and
find the rain blowing in. It was appointed
that he should turn over and go to
sleep again. But I have appointed that
he shall get up and close the window first.
That trifle will change his career entirely.
He will rise in the morning two minutes
later than the chain of his life had
appointed him to rise. By consequence,
thenceforth nothing will ever happen to
him in accordance with the details of the
old chain.*

—MARK TWAIN
"The Mysterious Stranger"

# Eighteen

The French liner *Antoinette* sat at its berth in the port of Barcelona, decked out in flags and streamers, having stopped overnight on the first leg of its trip from Marseilles to Dakar, via Casablanca and Tenerife. I stood blinking in the cold morning sun with a headache and a mouth that tasted like cheese.

I'd spent the night before in semisleep, cradled around my third and fourth liters of *tinto*. How much time had elapsed since I'd found Sean? I knew that somewhere the big holiday season was getting into full swing. Or had it passed? The night before, I'd gone to the market and bought some snails in tomato sauce, a wedge of Camembert, or so it was called, and a loaf of bread, along with the aforementioned *tinto,* and had come back to the tiny, airless room I'd rented just back from the *ramblas.* On one of my several trips to the bathroom, I was stopped by a skinny, dark youth wearing a pair of bright orange bikini shorts. He asked me if he could have some of my wine, or maybe come to my room and share it. I declined. Later I heard some scuffling outside my door, but didn't get up to examine it.

There was one window in the hall leading to the john, and through it, I noticed that somehow it had gotten light. I put on a clean shirt, made an attempt at shaving with cold water, and finally got out to the street.

I'd bought my ticket in Barcelona on the day before the funeral, but that seemed so long ago that I could scarcely believe I was finally going on board, getting out of this place at last. The girl who sold me the ticket spoke a bit of English and explained to me that in the French system, there were ten classes on a liner: three in deluxe, three in first class, two in economy, and two others, standard and *dortoir,* or dormitory. Since I was by now getting used to counting my pesetas, I'd elected to go lowest class. I'd lived in dormitories before. There was a remarkable difference in price. The girl assured me that there would be three meals served daily, lunch and dinner with wine. So I booked into *dortoir* as far as the Canaries. I wasn't quite ready for Africa yet.

At the pier, I waited in line silently while the travelers in front of me checked their baggage, but when I showed my ticket I was ushered around and brought, still carrying my suitcase, past the others and onto the ship.

A steward accompanied me down the first four levels. The ship was really something. Soft music was piped in. Everyone passing was friendly. This would be just what I needed for a couple of days, three days, whatever. The carpets, I noticed, were especially soft. There had been only throw rugs on the hardwood floors in Tossa.

We passed through a door, then, and the steward left me. Suddenly I was in the belly of the ship. There was no music, no carpets, and the lighting was by bare bulbs. I looked around, and decided to keep descending until I met someone who could direct me to the *dortoir*. Two floors farther down, it was much hotter, and a locker room and vomit smell began making me nauseous. But the second flight of stairs ended in another door, and I walked through it to a tiled, well-lit and friendly, though crowded, lobby. This wouldn't be so bad, after all. I checked my ticket as I went down the hall, checking the room numbers. Most of the people down here were Africans, I gathered, on their way home from vacationing in France. There were a few Moroccans and Europeans, who nodded at me without much enthusiasm as I passed, but my most vivid memory is of the black women in their bright dresses, sitting for the most part on the floor, weighing three hundred pounds or more. There must have been ten of them blocking the hall, chewing on some kind of sticks, and talking animatedly to one another. I looked again at my ticket, confused because it had no room number. Several of the room doors were open, and this was clearly the dormitory section, since each of the small rooms had six beds in it.

I had traveled down one length of the hall, and was making my way back on the other side of the ship, not yet having seen a porter, when my path was blocked by two women playing a game with stones in the middle of the hall. Stopping, I looked around, perplexed. My head was beginning to throb again. I swallowed twice to keep down my bile, and wondered if the bar was nearby. A young man appeared at the opposite end of the hall and stopped on the other side of the women. He looked at me and smiled.

"*Bonjour,*" he said.

I nodded.

"*Vous êtes français?*"

"No. American."

His face lit up. "Goddamn. No shit? I'm glad to meet you." He stepped over the women, excusing himself in polite French, and extended his hand to me. "You just get on here?"

"Yes," I said. "I wonder if you could help me. Do you know your way around here?"

"Sure. I've been here a whole day."

"Well, I haven't seen any porters and can't seem to find my room."

"Let's see your ticket."

I handed it to him. He stared at it for a minute and then looked at me.

"You're in the wrong spot. This is standard." He laughed out loud. "You've got a surprise coming, but it'll be nice having company."

He led me back the way I'd come, into another hallway, past the bar and dining area, and opened a door at the top of another stairway.

"How far down does this ship go?"

"All the way to the bilge."

We walked down the starkly lit metal steps. On the next landing, the smell of sulfur and burned oil nearly bowled me over. The final staircase was a metal ladder not eighteen inches wide.

"Watch your head," he called.

We were nine levels belowdecks.

Stepping off the ladder and turning around, I saw a room about sixty feet square, lit by eight or ten bare bulbs. The ceiling was under seven feet high, and my first impression was one of noise. It sounded as though a hundred radios were playing at once. And the odor was overpowering.

"Welcome to *dortoir,*" said my companion.

The room was filled with Africans and double bunk beds, eight to a unit. It was unbelievably crowded. My body started to respond to the high-pitched, thin voice of panic.

He took my suitcase. "Come on," he said. "I'll show you the bunks."

He walked through the men, smiling and clapping a few on the back, and I followed meekly. The bunk was a mattress that had seen better days. Stained and thin, its stuffing seemed to struggle everywhere to escape.

"You're welcome to be my mate," he said.

Still out of my depth, I nodded. "Sounds fine."

He put my suitcase on the floor under the bunk next to his.

"You have some rope in there?"

"No. Why?"

"You really ought to tie it under the bunk." He lowered his voice. "These guys'll rob you blind. They're nice enough, I mean, but you gotta be careful. Wouldn't hurt a fly, you understand. Very peaceful people. But stealing's another thing."

"Well, I don't have any rope."

"That's OK. Maybe I've got some extra. By the

way," he said, straightening up, "my name's Jay Dorney."

Again we shook hands.

"Doug Koenig."

"Good. Nice to meet you," he said. "Now, you have a bag?"

"What?"

"Sleeping bag? Something to cover the mattress. You don't want to get the scabes."

"Scabies?"

"Yeah. They're a bitch."

"I don't have anything."

"Well, I might have another blanket, or maybe we can get one from one of these guys. They sure don't need it for the heat."

"Is it this hot at night, too?"

"Oh, yeah. Pretty bad, isn't it?"

I looked at Jay. In his midtwenties and very hairy, with a full beard, he didn't seem the tour-guide type.

"What are you doing here?" I asked.

"Hanging out. Going down to Dakar."

"Well, thanks for your help. Can I buy you a drink?"

"Maybe later." He lay down on his bunk. "I think I'll rack it for a while right now."

"How do you sleep with this noise?"

He looked around. "Oh, the cassettes? It does seem like every African that goes to France comes back with twenty cassettes. Must be some kind of a quota thing." He shrugged. "You live with it, like anything else. Learn a lot of James Brown tunes." He smiled. "See you later. Take a look around."

Coming back up to the main deck, I was again amazed at the change. This was a luxury ship, with a pool, shuffleboard, nightclub, library, movie theater—the works. And below I felt I was in Africa, or what I assumed I would feel like in Africa. I wondered why the men down there stayed below, and resolved, with a guilty feeling, that I would descend only for meals and sleeping. The place had scared me.

The men down there were not American blacks. They were African blacks, and not a minority here. They'd seemed childlike, listening to their cassettes. I'd seen some of them dancing with one another. Maybe two steps removed from what I'd call sophisticated, they were unpredictable. It was another culture, and I didn't have any idea how to act, and it terrified me.

I sat at the bar and ordered a Heineken, still feeling too rocky to make small talk with the other patrons. The tugs were slowly pulling the ship out from the pier along the channel buoys. I wondered if there was an angle from which Barcelona didn't look impressive. Now, heading out past Montjuich, I ordered a second beer and looked at the receding skyline, trying to let the events of the past months also begin to recede, but without any luck.

Where was Lea now? In Marseilles, I supposed, with Mike. I sipped at my beer.

The bartender asked me if he could see my ticket, and I produced it. He then motioned to a steward, who came over and explained to me that after we cleared the channel markers, I would have to return below until we reached Casablanca. He was only marginally polite, saying he would escort me. His meaning was clear.

"Do you mean we're not allowed on the deck?"

"There is a separate deck for standard and *dortoir*, sir."

The tugs' horns blared their good-byes. The steward hovered condescendingly at my elbow. I wanted to strike him.

"Please hurry with your beer," he said.

After, from God only knows what reserve, I'd found the strength to walk again, away from the window of our room at Sean's. I knew I'd have to get away for a while, if only to give Lea the impression that I'd been gone. Still, for quite a few minutes I had been in a daze, and had gone back to sit on the bed, looking out the window at the black clouds. Then I'd gone out to the hall, quietly, not daring to break the awful silence of that day, and down the stairs, turning back to Sean's office. It had been empty, the door standing open. I'd crossed the courtyard and turned the corner, to be out of sight from the windows in Sean's room in case Lea opened them, when I'd seen him, hanging.

Then I hadn't been able to move. My legs gave out and I sat down on the ground, staring. I realized I had to get him down, and sprang up, going to the toolshed for something sharp, returning with a rusted pair of pruning scissors. As I mounted the steps, a tremendous clap of thunder rent the air and rain started falling in huge drops. I had to shimmy out along the beam to get to where the rope was tied. A bottle of Jack Daniel's, nearly empty, lay a foot beyond the rope, and I angrily knocked it to the ground. The rain had really been coming down as I reached around the beam and started cutting with the shears.

Then it had struck me that I couldn't let him fall to the ground from there, though of course it could make no difference, so I took the rope below where I was cutting through it into my hand to try to hoist him back up to me. But he was far too heavy. As soon as I'd gotten halfway through the rope, the weight of his body began ripping the strands, and in a moment he'd fallen and lay in a hump on the wet dirt.

Still, I had no time for thinking what I should do. I backed carefully off the beam and descended. He lay on his side, with one leg curled out of joint under him. I turned him onto his back and, as gently as I could, took the noose from around his neck. His body had still been warm. He must have gone out just after Lea and Mike . . .

I pulled the lids down over his eyes and sat holding them until they stayed closed, letting the rain soak us both, and beginning to understand the irony that had driven him to it. I hadn't been able to bring myself to take him inside. Somehow, it had seemed better to let him stay where he was.

The aftermath had been a nightmare. First Lea, and then Berta, after she'd come home, had gotten hysterical. Surprisingly, Mike had been a help. The new boundaries had been drawn, and I found myself without the energy to dispute them. Kyra had gotten back later, buoyant from drinking to Franco's death. The authorities had already come and gone, taking the body with them. She'd taken it well, considering. But what did that mean? Where the other women had cried and needed comforting, she was beyond that. Her face had gone white for a moment; then she'd lost control of her bladder and, with a pathetic little giggle, had excused herself to change. Coming back to where we'd gathered in the living room, she'd been externally composed.

Throughout the preparations for the funeral, I'd stayed on at the house, but slept down in Sean's office. Naturally, Lea and I had talked, but I hadn't the honesty or cruelty to clear up the mystery of why he had done it. It was tacitly understood that we were splitting up. She'd come in and told me on the day after Sean's death that she felt she had to get away from all this, and was going to Marseilles. The only time I'd come near to losing my temper with her was when she'd asked if I wanted to go with her.

"At least we've always been honest, Lea. Don't take me for a fool. I don't want this to drag on until I can't help but hate you."

Also, I hadn't wanted to make it any easier for her. I admit it.

The funeral had been held at the house. Sean had stipulated in his will that he wanted to be buried on his own land, and to my amazement there had been no bureaucratic problem with that. When he was buried, Tony took the bottle of champagne, which was supposed to have been for Franco, and poured the contents over the newly packed earth. Then he took Kyra back to her old *pensión* in Tossa, and me to my airless room in Barcelona. Lea had asked Berta if she could stay for one or two more days to straighten up some things, and of course the distraught housekeeper had been happy to comply.

Neither Berta nor Kyra had seemed to care for their inheritances, though Berta had been stunned to find herself so handsomely remembered.

Sometime before I left, I took Sean's unfinished novel and sent it along to his lawyer in Blanes. I hadn't been able to bring myself to read any of it.

I'd been tempted to tell Kyra what had happened that day, and let her draw her own conclusions, but after some thought decided that it would have accomplished nothing. Let her think what she would. She hadn't understood at all, but Lea had told her that maybe Sean had decided he was at the peak of his happiness, and it would be a good time to die. Maybe she would find some comfort believing that. I don't know.

The deck for standard and *dortoir* passengers was about forty feet square, wedged between the bridge, which rose menacingly in a wall behind it, and the lifeboat stations on the bow. There were three ten-foot wooden benches to accommodate the two hundred or so people who had access to the deck.

No sooner had we cleared the port than a fog

settled on the ship. I still hadn't been able to force myself below, so I stood leaning against the railing watching the gray water slip by at twenty knots. They were taking it slow. This was a luxury cruise.

The deck was not entirely deserted, with perhaps a dozen other men scattered about. There wasn't a woman to be seen. Though the beers had helped, I was still on the verge of nausea. Lunch might do me some good, and then a nap. I went below.

Jay was still on his bunk, propped up against a pillow, reading *Henderson The Rain King,* a good novel for someone on his way to Africa.

"You know we're not allowed run of the ship?" I asked.

He looked up and nodded, his face amused. "You missed lunch," he said, "such as it was."

I looked at my watch. "It shouldn't be for another half hour."

"That's for the other classes. We eat first here."

"Why don't they let us know?" I was whining, annoyed. What the hell was I doing here?

He put his book down, motioning me to sit on the bunk beside him. "You've gotta understand something, Doug. This here is really nameless class. Bottom of the rung. The goddamn frogs would probably treat animals better. So what if you miss a meal? You think anybody gives a shit?

That's why most of the men stay here all the time. Meals are served when they arrive, and that's that. See? The only people who go *dortoir* are African blacks, except for people who, generally speaking, don't know what it's like and decide to save a few bucks, like I suppose you did. But you know, a few days here and you'll be glad you did it. It's an eye-opener, I tell you."

But I didn't want an eye-opener. I needed some rest, a few days when I wouldn't have to deal with things. I went up to the bar and ordered another Heineken and a bag of peanuts, but they served only an African beer called Stork—not bad, considering. The peanuts were the best I'd ever had. I sat near a porthole, just about at the waterline, and nursed the beer, feeling that afterward I would go and lie down.

Two men came up and greeted me cordially in French, asking if they could sit at my table. There weren't any other free chairs, and I motioned that they were welcome. After a short conversation of many smiles and halting French, they began chatting with each other. I finished the beer, descended to my bunk, and lay down. Jay had gone somewhere. I dozed off.

I was awakened later by two men passing my bed, holding between them an enormous pot and banging a heavy ladle against it. It was a far cry from our half-hour bell at Tossa, and it woke me with a start. A large area had been cleared in the room, and makeshift tables had been set up—sheets of plywood laid across wooden workhorses. The men were lining up to the pot and accepting the food, which was dished into shallow tin pans. I got up, groggily, and waited my turn. Jay appeared from out of nowhere and stood behind me.

"Chow time," he said happily. "Feel better? Get any sleep?"

"A little."

The man at the pot handed me a spoon with the dish, and ladled some slop onto it.

"What is this?" I asked Jay.

"Better not to ask."

The table was set with tin cups and metal pitchers full of wine. I remembered the salesgirl's comment that wine was served twice a day, and wondered if she'd ever seen *dortoir*. There were also lumps of what appeared to be mildew on plates spaced every couple of feet. This, I found, was cheese.

It was a very noisy meal. One of the men at another table was standing on the bench and apparently auctioning clothes.

"Best time for it," Jay explained, "with everybody gathered around."

Somebody down the table from me asked me to pass down the wine pitcher, and I grabbed for it and picked it up with my left hand. The man next to me slapped my arm and forced me to put it down. Everyone was scowling at me. I looked around quizzically.

Jay picked up the pitcher and passed it, saying a few words in French and gesturing at me. In a moment, the tension had passed and everyone began talking again. He spooned himself a mouthful of food, then said to me, conversationally, across the table, "Don't use your left hand. That's your ass-wiping hand."

"But I'm left-handed."

"Doesn't matter. It's no joke. They take it seriously."

I transferred even my spoon then to my right side, and looked at the dish before me. It was a mixture of lentils and something, but I was hungry, and dipped my spoon in.

"They must be having squab upstairs tonight," Jay said, looking down into his tin.

"Why do you say that?"

He took something from the lentils and held it out for me to see. It was the head of a pigeon, its feathers still intact. I swallowed hard, got up, and went back to my bunk.

The next morning, I felt better. Somehow the thought that I'd spent a night there made the place less terrifying. When I'd opened my eyes, the lights had been off, and it might have been the middle of the night. Within minutes, though, I heard sounds on the steps and then saw the cooks coming through with another pot and something steaming. The lights went on, followed almost immediately by the cassettes.

Breakfast wasn't much better than dinner had been, but I was getting hungrier. There was a brew resembling coffee—a thin, brown mixture of water, sugar, coffee, chicory, and chocolate—and bits of the last evening's cheese, and some stale bread that had all too obviously been served to the better classes some time in the past. I did drink some of the coffee, and ate a bit of the bread.

To my surprise, I found that there were showers, and although they were open, dormitory style, they were fine. Hot water, even. A real pleasure after Tossa. The toilets, however, were simply holes in the floor with footrests lifted maybe an inch from the level. I squatted, dripping from the shower, while an African came in and, groaning majestically, performed naturally the same act which caused me so much embarrassment. When he finished, I realized that Jay had not been kidding about my left hand. The man dipped his in a water-filled Campbell's soup can, and wiped himself. Then he stood, arranged his robe, and smiling broadly at me, left the room. When I finished,

I turned the shower back on and stepped under it, feeling foolish—foolish for the way I was—but perfectly justified nonetheless.

The day turned out to be a good one. I felt so much better than I had the day before that I found myself taking pleasure in little things—a moment of sunlight through the fog on the deck, the taste of peanuts in the bar, Jay's conversation. We did stick together after I came back to the *dortoir* after breakfast and my shower. It turned out that he'd been in Africa for two years in the Peace Corps, and was returning from his vacation.

"You know what's funny about this *dortoir* thing," he said, when I'd asked him how he'd come to be there, "is that the Africans are used to this sort of thing. Maybe it's presumptuous of me to say so, but I think they've got it better here than most of them do in their villages. At least here they get three meals a day. That's outrageous. Nobody eats that well in the bush. It's only we Anglo-Europeans that take it hard, and not even me so much anymore. The only reason it got to me, the first time I came *dortoir*, was that I was looking forward to a bit of Europe, and didn't want to see any more of Africa until I got back. But it's interesting to me to see how the frogs really treat them. Look at the bastards now."

We were up on the deck. Above us, on the

bridge, a group of the "upper-class" tourists had gathered to look down at us, as though we were in the zoo.

"Pricks," he said to me. Then he cupped his hand over his mouth and looking up, yelled, "Hey! Never seen humans before?" Then he laughed.

It was still cold on the deck, as deserted as it had been the day before. Jay took something from the jacket he wore and put it in his mouth.

"Want some dope?" he asked. "Moroccan kef. Good shit."

I'd be a liar if I said I'd never been around marijuana. I'd lived in L.A. and knew that the major component of its smog was not automobile exhaust, as was generally believed, and I was in that kind of mood, so I took a few tokes. The blacks on deck with us didn't even seem to notice. After a while we went below and I bought Jay a few beers and told him a little about my time in Tossa. Then, once again, I became the center of attention when I started writing a letter to a friend in California. A crowd of the *noirs* gathered, amazed to see me writing left-handed. Apparently this was a serious thing, but since it involved no one else, everyone only laughed and seemed to think I was some kind of magician.

I ate lunch in a haze. Between the beer and the marijuana, the food didn't bother me, and I ate heartily. I forget what it was, but the main ingredient was rice. Afterward, I took another nap, and sometime late in the afternoon rejoined Jay in the bar. He was still reading.

"Good book?"

"Yeah," he said, not very convincingly. "I've read it four times already."

"Then why are you reading it again?"

"Why not?" he said. "Want a beer?"

We got to talking about what I was doing on the ship, and where I was getting off, and what I did when I wasn't traveling.

I laughed. "I don't do much traveling."

"You're here."

"Yes."

"And you've just spent five months in Spain."

"True."

"So what do you do when you're not traveling?"

I told him a little more about Lea. I don't know if it was good or not, but I felt better talking about it. We drank a lot of beer, and by the time I went down to dinner I felt completely comfortable with *dortoir*, with Jay, and with the men there. The next day we'd be docking in Casablanca, then leaving for the Canaries in the evening.

There was an American Western, dubbed in French, shown after dinner, and Jay translated the translation for me. One of the men near us got sick near the end of the movie, though, and we decided to clear out and let the smell subside. The bar was closed, so we worked our way up the floors to the deck. Jay smoked some more dope, but I'd had enough. The water had an eerie phosphorescent glow and seemed to reflect itself back on the fog. After a few minutes, Jay got cold and went below, leaving me pacing with my thoughts.

Sometimes it seemed to me that the whole thing had been planned. By whom, I hadn't the slightest idea. It just seemed somehow contrived. Maybe Lea had made all her important decisions before leaving California, and had latched onto Mike as a vehicle.

You bet.

The thing was, I became aware, or was becoming aware, that I was starting to feel again. I didn't know how long it had been since anything had mattered to me, but now I couldn't deny that, no matter what else I could say about the whole thing, it had made a difference.

The ship belched, and the noise brought me back to the deck. The fog had lifted, and I could make out the faintest lights just on the horizon. I wondered if they were Africa. Maybe Gibraltar.

Or maybe just the phosphorous where the clouds licked down near the water.

It was cold. I hadn't yet let myself really think about Lea being gone. I could say it, but it hadn't sunk in, and suddenly I found myself visualizing her getting ready for bed, her slim body quickly graceful without clothes, moving like a skittish doe. But really, at base, not at all timid. Just careful, watchful.

What the hell had gotten into her?

And suddenly it was clear to me what I should do. I should get off the ship tomorrow and fly to Marseilles and find her. Now I was getting better. The despair had lifted a little and I'd try to live again. We'd work it out. This thing with Mike was only a silly infatuation, and she'd outgrow it eventually.

But no sooner had I thought that than I began to feel that old constraint again, that deadening calm that had as much done me in as Sean's passion had him. Sean had, at least, if you'd excuse the expression, gone out alive. Feeling something. Pain? Maybe there's something ennobling about that keen a pain. With Lea, I'd slowly turned into a nothing. Who could blame her for leaving me? Mike offered something, even if it turned out not to be there.

Then I realized how strong a part of our early love had been the dreams we'd believed in, even if they hadn't been realistic. We'd planned things together. First the house, and then trips, classes, anything to keep us looking ahead. When had it stopped? Two or three years ago. And then Lea had suggested this vacation. Was believing that I would finally start writing a novel any more ridiculous than believing that she and Mike would find his girlfriend?

The wind felt good against my face. We were making pretty decent time, and the sea was picking up somewhat. I grinned and breathed in the cold and salty air through my teeth. We dipped and I heard a wave smack against the bow. Those definitely were lights off to port.

I can trace it all back now pretty easily. I mean how I'd come to stop thinking anything made any difference. It had begun, innocently enough, with an article I hadn't wanted to write. Of course, that had happened before, but this time it had been different. It really had been quite a long time ago. I remember it was one of those lifestyle stories that you now see in every magazine you pick up. I'd realized as I was pecking away at the keys that everybody we knew had this commitment to the way they lived their lives rather than what they did with themselves. We'd all dressed right, and talked right, and went to parties and either drank or did drugs, and laughed a lot, and it had all been routine. But worse had been the kind of hip cynicism that had gone with it, that had bored in under the routines, and left you with nothing.

And that had been it. I'd started to examine everything I did for motives, for truth, for meaning, and more often than not had found that cynicism was the overseer of my life. There was no other underlying principle. Above all, nothing was sacred, and I was cool enough to handle it.

Maybe that was what Lea had come to sense. I'd still acted like my old self, but somehow the connection had been broken, and not just with her. I'd stopped hoping and planning and dreaming because it couldn't matter much. We would go on in our routines and do things together, but the spark was gone. I hadn't been able to get excited about anything. There had been no continuity, no link between things, and with everything broken down and isolated, there had been no resonance in my life. No magic, no mystery, no hope.

But things had turned around now. I felt at home among people. I couldn't get out of my mind the thought of what the tune Mike played on the guitar that night had done to all of us. What if he hadn't done it, just put the guitar down after Marianne's dance and said good night? Would Sean still be alive? Or Lea with me?

A shooting star cut an arc across the sky. I almost wished on it.

# Nineteen

Normally, Lea didn't wear hats, but she had picked up one in Barcelona on the day of her flight to buoy her spirits. It was a light blue, tiny-brimmed and very fashionable hat that might be described as pert. It went well with her coloring.

At the airport, she paid the driver and had him transfer her bags to a porter, who carried them to the loading platform for her plane. Then she went to the bar and ordered a sandwich of very salty ham and a full bottle of white wine, which she finished.

She had never felt more alone. Her fingernails were bitten to the quick and, as she sat eating, she darted looks from time to time around the room as though she expected to see someone. But really she expected no one. When she had nearly emptied the wine bottle, the sun finally cleared the deck surrounding the airport and flooded the room with afternoon light. Immediately, one of the waiters went to pull the shades across the wide windows, but she didn't wait for that. She gulped the wine, and got up and left the place.

The plane loaded shortly afterward, and she took a window seat near the front. Pulling down her window shade, she took off her new hat and put it on the rack above her head. Then she settled down, intending to read a novel during the flight. But her eyes were heavy from the wine, and even as the plane taxied for takeoff, she found herself unable to concentrate. She opened the shade, and watched as Barcelona receded and the Mediterranean spread out below her. Luckily, the man next to her did not seem disposed to talk. She felt that she would have been rude to him if he had. It would not be a long flight, and she wanted to hug her solitude to herself. She slept on and off, and started when the stewardess announced their descent into Marseilles.

When they landed, she went into the bathroom and patted water on her eyes to revive herself. Mike should be waiting outside for her and she didn't know how anything would be with him. It had all been so strange and horrible with the funeral and Doug's good nature.

She'd hated herself, and him. And Sean was gone.

She wouldn't let herself think about that. She'd gone over and over it in her mind, and it could do no good. But she wanted to talk to him now. She was so confused, and it had just gotten so they were talking again for the first time since they'd been kids.

No, she wouldn't think about it.

Mike hadn't come up for the funeral. She really hadn't wanted him to, but had also been bothered when he'd suggested that he pass on it. They'd met the day before it for the first time since the day Sean had died. They'd gone up to Mike's shitty room and made love, and she'd cried the whole day, and he'd tried to be kind, but didn't really know what would help, or how to reach her. And he'd hurt her physically. She hadn't been quite ready and he was young and too fast. He hadn't forced himself on her. She'd wanted him, but at a different pace.

But then he'd told her about his plans, about their plans. He was going to drive to Marseilles the next day and he'd meet her there when she felt she could travel. He'd given her the address where he'd be staying. It was the old dive he'd known from years before, and he told her to write to him and he'd pick her up at the airport or the train station.

And now here she was. Two weeks had gone by. Berta had been good to let her stay, and they had stayed up late almost every night, talking about Sean. She was a good woman, not so simple as Lea had earlier imagined. She was different in what she thought about. When she'd talked about Sean, she spoke of the things he'd done, in a practical sense, whereas Lea had gone on about the kind of man he'd been. They'd complemented each other, and it had been a comfort. In the end, she wasn't sure she wanted to leave, but she knew she had to follow through with the thing with Mike. After all, she'd lost Doug over it. Wouldn't it be stupid to give up on it now?

The sun had just gone down as she stepped onto the boarding platform. It was cold and windy, especially after the warmth of the plane, and as soon as she stepped outside the wind picked up and whipped her hat off and into the air. She watched it being tossed and then land way back beyond the tail of the plane. Then it skidded and rolled in the wind, getting smaller and smaller as it crossed the open airfield, until it was the size of a pebble to her eye. The hat hadn't really meant anything to her, but she found herself on the verge of tears. Then she straightened her shoulders and looked back into the wind, telling herself she wouldn't let herself cry. Still, she bit her bottom lip until it bled.

Mike met her just beyond customs. At first, she was surprised at his appearance. He'd cut his hair quite a bit and looked much younger. His clothing had improved. Before, he'd always been neat, but now he looked almost elegant, in a way that didn't appeal to Lea. He wore brown loafers and beige, highly pressed slacks, and a pale yellow turtleneck pullover. She'd stared at him when she waited in line, smiled nervously when he'd caught her eye, and then looked down, pretending to be checking her bags. She felt awkward, embarrassed to be seen with him. This was the first time she was with him as his woman. She felt uneasily that she must look like one of those rich women who hire young gigolos to escort them. And he certainly looked the part.

In Tossa, even when she'd been with him, it had been easy to imagine that everyone knew they were only friends, that everyone knew she was Doug's wife, and that it was perfectly legitimate. Here she was with Mike. But then she thought of the other side—that she on her own had attracted this younger man, and was pleasing him. The thought made her feel better. Certainly, that was how it must look. She was too attractive to have to pay someone. But still she wished he had not cut his hair, and that he had dressed more casually.

When she'd been cleared, he was waiting just at the gate, and took her things. She kissed him on the cheek in greeting, and then walked beside him out to the parking lot. They didn't speak. When he put the bags in the Citröen, he turned to her and put his arms around her, and she pressed herself against him. She was with him now, and she would be with him, damn it. She hugged him closer, forcing herself not to think.

They got in the car and started driving. Finally, she felt a little relaxed. It was just the two of them again. He got out a cigarette and lit it, looked over at her, and smiled.

"I'm glad you've come."

"So am I."

"How do you feel?"

"Good. Tired."

He reached out his hand and took one of hers. Their fingers intertwined. Was he nervous, too? she wondered.

"We should be at the hotel before long. Why don't you lean back, close your eyes?"

"I feel like I've been trying to sleep all day long. Especially on the plane. I'm OK. I just think I want to stop . . . oh, nothing."

"Stop what?"

"Nothing. I'm just drained. I'd like to stop having everything be so intense for a couple of hours, is all."

"With me?"

She looked over at him and squeezed his hand. He was so much younger.

"Who's being intense with you?"

They drove now into the city, talking in bursts, not saying anything important, then lapsing into silence.

"Would you like to stop for a drink?"

"That would be good," she said.

"Have you eaten?"

"Yes. No. I don't remember."

He pulled the car over to the side of the road, and turned to face her. She looked at his face now in the dark. The only light was from the streetlamps outside. It was not the face of such a young man. She was getting used to it again. He put his hand on the nape of her neck and held her facing him.

"Come on," he said. "Stop this. What's wrong?"

She looked down. "Nothing. I don't know."

He pulled her face up and leaned over to kiss her.

"Give yourself a chance," he said. "Why don't we have something to eat?"

He started up again and turned onto one of the backstreets behind the port. The streets here were lit only at the corners. Women stood singly in doorways and the pedestrians seemed to hug the walls as they drove past. They came out into a pleasant street, well lit and open, and Mike parked in front of an open-air café. Heaters burned between the outdoor tables, but most of the patrons preferred to eat inside. Lea linked her arm through Mike's. She felt funny holding hands while walking with him.

The restaurant specialized in shellfish on the half-shell, but Lea had a fillet of sole. Mike ordered a couple dozen assorted oysters, clams, and mussels, and a bottle of wine, and halfway through the meal they began talking naturally with each other, at least from Lea's point of view. She was feeling much better. Warmer. The wine helped.

"I'm sorry," she said. "Sometimes I feel that I just can't get my balance back. I don't mean to take it out on you. This has been an awfully hard time."

"I know. I don't know how you've done it."

"I don't think I have. I feel like this past month I've been sleepwalking, just trying to make it to the next morning, and always waking up in the middle of something I can't control."

"Would you like to take a few days off here and just kind of get to feeling back to normal?"

"But you see, that's just it. I don't know what normal is anymore. I've been taking days off to myself now since you left Tossa, and trying to sort things out, but getting nowhere. What I'd like to do is be able to not think about anything for a week, but I can't get Sean out of my mind, or Douglas, for that matter. They're both just as surely gone. And now you're really all I have, and I don't know you at all."

He didn't answer, and took a drink of his wine.

"I'm sorry. I don't mean that the way it sounded. But do you know what I mean?"

"What more do you need to know about me? I didn't force you here."

"Oh, God, Mike, don't get mad. Please. I didn't mean to make you mad."

"I'm not mad, but you know me enough. How well do I know you?"

"Yes. I know. You're right. Let's not fight, all right? I couldn't take a fight now."

"I'm not going to fight you." He pointed down at her plate. "Eat your fish, and just try to concentrate on how it tastes. We don't need to talk for a while."

And she did what he told her, calming herself. He ordered coffee for them both, and then brandy. She just wanted not to care, to let things go on for a while, and even to enjoy herself. She wished she

271

were with Douglas, so they wouldn't have to talk, to explain things. Although Mike wasn't forcing her to talk, she felt pressure. But Douglas really would be worse. He wouldn't care about her, or anything else, and he would appear to. That was why she had left him. Or was that true? She hadn't so much left him as gone with Mike. When it had come to it, you could almost say that Doug had left her. Certainly he hadn't given her much of a chance to reconcile.

Then she thought of why she was really here, to help Mike find his lost love, and she felt like a fool. Why did he need her? And why was she going to bed with him? She glanced toward him.

He sat drinking his brandy, turned half away from her in his seat, looking out at the people passing. It was the sharing, she decided. She didn't know that they ever had a chance of finding Sharon, but that didn't matter. They were looking together, and he had something he had to do. As long as there was that, she would be with him, and if they found her, and he went with Sharon, then she would be prepared for that, too. She loved him, she thought. And he took her because he needed someone. He could never love her. She knew that. Maybe she loved him more because it was so clear to her. But what if they spent a year or more looking and never found Sharon? Then what would she be left with? Would she love him without that? At least, she thought, by then I'll know him and be able to say.

Abruptly, Mike finished his brandy and said they should go. She gulped what was left of hers and stood. He came around the table and helped her with her coat.

Back in the car, they drove back through the red-light district and pulled up in front of a sleazy doorway across from a bar. Mike got out his side and opened the back for the bags. Lea looked at the building they'd parked in front of and suddenly wanted to be far away. Mike came to her door and opened it.

"We're here."

She got out slowly and followed him through the entranceway, which was cluttered with old newspapers and smelled like dog. The concierge looked up as they passed through what passed for a lobby, and Lea thought she saw a leering smile on his face for an instant. She wanted to go over and tell him she wasn't one of the neighborhood tarts, but what would that do? He wouldn't care either way.

The room was up two winding flights of stairs. There was no elevator, and she followed Mike silently, with her head down. Inside, the room had two windows facing the street, a dresser, a sink and bidet, and a run-down double bed.

Mike put the things down and turned to face her.

"What do you think?" he asked with a weak smile.

"I won't stay here."

"Now, Lea, sit down."

"No. I won't stay here."

He grabbed her by the shoulders and forced her to sit on the bed.

"What did you expect, the Ritz?"

"Anything," she said. "I don't know, but not this."

"What's wrong with this?"

"It's a dump. It's horrible."

"It's not so bad."

"It is. Look around you. Smell it."

He sat next to her, putting his arm around her.

"Look," he said, "you're tired. Why don't we get into bed? You'll feel better after you've slept a little." He began kneading her shoulders and felt her muscles loosen. "Come on, lie back. Relax."

She did what he said. He took off her shoes and rubbed her feet.

"I just want to sleep," she said. "Would you get out my pajamas? They're in the suitcase."

She sat up and, while he was looking for the pajamas, took off all her clothes. He turned around then, and saw her.

"Are you sure you want these?"

"Yes."

She stepped into the pants. They were like men's flannel pajamas, with a floral design. She didn't put the top on, but flung back the blanket and arranged herself in bed, tucking the covers up just under her breasts.

"Come," she said. "Aren't you getting into bed?"

She watched him taking off his clothes through half-closed eyes. He was aroused when he got in beside her, and she crossed her flanneled leg over his, taking him in her hand. She kissed his neck, and liked the way he smelled.

They kissed deeply, and his hands began to move over her body, but she stopped him.

"Do you want to sleep?" he asked.

"Let's talk a little first."

"OK," he said, his hand resting on her flat, warm stomach, "talk."

"I really just wanted to find out a little of how it's been going since you've come here. I've been so wrapped up in myself, I keep forgetting why it is we're both here. Have you had any luck?"

He put his arm under his head and rolled onto his back.

"With Sharon, you mean?"

"Yes."

"I haven't started to look."

She felt the beginning of fear, or anger, building up in the pit of her stomach.

"Why not?"

He took a deep breath. "I might as well tell you now as later," he said. "I'm not sure that I want to find Sharon anymore. I've thought so much about it in the past couple of months, I don't know what I'd do if I did run into her. We wouldn't know each other anymore. It's been so many years, and I've got to believe that she's dead."

"And you don't care if you find her?"

"I don't see what would be the point."

"Then why did you bring me here?"

"I didn't bring you here," he said, raising his voice. "You came here yourself. Today. Remember?"

"But why? Why did you let me?"

"What are you, crazy? I wanted you to come."

"But why?"

"To be with me, goddamn it. Why do you think?"

She was crying now, and turned her back to him.

"I don't know. I don't know. Just leave me alone."

"Well, fuck, Lea, what's the problem? You wanted to come."

"No. I had to come. I had to help you."

"Bullshit. Why are you in bed with me then?"

"I don't know." She was sobbing now. "I don't know."

Someone knocked on the door and yelled something angrily in French.

Mike put his hand on her shoulder, and pulled her around to him.

"Don't you understand?" he whispered. "I wanted you to come because I didn't want to lose you. We can get to know each other here. What difference does it make so long as we're happy together?"

She let him go on, and let his hands start to move over her body again, but she felt dead now, used up, lied to. He kissed her, and she let him, trying to let her body take over. His hand went under the elastic of the pajamas and she began thrusting her hips rhythmically. Yes, she would just forget about him. It was her body now. That was all. His mouth went to her breasts and down her belly. Then she came out of her trance and grabbed his hair, pulling him up.

"No. You can't do that. Not tonight. Here. Just come inside me. There, that's a good boy. It'll be fine now. Okay. Good. Slower, now, slower."

Then she was talking to herself. *Okay. Steady, now. Fast. Not too fast. Okay. Faster. Harder, now, and harder . . .*

Before she went to sleep, she made a mental note to stop at a bank the next day. She'd need more cash for a better hotel.

# Twenty

"What's on for today?" I asked Jay as we walked down the gangplank.

"I've never been laid in Morocco," he said, "and I try to make it a point to get laid in every country I visit. You never know but you might not make it back."

I laughed. The sun was out and it was warm, even though still before eight in the morning. We'd been docked already when I woke up, and both Jay and I had decided to skip breakfast on the ship and spend as much time as possible ashore.

"I'll see you this evening, then."

"I could meet you somewhere in the afternoon," he said.

So we decided to rendezvous at the gate to the port at around two, and I went to a café while he went off with a smile to his other pursuits. I had a delicious breakfast of ham and eggs, three glasses of orange juice, and the most enjoyable couple of cups of coffee I could remember in a long time. Then I sat at an outside table with a copy of the *International Herald Tribune* and passed another fine hour, watching the city come to life around me.

The café was on the main street leading up from the dock—a broad, palm-lined avenue nearly empty of automobile traffic. The men who walked by were dressed in everything from caftans to business suits, and I was surprised to see several women in veils. They didn't seem to jive with the modernity of the Casablanca that fronted this main street, but after I'd finished the paper, I walked through the crowded markets off the main road, and those veiled women seemed perfectly in place.

It was a strange city to me, after the months in Spain. While it wasn't especially clean, it lacked the gutter smell that I'd come to associate with cities in Spain, and its overwhelming whiteness, living up to its name, left me with an impression of a nearly anti-septic, heat-dried cleanliness. Then, too, it was hot. The sky was perfectly blue, and the heat seemed as though it must permanently reside there. I couldn't imagine a different kind of day in Casablanca. At the markets, the crowds were large and noisy. Children ran about freely and there seemed to be constantly the sound of tambourines and bells, wafted on the air along with the smells of spices and hashish, and occasionally what I came to recognize as the green, foul, mucky breath of a camel.

I walked my way around through the backstreets and came out on a cliff overlooking the public beach, which was filled with bodies. For a moment, I thought of going down and taking off my shoes, but decided I had better start back to the dock, since by the way I had come it was about four miles. I checked my wallet, which I'd stuck into my front pocket in the market, and still had several hundred pesetas, which were accepted here, and so I realized there was nothing I had to do, and began ambling back toward the port.

I'd been expecting, ever since Franco's death, to hear news of the revolution in Spain, which I'd come to believe was inevitable. Though it had been only two days since I'd been in Barcelona, somehow it seemed much longer, and I expected events to have moved along. But the paper that morning had had no news of Spain at all, and as I walked under the Moroccan sun, I thought of Tony and his plans, and the passion with which he'd discussed them. He must be frustrated now. But he was young, and there would be time for his revolution. Spain might even become modern without it.

I met Jay and we went to eat at a place he'd passed coming back to meet me. Small and hot, it was not a restaurant I would have picked myself, but the food was good. We had a hot chicken and cinnamon pie covered with sugar, and some dish made with mutton and honey. The bread was flat and tasteless, seemingly there only to mop up grease and to dip in the mouth-burning red relish they served. We drank a lot of wine, and left in high spirits, though the thought of another night on the *Antoinette* loomed menacingly before us. We walked back slowly, savoring the warm dusk. Stopping once, we bought a large sack of oranges and carried them back with us.

"This has been great," I said.

"You sound almost surprised."

"I guess I am. A couple of days on that ship and you don't feel like you'll ever be out in the air again, walking along more or less carefree."

"You know," he said, "I really don't feel that way. Oh, I know where you're coming from, but somehow the ship isn't negative for me. I mean, it's a drag in some ways, but it's also a good counterpoint." He took out one of the oranges and began peeling it. "Look. There's a lot of shit everywhere, and it seems to me there are three ways to deal with it. You either concentrate on it, or you deny it altogether, or you're aware of it, but don't let it become the focal point of your life. There's also good things, you know, and I find they all sort of balance out. But," he said disarmingly, breaking the orange and handing half to me, "I am but a callow youth, and defer to your experience. Good orange, huh?"

I thought about what he'd said, and about the past few months, and there was no way that the good and the bad balanced out at all. But then, I had to admit that a few months was not exactly the long run.

"Look," he said. "Didn't you find that today you were, I don't know, more aware of things than you would have been if you'd, say, flown in?"

"It's possible, I guess."

"Well, just take this orange. Can you believe how good it tastes after what we've been eating?"

"That's true."

"Sure. The main thing you want to avoid is the rut. That's the killer. Everything becomes the same and the good and the shit kind of blend into gray and nothing means anything."

"I've noticed that."

He clapped me on the back. "Hey. Who am I to be telling you anything? But it's been a hang-up of mine and I get off talking about it."

"So talk. Who's stopping you?"

"What I don't understand is why everybody

seems to view the rut as the ideal. I mean, get a job and stay at it and avoid highs and lows, right? Fuckin' A. I got a job right out of college and had zoomed right on through college and was a good little boy, but after two years of that, I thought I had lost it forever. I mean, everything was so fucking bland, and all the people I hung out with were bored and boring and talked about how they were going to quit soon and do something else, and nobody ever did. Kee-rist! Nearly sent me over the edge. I'm not kidding. So I decided to quit and do this Peace Corps thing, and not 'cause I'm idealistic, and I didn't talk about it at all. Didn't even give notice. Just got on the plane when the time came and took off. And even this is structured, but it's better than it was. But in six months I'm through and then I'll try something else."

"Do you know what you'll do?"

"Not really. Probably travel for a while. I don't really care that much."

I laughed. "That's amazing."

"Why?"

"Where's it all leading?"

"Where should it lead?"

"I don't know. You're a smart guy. Seems like you could really do something."

"I am doing something."

"No. You know what I mean."

"Yeah, but what you mean is crazy. I mean, it's not like you win a prize or something at the end. You just go on doing what you're happy with. Maybe someday I'll get into something I really enjoy that makes me stay in one place, and then I'll stay in one place. Besides, it's not really what you do that makes any difference. The worst thing is that feeling that you're finished. That you've done all you're going to do. That's why that job drove me crazy. It wasn't the job. There were a few guys there that were thrilled and delighted every day, but it wasn't for me. I wasn't me, and if you're not you, then what do you have to offer to anybody, right?"

We arrived at the dock and went aboard. The ship was trimmed out in lights and streamers to impress visitors, and we could wander on board, so we decided to go to the upstairs bar for a drink. I don't know if the bartender recognized me as the crasher, but Jay stood out clearly from the other patrons. There were a few other people his age, but they were all very well dressed. Jay seemed to enjoy his black-sheep status, and smiled happily at the porter who hovered near us, waiting, I know, for the moment we could be evicted.

We sat at a table near the pool, which had been uncovered after we hit the warmer weather, and I drank off half my bourbon in one gulp.

"You know what got to me the most when I started this vacation?" I asked.

"Time."

"That's it."

"Sure. That's what gets to everybody."

"Yeah. It was pretty bad. I kept wanting the days to end, so maybe something would clear itself up, but instead the next day would begin in that same void."

"It's a bitch," he said. "I remember the first couple of months out in the bush I really thought I'd blown it. I mean, there was nothing to do but sit around and think about things. And then that emptiness that comes whenever you break a habit started really to get to me. I mean, when your whole life is a habit?"

"Yeah, I know." I sipped my drink. "How did you get out of it?"

He shrugged. "I don't know. Got into little things, I guess. Studied French, read a lot—but mostly, you know, I don't think it's a question of doing anything special. I think that with me, I just got to a point where my body sensed that things had to change, almost like what was going on was a disease it had to take care of. And I just found myself feeling more at home with myself.

"It wasn't that big a deal, like a revelation or anything. Suddenly little things got to be important in themselves. It was kind of like I was starting over completely and answering what I thought were the big questions became not so important. I mean, who really cares if you've figured everything out? You're not living a study, you know. You're living a life. And so I concentrated on details, on what naturally felt right, and pretty soon they added up to a whole different picture of what life was about. And all that other stuff, like my job, and what was I doing with my life—you know, the big picture—all that just seemed stupid. I mean, it didn't work, and that's the thing. Maybe for some people it does, but I tend to like enjoying things if they're fun instead of wondering what it is in me that would like something so nonprofound."

We were silent for a while, and I ordered another round from the porter. The first stars were becoming visible, and around us I was becoming aware of the bustle of people getting ready to leave. There was a warm evening breeze off the sea. It was a beautiful moment.

"You know," Jay finally went on, "when I first

got to my post, there was nobody there to meet me, and no hotel and no restaurant, needless to say, and so I just walked up to this hut and asked the father there if he could tell me where the *préfet* was, so I could get settled, or start something. But he wouldn't even talk to me until he'd had me in to meet his family, and I'd finished dinner with them." He shrugged again. "I don't know if that means anything, but it made all the difference in the world to me at the time. I mean, here's a guy who is poor as sin and doesn't know me from Jesus, and he has me eat with his whole family. I don't know. Maybe that was the first detail that got to me. It was so immediate. He didn't expect me to ask him back, or to pay him, or to owe him something. It was just the natural thing to do for him." He looked at his drink. "I'm rambling. Must be the booze."

"No," I said. "That's the thing that's been getting to me—that I can't seem to get the details to mean anything."

"Well, they don't at first. That dinner didn't mean anything more to me at the time than that it was damn nice of the guy to put me up. But it's kind of like learning a language. The first words mean nothing. There's no pattern, but you remember them because you know they mean something, even if you can't define it, or it's unrelated to anything else you know. So you just let the words build up and pretty soon you've got some sentences, and then you find that you can talk to hundreds of other people you might never have been able to know, and then one of those people, maybe, you fall in love with, or kills you, or leaves you a fortune, and it's all traceable back to that first word. Woo. I must be getting loaded."

"We might as well get below," I said. "The penguin's getting nervous."

Down at our bunks, I once again felt uncomfortable with the crowd, the heat, and the noise. Jay was lying down, his eyes closed, and I was sitting hunched on the side of the bunk, thumbing through one of his books.

"Jay?"

"Huh."

"What do you do if all the details—the first ones, I mean—are all bad? I mean really shitty?"

"What the hell," he said. "They're only details."

I passed most of the next day on our deck. The air was cooler than it had been in Casablanca, but still quite pleasant. Jay stayed below. We'd pretty much talked ourselves out the day before, and I was content to stand by the side of the ship and look out over the expanse of water.

Once, around midday, a school of dolphins kept us entertained as they broke water in front and on the sides of us.

I got to know a few of the other men on board, and talked at length with one of them, a gaily dressed giant black man named Minta. He talked in the same broken French I did, and we got along very well, smiling and nodding to each other while we tried to make ourselves understood. He taught me the game called *oware* that I'd seen the women playing with stones, and beat me handily four times.

Later in the afternoon, I went to the bar and did write a few letters, one to Lea in care of a mutual friend. I told her where she could reach me in case she wanted to be in touch. There were still many practical things to clear up. I felt good about writing to her. I didn't really have the sense that I should hate her, or she me, and I restrained myself from saying that I loved her. She probably wouldn't get the letter anyway for a couple of months, and by then maybe her whole world would be different. Still, it was a start and, at the same time, didn't lead anywhere. I didn't want to offer more than that.

Dinner was again lentils with some kind of meat. I ate a lot, talking to Jay and Minta and the others. After dinner, we gave out what oranges we had left. I was tired from a day outside on the deck, even though I had done nothing, and when they disassembled the tables, I walked over to my bed and lay down. Tomorrow we'd put in at Tenerife.

The ship rode easily, and I was aware for a while of its steady rise and fall, but before long the gentle rocking had its effect, and I slept.

# Twenty-one

Mike sat at the edge of the pier in Marseilles trying to decide where he had gone wrong. He'd been there since early in the afternoon, when he'd come back from shopping for lunch to find Lea gone. She'd left a terse note. There was no mystery this time.

So he'd come down to the waterfront. It was cold. The wind blew in off the water. He didn't know what to think. In the evening, there was a cloudburst, a sun shower, with the cold rain soaking him even as he watched the sun going down. The squall passed. It got dark quickly, and then he was really cold. He considered getting in his car and driving back to Tossa. But what waited for him there?

He got up stiffly and began walking back to the

hotel. He needed some dry clothes. That was the first thing. As he walked, he cursed Lea.

The streets shone with the wet. He was more comfortable in the back alleys, and walked with his hands shoved deep into his pockets, hunched over. Occasionally one of the girls would call to him, but he wouldn't look at her. To fight the cold, he started jogging down the middle of the street. When he was nearly back to the hotel, he stopped at a corner to get his breath. The street looked to him like a cheap movie set, the lights doing nothing but making him feel how dark it would be without them. His breath curled up out of his mouth as he leaned up under a doorway and panted.

Across the street, a door opened and a girl stepped out, framed in the light from inside. Mike could see that she was not old. She wore a heavy, dark coat which stopped far above her knees, and she looked sullenly across at him, and lit a cigarette. When the match glared briefly, he saw her face and couldn't believe his eyes. It was Sharon's face. Her hair was blond, not the dyed red most of the whores had. He stared at her while she looked vacantly down the empty street and dragged again at the cigarette. Behind her, the door opened again and a man stepped out, patted her on the rear, and walked off. Mike came out of the shadow of the doorway and looked at her. She paid no attention to him. It was amazing. He wanted to speak to her, but couldn't say anything. He'd like to hear her voice. Maybe it was her, after all this time.

She threw down her cigarette suddenly and disappeared inside the door. He stood looking at the spot for a second, and then turned the corner and went back to his hotel.

The concierge didn't want him to enter looking so wet and mangy, but Mike shut him up with a look before he could say anything. He took the steps two at a time and let himself in his room.

Fuck her, he thought. I don't need her.

He picked out some of the new clothes he'd bought, and carefully checked to see how he looked in the mirror. His mind raced. He didn't know what he would do, but he'd do something. Outside, he went down the street to a large bar at the corner. He sat down, conspicuously facing the center of the room, though off to one side. The bar wasn't crowded. He ordered a good bottle of wine and a bottle of Perrier, and settled down to wait.

After perhaps an hour, the girl he wanted came in alone. Except for the fact that she was slim and had dark hair, she didn't look much like Lea. She was young, probably not yet twenty, maybe a secretary somewhere. She dressed well, conservatively. Nylons with a seam down the back of her legs, light gloves, a dark sweater, a wrap-around skirt of fashionable length. That wasn't what made him sure she was the right one, however. There was a brooding quality about her, even as she stood by the bar. She looked around too much, not as though she were expecting someone, but rather as though she needed to know she was missing nothing that might threaten her.

Mike stopped the waiter and asked him if he would invite the girl over to share some wine. He knew she wouldn't refuse. He looked presentable, and she had come into the bar unescorted.

When she came over, Mike stood, all manners, and held her chair. They introduced themselves, and he poured wine.

At first they made small talk. How well he spoke French. He told her the same thing, and they laughed. She hadn't known many Americans. What had brought him to Marseilles?

But he evaded that. Instead, his eyes clouded briefly, and his face hardened. Then, immediately, he brightened again and asked her about her work, her family. Then, as they started the second bottle, he quieted himself. The laughs became scarce and then, when he felt she was ready, he began.

"You ask why I'm in Marseilles. I want to tell you."

"Do," she said. Her eyes were wide, focused on him. He lifted his glass to his mouth and she followed it with her eyes.

"I don't want to bore you." All seriousness now.

"No, go on. Please."

"I came here to Marseilles for the first time when I was eighteen. But I was younger than that. Too young, I supposed I believed, then, in love, and I came with my lover. We were on vacation, and . . ."

It had worked with Lea, although then he had meant it. And it would work with this girl. He would show them. He understood now what it had all meant to her, and if she hadn't wanted him for himself, and he knew that, then he would at least learn something from what she had wanted. This girl would be easy, and then there would be more. And he went on and on, and her eyes grew wider with sympathy, and when he felt himself near to crying, he stopped.

They finished the wine. He was here to look for her. Did she understand how hard it was?

Getting up, they left the bar, walking down the near-empty street toward his hotel. He talked quietly now about his hopes, his future, his forlorn and lonely past. The wind made a siren sound between the buildings, and she let him put his arm around her so they both wouldn't be so cold. The tears came, and she brushed them away with her gloved hand, looking up at him, believing. He kissed her, touching her lips gently, then forcing her easily until they were sucking in each other's breath on the cold street, their tongues deep in each other's mouths.

And then, when it was so certain, so easy, he knew he couldn't do it. It would only be a matter of taking her back to the bar and excusing himself to go to the bathroom. It had been a rotten plan, leading nowhere. He had been hurting and had wanted to hurt. He still did, but not this way. This girl had never hurt him, and never could.

He turned her around, and suggested another bottle of wine. He sat her so she'd face away from the door, and then told her he'd be right back. Was it all so stupid? he thought. He felt abandoned. He turned quickly off the street back into the alleys. Maybe this would not have to be such a horrible thing. He hadn't loved Lea. There hadn't been time. Maybe he'd needed her, but for what?

He felt sick for playing with that girl. What had been the point of that? But he wouldn't let himself dwell on it. So he'd made a mistake, and perhaps the girl would be upset for a day or so. Big deal.

He thought about Lea. He didn't really miss her, since she'd never been constantly around anyway. It was just that she'd come to be what Sharon had been—some ideal he could use to hide out behind. Maybe it was time he laid to rest a ghost or two.

He knew where he was. The streets were the ones he had walked in his mind thousands of times trying to figure where Sharon had gone. So now he walked with his head up, knowing where he wanted to go, letting the wind cut through his jacket. It didn't chill him so much now.

He came to the corner, and sat on the stoop across from the door. At least here it wouldn't be a matter of lying, and it would come to an end once and for all. He waited about a quarter of an hour and smoked two cigarettes. Then the door opened and the girl who looked like Sharon came out again.

His heart beat violently, but with a clean fear-beat that he knew how to live with. After this, after tonight, it would be different. OK, he'd learned. No more trying to plug how he'd felt at eighteen into how he was now. He had better things to do than that.

The door opened again and the other john came

out. He pecked the girl on the cheek and squeezed her breast. When he had gone, Mike stood and crossed over to her. Her eyes were stone cold, but she smiled at him.

*"Combien?"* he asked.

# Twenty-two

Tenerife is the largest of the Canary Islands, spared the overwhelming bustle of tourism because its largest city, Santa Cruz, does not pretend that it is solely a resort town. It leaves its tourists to Las Palmas, which is happy to have them. Tenerife produces a fine, Madeira-like wine called Teneriffe, and bananas, but it is not by any means a commercial center. Santa Cruz is a beautiful and very small city, lush and well scrubbed, set at the base of a small mountain that extends nearly to the sea. From a mile out, it was breathtaking, and seemed to get better as we approached.

I'd retired so early the night before that I was up well before dawn, and I reached under my bunk after showering, made sure that I was packed, and walked up to enjoy the sunrise on the deck. Even our deck didn't bother me anymore, and standing there alone in the early morning I thought that I had never felt so free. As soon as there was enough light I saw the island, though we were still quite a ways off. Irrationally, I felt I couldn't be arriving at a better spot.

When we docked, I went below and found that Jay would be coming ashore until the ship disembarked again at two thirty. He knew a place at San Andrés, at the other end of the island, he said, where they made the best paella in the world, so I decided I'd spend those few last hours in his company, and then set about finding a place to stay.

We went ashore to find most of the town still closed up, so we decided to walk around before having breakfast, while the streets were quiet. The sun was shining brightly in the deep-blue sky, and the day was still except for an occasional wisp of warm breeze. Santa Cruz itself was only about ten blocks deep and twenty-five wide, so we had explored it pretty thoroughly within an hour. Then we stopped and had some coffee and milk in one of the cafés, and bought a box of good Las Palmas cigars.

All of the Canaries are part of Spain, and I felt immediately at home with the money and the language. Still, it was not really a Spanish setting. The African influence was strong. There were more blacks around than I'd ever seen in Spain, dressed in anything from the bright-colored *boubous* of the men on the *Antoinette* to more continental styles. It was a good blend. I didn't sense, even from the first, that mood of intolerance that had seemed to pervade mainland Spain. It was odd, I thought. The Canaries were a Franco stronghold. He'd come from here. Yet the whole feel of the town was freer, more open than Barcelona had been. Maybe it was only a matter of size, though.

We read newspapers in the park for a while, and then Jay flagged a taxi to the curb and we rode five miles down the island to San Andrés de Tenerife. The ride, along the water, was interesting mostly because after we left the town, the island seemed extraordinarily barren. In Santa Cruz, everything had been well watered, almost tropical, and here, less than two miles away, once again we were bounded by a stony, Spanish whiteness on our left, and the sea on our right. The road out to San Andrés was nearly deserted. We passed only one car coming the other way.

San Andrés itself was a sleepy, typical Spanish village. There were no roads to speak of. The driver left us down by the beach, and I was surprised to see, after all my months of white-sanded resorts, that it was covered by pebbles and debris. That didn't seem to bother the several children who were out in the water, but it didn't look very inviting. A few boats were tied up at the breakwater, which extended perhaps two hundred yards out. Here and there on the breakwater a fisherman would tug at his pole, but in spite of that and the children in the water the whole place had a deserted, abandoned feeling.

Jay led me back into the town, which consisted of no more than a hundred white stucco buildings clustered together, and turned into what looked like the door to a house. Inside, a small room contained a bar and some men sitting around drinking. Jay ordered us a couple of beers and talked to the bartender for a few minutes, while I lit up one of the cigars and sat back to relax. He came back from the bar with a plate containing a bunch of deep-fried squid and the biggest lobster claw I'd ever seen.

"He says it'll be two hours, which is just right."

"Why so long?"

"He's got to go down to the pier and get all the fish before he puts it on. Meanwhile, this stuff ought to tide us over. Go ahead, you can have the claw. I've had lots."

"How do you know about this place?"

"Oh, I came here my first-year vacation. Flew to Las Palmas, but the crowds got to me, so I took a ferry over here and loved it. Some German sailor I met turned me on to this place, and it really is the best."

I had no complaints with the lobster. The claw must have been seven inches long by two wide.

"By the way," Jay asked, "do you have any money?"

"Sure."

"Well, he's in the back now, and wants to get paid before he goes out, and I just realized I've got no pesetas." He grinned, and did a kind of shuffle in his chair. "Yes, I've got no pesetas," he sang. "I have no pesetas today."

Laughing, I got out my wallet. "How much is it?"

He was still humming the tune. "Pretty expensive."

I looked in the wallet. What with the cab and last night's dinner, I was getting down pretty far. "How much?"

"Two hundred."

"You're kidding?" Two hundred pesetas was about three dollars.

"No, but that includes all the wine we want, and salad, and coffee, and these first *tapas* were on the house."

"Jesus. How can he afford that?"

"I don't know. Just be glad. I'll give you my half in traveler's checks."

"That's OK. It's on me."

We finished our beer, paid the man, and decided

to see a little more of the town while we waited for the paella. Our tour lasted only about twenty minutes, however, so Jay decided to show me another bar.

"I'm pretty much out of money," I said, "if we want to cab it back."

"No sweat. Let's see if we can work something out."

The other bar was similar to the first. It was smaller, and there were more bottles on the counters behind the bar, but again it was just a room with a few tables, a dirt floor, and some faded pin-ups on the walls.

"Pretty risqué for Spain," I said.

Jay looked around for a minute. "There's a lot of little differences here."

We went up to the bar, and Jay asked the man if he would take traveler's checks. He said he didn't know what they were. I thought he was kidding, but Jay explained it to him carefully, and the man then said he'd be happy to accept them if we knew the exchange rate. I thought we were getting the old runaround, but Jay patiently pulled out the paper he'd been reading that morning and turned to the foreign exchange listings. When he'd shown the man the dollar and peseta values, the man smiled and said he'd give him ten dollars' worth of pesetas at the morning's price. I couldn't believe it, since I'd heard stories of people having trouble cashing traveler's checks in major hotels. I was really starting to like this place.

We both had gin and tonics and talked with the bartender about Franco's death and what it had meant to him. He didn't seem to think it would make much difference.

"So you don't think there'll be a revolution?"

He laughed. *"¿Dónde?"*

"In the north," I said. "Barcelona."

He looked puzzled. "Why should there be?"

He bought us both another drink, and we talked for another hour about sports and other things. When I asked him why he had the pinups on his wall, he answered that he liked to look at pretty women.

"Pretty good reason," Jay said when we left.

Back in the first bar, we were escorted behind the counter to a hall leading to an outdoor dining room. There was a striped red and white awning stretched over a trellis, serving as the roof. The floor was lovely, bloodred tiles. The trellis was hung with grapevines, and the foliage let just enough breeze through to leave us aware that we were on a patio, and not in a room.

In the center of the table was a large carafe of rosé, beaded with condensation, and a plate heaped with artichoke hearts, olives, green and white onions, and radishes. We had barely begun when the bartender-chef brought in the paella, covered, and a loaf of bread. From the size of the pan, we could see it would easily feed six people. We moved our salad plates aside while he spooned out monstrous platefuls of lobster, squid, chicken, *merluza,* and sausage, not to mention the rice and pimento and peas. We looked across the table at each other and laughed at the size of the servings. The amount left in the pan didn't seem to have been diminished.

"I bet everybody in there eats on what we leave."

"Wouldn't surprise me if it lasted a week."

We asked the bartender if he'd join us, but he said no; he had his customers inside to watch.

An hour later, stuffed and happy, we walked down to the beach and caught a cab back to Santa Cruz. I told Jay I'd be here at General Delivery if he felt like writing. Then I wished him good luck. He embraced me, and was gone.

I easily got a room at full-pension in an old but very clean and charming hotel. My room had a hard bed and a sink and dresser. Right across the hall was a bathroom with a hot shower. Downstairs, the dining room was well lit and had a full bar. I still didn't know what I would do, or how long I would stay here but, above all, I felt hopeful.

It was still only early afternoon, so I decided to walk to the top of the mountain behind the city. There was a paved road that wound up it, and it was really no more than one thousand feet high. I'd barely left the buildings of the town behind me, though, when the landscape again changed dramatically. I passed a grove of broad-leafed banana trees, looking cool and inviting in the afternoon sun. Then, before I knew it, suddenly I could have been back in California or even Tossa. Low brush dotted the hill on either side of me. This was rough land. As I got higher, I noticed more and more dwellings I hadn't seen from the town—shacks of plywood and corrugated iron with a goat or two tethered in front. An old man crossed the road, driving a few sheep before him with a switch.

I began to sweat. This was quite a steep climb. Where the shacks were nearer to the road, dogs ran snarling toward me until their leashes choked them off.

Finally, I reached the summit, breathless but invigorated. The road ended in a paved vista point, around which a low white wall had been built. I sat on it and looked below.

To my left, behind the first ridge of the hill, was

a group of houses I hadn't been able to see from below. They looked as if they'd been moved out from Malibu Canyon, with their sculptured lawns and swimming pools. The afternoon shade was beginning to move over them now, and they were like a bit of fairyland—emerald green, refreshing, carefree. I wondered if the peasants in the shacks I'd passed ever came up here just to look.

Maybe once.

In front of me, the hill sloped down to Santa Cruz, and out to the ocean beyond. From up here, I could see the next island on the horizon, but I didn't know which one it was. It wasn't visible from the beach.

The wind picked up slightly. I thought back to what Jay had said the other day about details, and how it had sounded so right. I closed my eyes and could almost bring back the melody of that song Mike had played that had started all this. And it had been that song. Just a detail. Might easily have been left out. But if it had, where would we all be now? I didn't feel any anger toward him. He was young and he'd learn. And I was now willing to see that it hadn't been all bad for me. I felt alive again. Maybe hurt in places, but better than before. I believed again that little things could make a difference, and maybe I'd been looking at it wrong, and things did fit together. I decided, at least, to believe that in the future. Believing nothing had gotten me nowhere. Start small, work up.

I stood up and shivered. My clothes were still slightly wet from sweating, and the breeze was getting stronger. The paved road I had come up led out behind the vista point and then curved around the hill, coming out again below me a hundred yards down before it continued on to the city. Between the white wall where I stood and the road below was a pathless, rocky terrain. It was with a kind of surprise that I watched my feet step over onto that slope. It was steep and slippery going down, and I picked up some nettle in my hand, but otherwise I got to the road feeling fine, and turned my steps to the city, there to buy some paper and start about this business of making myself a living.

# Twenty-three

The bell on the cheap clock rang shrilly, and Kyra turned over and reached for the button to turn it off. She opened her eyes and looked at the dial until it came into focus. Six thirty. She threw back the covers and stepped onto the wooden floor.

She lived in a small apartment on the Calle Siracusa in Barcelona, very near the center of the city. She'd moved out of Tossa sometime in late February and now, four months later, was starting to feel that she belonged here. She hadn't made any friends, but Tony would occasionally come by to visit. She wasn't lonely. There had been a lot of work to do.

The apartment was nothing special, but she liked it. The building was of red brick, and the street was a quiet one, even so close to downtown. She had three rooms up on the third floor, and the afternoon sun lit the place up nicely.

Absently, she went to the sink and filled a pitcher, then crossed to the full-length window facing the street and opened it. There was a small, grilled-iron fence surrounding the tiniest of patios, and she'd bought several pots of plants and set them out there. After she watered them, she straightened up and looked at the surrounding roofs. The sun was up, but it was still early enough that the whole neighborhood was in shade. Over the buildings, a couple of miles away, she could see the amusement park on Montjuich bathed in sunlight. The air was warm and soft, and it would be a hot day.

In half an hour, she had dressed and left the apartment. She'd lost some weight since the winter and hadn't needed to, but men still stopped and looked after her when she passed. To her own mind, she'd gotten rid of the last of her baby fat, and she was glad of it. She did look older.

She went, as she did every day, to a café on the Avenida del Generalisimo Franco, and sat outside, with her back against the building. The waiter knew her and without her having to ask he brought out a croissant and a cup of *café con leche*. She smiled at him and exchanged some pleasantries about the weather and the summer influx of tourists.

"It will be good for you," he said, "for the business."

"I hope so."

"You'll see. You will do well. Today's the first day, isn't it?"

"Yes."

They spoke in Spanish. She had decided she had better know the language if she was going to live in Spain, and had started studying seriously even before she had left Tossa.

When she finished her breakfast, she paid the man, tipping him more than usual, and walked up to the Paseo del Gracia. This was her favorite time of day. She loved the fresh smell of the streets as she walked to her shop. The flower stalls were opening as she passed them, and she nodded to the old men and women in their black clothes. Occasionally, one of them would give her something to put in her hair. More often, she'd buy several small bouquets and put them around her shop although construction was still going on. They had made her feel settled.

Her style of dressing had changed. There was a muted feel about her now. She wore browns and yellows, and pastels. The cuts were European and businesslike. She'd cut her hair, but not too short. Where before her waving hair might have made you notice her, now it only made her more attractive once you had noticed her.

The sun was full up now, the streets busy. Holding a large bunch of assorted bright flowers in her hand, she turned onto the Rambla de Cataluña and looked up at the sign that hung above her shop.

She took out the key and opened the door, then pulled up the shades and turned the sign over from *Cerrado* to *Abierto*. When the flowers had been put in their vases, she went to her chair near the counter and sat down.

It was a small shop, but it was in a good location and very well done. Books, mostly in English, lined the three walls from floor to ceiling, and there were two tables in the middle of the room, laden with "coffee-table books." The entire front of the store was glass, and it was always light and pleasant inside. She'd discovered she had a gift for decorating, and the select prints and scattered greenery made the room easy to spend long periods of time in it. The big problem had been stocking the books—the letters, the connections, the credit. But at least she'd had enough from Sean's will to pay the first year's lease and get started. She knew her stock was still small, but in the summer she might make enough to keep it going. That was all she wanted to do, really, keep it going for a year or two. And it had a chance. It was close enough to the university to draw customers from there, and the road was certainly well traveled by tourists.

Time would tell, she thought. She pulled down a book and began to read, but her mind drifted.

At first, she hadn't wanted the money. She hadn't wanted anything but to be left alone. She didn't understand why he had done it. Everything had been going so well with them, and for the first time. She had tried over and over again to remember if she had done anything to hurt him, but she could think of nothing. If it had been because of her, she did not know why. It couldn't have been. But gradually the concern over why had receded, and she knew it didn't matter. He was dead, and she would never know why. She had loved him. In her sorrow, she had hated herself for that, and hated him for having let it happen. She missed him. That was all. She didn't care if it was anybody's fault.

She wasn't in mourning. In a strange way, she had finally come to realize who she was. She no longer had to prove herself to men. She felt whole by herself. She was lonely from time to time, but she could take it now. The shop was important to her, and she had kept busy getting it ready, and she would now keep busy making it go. But she knew that the keeping busy was not a way of hiding. She was interested. Being her own woman fascinated her. She supposed she would meet someone she might love again. But that was how she looked at it—not as a necessity, but as something she more or less expected to happen. She wouldn't live waiting for it. If it came, she would let it. She was open, but not hungry. There were many other things to do.

An elderly couple from Britain stopped in the doorway and she looked up and smiled at them. They came in. Before they left, a girl from the university stopped in and said she needed a book for a class. Luckily it was in stock. All the morning long, people entered in a steady stream, and Kyra enjoyed herself immensely, talking to them or just watching, smiling. Tony came by and offered to take her to lunch during siesta, and she was happy to go with him.

In the afternoon, two of the workers who'd helped her set up the shelves and do the painting came by with flowers for her. She kissed them each warmly on the cheek, thanking them, and they left, blushing. They were very young and she knew they both had crushes on her.

Customers kept stopping in, and though there was never a rush, neither was the shop ever empty for long. When she pulled the shades down at seven thirty and turned the sign back to *Cerrado*, she felt she'd done a good day's work.

Back in her apartment, she ate a light dinner and then sat by the window that looked out over the city. She intended to read a little and then see how the ledger looked for the first day. She moved the chair over enough so that she could see the lights outside. A strong smell of rotten flowers came in on the hot breeze. She could see the bright red and green lights of the funicular moving up to the amusement park on Montjuich. She closed her eyes and imagined that she heard the couples laughing on the rides. She leaned back in the chair then, and decided to let herself cry.

It would be the last time she'd cry in a long time, and she knew that she wanted to. And she knew why she wanted to, and that it was all right.

# Twenty-four

Berta finished doing the dishes that had piled up from the day before. She had been so excited that she hadn't remembered to do them. It hadn't been easy, all this time, to convince Pedro and Ramon that they should come up and live with her. They hadn't trusted the money—death money they had called it—but she had refused to turn it down. It was from God, she'd argued. She'd done nothing to get it except do her job. She had liked Señor Sean. She would rather that he was still alive than that she had the estate, but once he was dead, it would be stupid not to take the money. But even from a man in hell? they had argued. She had flown into a rage. Who were they to say a man couldn't repent even as he fell ten feet to his doom? God would always forgive, as he would forgive all of them. She had looked meaningfully at Ramon.

And finally, yesterday while they were up visiting for the day, they had said they would come and stay if she wanted them to. Then at night Ramon had said they would find some way to marry in the Church, as it wouldn't look right if he lived in the same house with her and they were not married.

She had stayed in bed and let the men leave early. Ramon still had his business and if he wanted to continue in the same place, she would say nothing. It was not her affair, anyway, what he did for a living. If he asked, she would help him open a place closer to Tossa, now that he'd be living here.

Then she had gotten up and knelt by her bed to pray that the Virgin intercede for Señor Sean, since in spite of her railings at the men, she realized that it was likely that he had lost his soul. Then she got dressed and went in to do the dishes.

Now she had her broom and was sweeping the house thoroughly. If Ramon were going to be here, then the house, their house, must be spotless. He would have it no other way, she knew. Not that she had ever been lax in her housekeeping with the señor, but from time to time in the past six months she had let things run down a bit. She hadn't been used to all the haggling about money, but Pedro and Ramon had helped her, and she was glad, now, that they had settled things with the lawyers and the insurance people, even if it had taken time away from the house.

It was summer, and it seemed that everywhere in the front and back courtyards, flowers were blooming. She went out to the backyard and snipped the blossoms that were ready, and then turned the water on to keep the ground moist. It was another scorching hot day, and she knew that it would remain that way for at least three more months. She laid the hose down in one of the small ditches she had dug, and walked back through the house to the front, her arms filled with the flowers. Over on her left was Sean's grave, marked by a stone, since a cross would have been sacrilegious. It was out of the way, over by the wall. After the winter rains the ground had been packed down so that there was no way to tell that it had been dug. It's hard to imagine his body lying there, she thought. She laid the flowers near the stone.

The sun beat like a mallet on her head. She straightened up too fast and got dizzy. For a moment she stood over the grave, but her thoughts were far away. She was thinking that in two weeks the men would be here, and it would be a happy house again.

Then she turned back, thinking of the preparations she'd make for them and, squinting against the glaring whiteness, went inside, humming softly to herself.

Read on for a preview of
John Lescroart's riveting novel

# BETRAYAL

Available now

"**M**r. Hardy?"

"Speaking."

"Mr. Hardy, this is Oscar Thomasino."

"Your honor, how are you?"

"Fine, thanks. Am I bothering you at an inopportune time?"

"No, but whatever—it's no bother. What can I do for you?"

"Well, admittedly this is a little unusual, but you and I have known each other for a long time, and I wondered if I could presume slightly upon our professional relationship."

This was unusual, if not to say unprecedented, but Hardy nevertheless kept his tone neutral. "Certainly, your honor. Anything I can do, if it's within my power." A Superior Court judge asking an attorney for a favor was a rare enough opportunity, and Hardy wasn't going to let it pass him by.

"Well, I'm sure it is," Thomasino said. "Did you know Charles Bowen—Charlie?"

"I don't think so."

"You'd remember him. Flashy dresser, bright red hair, big beard."

"Doesn't ring a bell. He a lawyer?"

"Yes—he was, anyway. He disappeared six months ago."

"Where'd he go?"

"If I knew that, he wouldn't be disappeared, would he? He'd be someplace."

"Everybody's someplace, your honor. It's one of the two main rules. Everybody loves somebody sometime, and you've got to be someplace."

During the short pause that ensued, Hardy came to realize that he'd overstepped. His tendency to crack wise was going to be the end of him yet. But Thomasino eventually recovered to some extent, even reverting to his own stab at not-quite-cozy informality. "Thanks, Diz," he said. "I'll try to keep those in mind. Meanwhile, Charlie Bowen."

"Okay."

"Yes, well . . . the point is that he was a sole practitioner. No firm, no partners, but a reasonably robust caseload."

"Good for him."

"True, but his disappearance hasn't been good for the court. Or for his wife and daughter either, to tell you the truth. She's hired her own lawyer to file a presumption of death claim, which between you and me has very little chance of getting recognized, in spite of the fact that it would be convenient for the court."

"Why's that?"

"Because when sole practitioners die and go to heaven, the bar inherits the caseload and has to dispose of it."

"What if they don't go to heaven?"

"Most lawyers argue themselves in, don't you think? I know you would."

"Thanks, I think. Your honor."

"Anyway, I know it's just housecleaning, but Bowen had a ton of work outstanding, and that work needs to get done. And while we're not going to issue any presumption of death until he's been gone a lot longer, last month Marian Braun"—another of the city's Superior Court judges—"ruled that his disappearance rendered him legally incompetent, and just yesterday the State Bar suspended his ticket at the court's request."

"So now they've got to farm out his cases. If he hadn't returned my calls for six months and I was his client, I would have fired him by now."

"I'm sure some of his clients may have done

just that, but not all by a long shot." Thomasino sighed. "Charlie was a friend of mine. His wife's going to need whatever he still has coming from his cases. I'd like to be sure that the bar puts those cases in the hands of somebody I know will do the right thing by her. Anyway, bottom line is that I ran into Wes Farrell today at lunch." This was one of Hardy's partners. "He said things at your place were a little slow. The good news is that you can probably count on some percentage of Mr. Bowen's clients hooking up with your firm. Not that any of 'em will make you rich."

Reading between the lines, Hardy knew what the judge was saying—that this was grunt administrative work. The court probably had appointed the majority of Charlie's clients, indigents up for petty crimes and misdemeanors. Nevertheless, the court would pay for every hour Hardy's associates spent on the criminal cases, and if the civil cases made any money, the firm could expect reasonable compensation. And it was, again, an opportunity to do a small good deed for a judge, and that was never a bad idea.

"You could probably get them all assigned out or closed in the next couple of months."

"I'm sold, your honor. I'd be happy to help you out."

"Thanks, Diz. I appreciate it. I know it's not

very sexy. I'll have it all delivered to your office within the week."

"How much stuff is it?"

Thomasino paused. "About sixty boxes." In other words, a lot. "But here's the silver lining. It's only half as much as it appears, since half the boxes are one client."

"Tell me it's Microsoft."

A soft chuckle. "No such luck. It's Evan Scholler."

Hardy hesitated for an instant. "Why is that name familiar?"

"Because you've read all about it. The two guys who'd been over in Iraq together?"

"Ah, it comes flooding back," Hardy said. "They had the same girlfriend or something, too, didn't they?"

"I believe so. There's a bunch of juicy stuff, but you'll find that out soon enough, I guess. But in any event, Diz, I really appreciate you doing this."

"I live to serve the court, your honor."

"You're already up on points, counselor. Don't lay it on too thick. Have a nice night."

Hardy hung up and stood for a moment, musing. The judge's line played back in his mind: "There's a bunch of juicy stuff" in the Scholler case. Hardy thought he could use some juicy stuff in his life about now. If his memory served, and it always did, Scholler's situation was even more compelling than the bare bones of the murder case because of its genesis in chaos and violence.

In Iraq.

A burnt orange sun kissed the horizon to the west as twenty-six-year-old Second Lieutenant Evan Scholler led his three-pack of converted gun truck support Humvees through the gates of the Allstrong compound in the middle of an area surrounded by palm trees, canals, and green farmland. The landscape here was nothing like the sandy, flat, brown terrain that Evan had grown used to since he'd arrived in Kuwait. The enclosure was about the size of three football fields, protected, like every other "safe" area, by Bremer walls—twelve-foot-tall concrete barriers topped with concertina wiring. Ahead of him squatted three double-wide motor-home trailers that Allstrong Security, an American contracting company, had provided for its local employees.

Pulling up to the central temporary building, over which flew an American flag, Evan stepped out of his car onto the gravel that extended as far as he could see in all directions. A fit-looking American military type stood in the open doorway and now came down the three steps, his hand extended. Evan snapped a salute and the man laughed.

"You don't need to salute me, Lieutenant," he said. "Jack Allstrong. Welcome to BIAP. You must be Scholler."

"Yes, sir. If you're expecting me, that's a nice change of pace."

"Gotten the runaround, have you?"

"A little bit. I've got eight men here with me, and, Colonel . . . I'm sorry, the commander here?"

"Calliston."

"That's it. He wasn't expecting us. Calliston said you had some beds we could use."

"Yeah, he called. But all we've got are cots, really."

"We've got our own on board," Evan said. "We're okay with cots."

Allstrong's face showed something like sympathy. "You all been on the road awhile?"

"Three days driving up from Kuwait with a Halliburton convoy, four days wandering around between here and Baghdad, watching out for looters and getting passed off around the brass. Now here we are. If you don't mind, sir, none of my men have seen a bed or a regular meal or a shower since we landed. You mind if we get 'em settled in first?"

Allstrong squinted through the wind at Evan, then looked over to the small line of Humvees, with M-60 Vietnam-era machine guns mounted on their roofs, exhausted-looking and dirty men standing behind them. Coming back to Evan, he nodded and pointed to the trailer on his right. "Bring 'em on up and park over there. It's dorm-style. Find an empty spot and claim it. Showers are all yours. Dinner's at eighteen hundred hours, forty minutes from now. Think your men can make it?"

Evan tamped down a smile. "Nobody better stand in their way, sir."

"Nobody's gonna." Allstrong cocked his head. "Well, get 'em started, then."

Read on for a preview of
John Lescroart's riveting novel

# A PLAGUE OF SECRETS

Available now

Friday, the end of the workweek.

On the small deck outside his back door, a lawyer named Dismas Hardy sat with his feet up on the deck's railing and savored a rare moment as the sun spent the last hour of its day lowering itself toward the horizon behind his home.

The house cast its ever-lengthening shadow out over the neighborhood to the east—San Francisco's Richmond District—and it threw into relief the bright west-facing facades of the buildings in the city before him as it stretched away to downtown. The random window reflected glints of sunlight back at him, fireflies in the gathering dusk, shimmering in the Indian summer air.

He sipped his gin and ice, placed the glass down on the meshed metal of the picnic table they'd set up out here, and was suddenly and acutely aware that he could not be more content. His wife, Frannie, whom he still loved after twenty-three years, was inside the house behind him, humming as she did whatever she was doing. His two children were away and doing well at their respective schools— Rebecca at Boston University, and Vincent at UC San Diego. The law firm of Freeman, Farrell, Hardy & Roake, of which he was the managing partner, was humming along as though it were on autopilot.

Hardy looked for a moment into the blue above him, blinking against a wave of emotion. Then, being who he was, his mouth cracked into a small grin at himself and he lifted his glass for another sip.

Inside, the telephone rang twice and stopped, which meant that it was someone they knew and that Frannie had picked it up. Her voice, with notes of sympathy and understanding, floated out to him, but he didn't bother trying to make out any of the words. She had begun to have a somewhat thriving career of her own as a marriage and family therapist and often would wind up counseling her clients from home.

Hardy drifted, not off to anywhere, but into a kind of surrender of conscious thought. For a long moment, he was simply there in the same way that his drink or his chair existed, or the light, or the breeze off the ocean a little more than a mile west of where he sat. So that when the door opened behind him, he came back with a bit of a start.

Frannie put a hand on his shoulder and he brought his hand up to cover hers, half turning, seeing the look on her face. "What's up?" he asked, his feet coming down off the railing. "Are the kids all right?" Always the first concern.

She nodded a yes to the second question, then answered the first. "That was Treya." Treya was the wife of Hardy's best friend, Abe Glitsky, the head of San Francisco's homicide department. Anguish in her eyes, Frannie held and released a breath. "It's Zack," she said, referring to Glitsky's three-year-old son. "He's had an accident."

Accompanied by her five-year-old daughter, Rachel, Treya Glitsky opened the gate in the Hardys' white picket fence. Dismas Hardy, in his living room watching out through the plantation shutters of his front window, called back to his wife in the kitchen that they were here, then walked over and opened his front door.

Treya turned away and, closing the gate, reached down for a small duffel bag. By the way she picked it up, it might have weighed a hundred pounds. When she straightened up, her shoulders rose and fell; then she brought a hand to her forehead and stood completely still for another second or two. With her tiny hand, Rachel held on to the front pocket of her mother's jeans while she looked up at her face, her own lips pressed tight.

Hardy crossed his porch and descended three steps to the cement path that bisected his small lawn. The sun had gone down behind the buildings across the street although true dusk was still twenty minutes away. Treya turned and saw him now, and her legendary composure threatened to break. She was a tall woman—nearly Hardy's size—and strongly built. Her mouth, expressive and normally quick to smile, quivered, then set in a line.

Hardy came forward, took the duffel bag from her, and put an arm around her neck, drawing her in, holding her for a moment. Finally he stepped back and whispered, "How is he?"

She shrugged and shook her head. Then her voice was as quiet as his. "We don't know yet."

Frannie came up, touched his shoulder, and came around to hug Treya.

Hardy stepped to the side and went down to one knee to face Rachel at her level. "And how's my favorite little girl in the whole world?"

"Okay," she said. "But Zack got hit by a car."

"I know he did, hon."

"But he's not going to die."

Hardy looked up at the two women. Treya gave him a quick nod, and he came back to her daughter. "No, of course not. But I hear you're going to stay here for a couple of days while he gets better. Is that okay with you?"

"If Mom says."

"And she does. Is that duffel bag your stuff? Here, let me get it. If you put your arms around my neck, your old uncle Diz will carry you inside."

Then they were all moving up the path and into the house. "Abe went with the ambulance," Treya was saying. "We don't know how long we're going to have to be down there. I don't know how to thank you for watching Rachel."

"Don't be ridiculous," Frannie said. "We love Rachel." She reached out and touched the little girl's cheek where she rested it on Hardy's shoulder. "She's our favorite little girl."

Hardy and Frannie walked Treya out after they got Rachel settled in with cookies and milk in front of the television. They stopped again on the path just inside the fence. "Was he conscious?" Hardy asked.

"No." Treya paused, then lowered her voice. "He didn't have his helmet on."

"What happened exactly?" Frannie asked.

"We may never know," she said. "Abe had

just brought down his Big Wheel bike and Zack was on it, but Abe told him to just sit still and wait a minute while he turned around and got his helmet. Which he'd set down, like, two feet away on the stairs. But then as soon as his back was turned, Zack got aboard and either started pedaling or just rolling down the driveway just as another car was coming up the street. One of our neighbors. He was only going, like, five miles an hour but Zack just plowed into him and got knocked off the bike and into the street." She flashed a pained look from Hardy to Frannie. "He banged his head." She hesitated. "I've got to get down there now. You guys are great. Thank you."

"Go," Hardy said. "Call when you can."


"The best bit of news," Treya was saying to both of them as they listened on the two extension phones, "is that he's out of his twos. Evidently the younger you are, the worse the prognosis. Three is way better than two. And this is a level-one hospital, so they had a neurological resident in-house, which is also lucky since he could go right to work." Her voice, while not by any stretch remotely cheerful, was strong and confident-sounding. Conveying facts, keeping to the bearable news, she was keeping herself together the way she always did, by sucking it up.

"They've cooled him down to make him hypothermic," she went on, "which is what they always do, and taken some scans and they've got him on a continuous EEG and his vital signs are good, so that's all heartening."

"But he's still unconscious?" Hardy asked.

Frannie and Hardy heard Treya's quick intake of breath and flashed their reactions to each other. "Well, that's really not so much of an issue now, since they've induced a coma. He's going to be unconscious for a while. Maybe a week or more."

"He's in a coma?" Frannie, before she could stop herself.

"It's not as bad as it sounds," Treya said.

Silence collected in the line as this bit of horrifying, yet perhaps good, information began to sink in. Finally Hardy cleared his throat. "So how's Abe?"

Treya hesitated. "Quiet. Even for him."

"It's not his fault," Frannie said.

"I know that. It might not be so clear to him." Again, a stab at an optimistic tone. "He'll get to it."

"I know he will," Frannie said.

Hardy, not so certain of that, especially if Zachary didn't make it, turned to face away from his wife. The women's words continued to tumble through the phone at his ear, but he didn't hear any of them over his own imaginings—or was it only his pulse, sounding like the tick of a clock counting down the seconds?

Bay Beans West enjoyed a privileged location, location, location at the intersection of Haight and Ashbury streets in San Francisco.

The large, wide-windowed coffee shop had opened in the summer of 1998 and from its first days became a fixture in the neighborhood. It opened every morning except Sunday at six o'clock, when it opened at eight, and stayed open until ten. Between the UCSF medical school a couple of blocks east, the University of San Francisco a few blocks north, the tourists visiting the epicenter of the birth of hippiedom, and the vibrant and wildly eclectic local neighborhood, the place rarely had a slow moment, much less an empty one.

The smell of its roasting beans infused the immediate vicinity with a beckoning aroma; the management provided copies of the city's newspapers—the *Chronicle,* the *Free Press,* and the *Bay Guardian*—for free on the honor system that they wouldn't be taken. The papers rarely disappeared before three o'clock. Even the homeless honored the custom, except for Crazy Melinda, who used to come in, scoop all the papers up, and try to leave with them. Until the patrons started setting aside a copy of each paper for her at the counter to pick up whenever she wanted them.

Comfortable, colorful couches were available as well as the usual chairs and tables; the ethic of the place allowed an unlimited time at your seat once you'd claimed it, whether or not you continued to drink coffee; for the past five years or so, customers could avail themselves of free wireless Internet service; and legal or not, pets were welcome. For many in the neighborhood, BBW was a refuge, a meeting place, a home away from home.

At a few minutes before seven o'clock on this Saturday morning, the usual line of about twenty customers needing their morning infusions of caffeine was already growing along Haight Street at the establishment's front door. A long-haired man named Wes Farrell, in jogging pants and a T-shirt that read "DAM—Mothers Against Dyslexia," stood holding in one hand the hand of his live-in girlfriend, Sam Duncan, and in the other the leash of Gertrude, his boxer. They, like many others in the city that morning, were discussing the homeless problem.

For decades, San Francisco has been a haven for the homeless, spending upward of one hundred fifty million dollars per year on shelters, subsidized rental units, medical and psychiatric care, soup kitchens, and so on. Now, suddenly, unexpectedly, and apparently due to a series of articles that had just appeared in the *Chronicle,* came a widespread outcry among the citizenry that the welcome mat should be removed. Wes finished reading today's article aloud to Sam and, folding up the paper, said, "And about time, too."

Sam extracted her hand from his. "You don't mean that."

"I don't? I thought I did."

"So what do you want to do with them? I mean, once you give them a ticket, which by the way they have no money to pay, so that won't work."

"What part of that statement—I hesitate to call it a sentence—do you want me to address?"

"Any part. Don't be wise."

"I'm not. But I'd hate to be the guy assigned to trying to diagram one of your sentences."

"You're just trying to get me off the point. Which is what you would do with these homeless people, who suddenly are no longer welcome."

"Actually, they're just as welcome. They're just not going to be welcome to use public streets and sidewalks as their campsites and bathrooms any-more."

"So where else would they go?"

"Are we talking bathrooms? They go to the bathroom in bathrooms, like the rest of us."

"The rest of us who have homes, Wes. I think that's more or less the point. They don't."

"You're right. But you notice we're loaded with shelters and public toilets."

"They don't like the shelters. They're dangerous and dirty."

"And the streets aren't? Besides, this may sound like a cruel cliché, my dear, but where do you think we get the expression 'beggars can't be choosers'?"

"I can't believe you just said that. That is so, so"—Sam dredged up about the worst epithet she could imagine—"so *right-wing.*"

Wes looked down, went to a knee, and snapped his fingers, bringing Gertrude close in for a quick pet. "It's all right, girl. Your mom and I aren't fighting. We're just talking." Standing up, he said, "She's getting upset."

"So am I. If you try to pet me to calm me down, I'll deck you."

"There's a tolerant approach. And meanwhile, I hate to say this, but it's not a right-wing, left-wing issue here. It's a health and quality-of-life issue. Feces and urine on public streets and playgrounds and parks pose a health risk and are just a little bit of a nuisance, I think we can admit. Are we in accord here?"

Sam, arms folded, leaned back against the windows of the coffee shop, unyielding.

"Sam," Wes continued, "when I take Gertie out for a walk, I bring a bag to clean up after her. That's for a dog. You really think it's too much to ask the same for humans?"

"It's not the same thing."

"Why not?"

"Because a lot of these people, they have mental problems, too. They don't even know they're doing it or where."

"And so we should just tolerate it? You send your kids out to play and there's a pile of shit on your front stoop? Next thing you know, half a school's got hepatitis. You don't think that's a small problem?"

"That's not what's happening."

"Sam, that's exactly what's happening. They've got to check the sandbox near the merry-go-round in Golden Gate Park every morning for shit and needles. Some of these people think it's a litter box."

"Well, I haven't heard of any hepatitis epidemic. That's way an exaggeration."

"The point is the alfresco-bathroom kind of

thing that's been happening downtown for years. I think you'll remember we had a guy who used our front stoop at the office every night for a month. We had to wash the steps down every morning."

"There," Sam said. "That was a solution."

"It's a ridiculous solution. It's insane. To say nothing about the fact that using the streets for bathrooms punishes innocent, good citizens and devalues property."

"Aha! I knew property would get in there."

"Property's not a bad thing, Sam."

"Which is what every Republican in the world believes."

"And some Democrats, too. Dare I say most? And for the umpteenth time, Sam, it's not a Republican thing. You can be opposed to Bush and still not want to have people shitting in your flowerpots. Those aren't mutually exclusive."

"I think they might actually be."

"Well, no offense, but you're wrong. Public defecation and homeless encampments on the streets and in the parks are gross and unhealthy and sickening. I don't understand how you can't see that."

Sam again shook her head. "I see those poor people suffering. That's what I see. We've got a fire department with miles of hoses. We could deploy them to wash down the streets. The city could get up some work program and hire people to clean up."

"What a great idea! Should we pay them to clean up after themselves or after one another? Except then again, where does the money to do that come from?"

"There it is again, money! It always comes down to money."

"Well, as a matter of fact, yes, sometimes it does."

"The point is, Wes, these people just don't have the same options as everybody else."

"And they never will, Sam. That's rough maybe, okay, but it's life. And life's just not fair sometimes. Which doesn't mean everybody else has to deal with their problems. They get rounded up and taken to the shelters whether or not they want to go, and I say it's about time."

Without either Sam or Wes noticing, several others in the line, both male and female, had closed in around them, listening in. Now a young hippie spoke up to Wes. "You're right, dude," he said. "It's out of control. It is about time."

A chorus of similar sentiments followed.

Sam took it all in, straightened up, and looked out into the faces surrounding her. "I just can't believe that I'm hearing this in San Francisco," she said. "I'm so ashamed of all of you."

And with that, she pushed her way through the crowd and started walking up Ashbury, away from her boyfriend and their dog.

Sam was the director of San Francisco's Rape Crisis Counseling Center, which also happened to be on Haight Street. Her plan this morning had been to take her early-morning constitutional from their home up on Buena Vista with Wes and Gertie, share a cup of coffee and a croissant at BBW, then check in at the office to make sure there hadn't been an overnight crisis that demanded her attention.

But now, seething, just wanting to get away from all the reactionaries, she had started out in the wrong direction to get to the center. Fortunately, the line for the BBW stretched down Haight Street, and not up Ashbury, and she'd gone about half a block uphill when she stopped and turned around, realizing she could take the alley that ran behind the Haight Street storefronts, bypassing the crowd and emerging on the next block on the way to her office.

But first she stopped a minute, not just to get her breath, but to try to calm herself. After an extraordinarily rocky beginning to their relationship, she and Wes hadn't had a fight in six or seven years. She'd come to believe that he was her true soul mate and shared her opinions about nearly everything, especially politics. But now apparently not.

It shook her.

And okay, she knew that she was among those whom conservatives would include among California's "fruits and nuts." She certainly didn't too often doubt the rightness of her various stances. She was in her early forties, and had seen enough of the world to know that the dollar was the basic problem. The military-industrial complex. Big oil and corporate globalism. Republicans.

But here now Wes, who had registered Green and hated the right-wingers as much as she did, was arguing for something that she just knew in her heart was wrong. You couldn't just abandon these homeless people who had after all flocked to San Francisco precisely because of the benign political environment. That would be the worst bait-and-switch tactic she could imagine. She would have to talk to him, but after they'd both calmed down.

She crossed back to where she wouldn't be visible to Wes or anyone else in the line as she came down the hill. It was the kind of clear morning that people tended to expect when they visited San Francisco during the traditional summer months. Those people often left in bitter disappointment at the incessant fog, the general inclemency of the weather. But today the early sun sprayed the rooftops golden. The temperature was already in the low sixties. It was going to be a perfect day.

She got to the alley, squinting into the bright morning sun, when here was an example of exactly the thing she and Wes had been talking about: a pair of feet protruded from the back door area of BBW. Not wanting to awaken the poor sleeping homeless man, she gave him a wide berth and only a quick glance as she came abreast of where he slept.

But something about the attitude of the body stopped her. It didn't seem to be lying in a natural position, the head propped up against the screen door. She couldn't imagine such a posture would be conducive to sleep. Most of the weight seemed to be on his left shoulder, but under that, the torso turned in an awkward way so that both feet pointed up, as if he were lying on his back.

Moving closer, she noticed a line of liquid tracing itself down over the concrete and pooling in the gap between the cement of the porch and the asphalt of the alley. In the bright morning sunlight, from a distance it could have been water. But another couple of steps brought her close enough to remove any doubt on that score—the glistening wet stuff was red.

Leaning over, Sam shaded her eyes against the glare and she saw the man's face—a face she recognized, had expected to see this morning behind the counter where he always was at BBW.

Her hand, already trembling, went to her mouth.

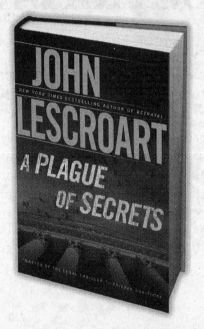

The *New York Times* bestseller from

# John Lescroart

# BETRAYAL

Dismas Hardy agrees to take an appeal to
overturn the murder conviction of National
Guard reservist Evan Scholler. Scholler had
plenty of reasons for revenge—but as Dismas
delves into the case, he begins to uncover a
terrible truth that drops him right into the
complicated world of government conspiracy,
assassination, and betrayal…

**"A tour de force of a legal thriller."**
—*Providence Journal-Bulletin*

Available wherever books are sold
or at penguin.com